'It's the same always. Huge trolls run rampant and unstoppable, village destroyed by fire, bloated corpses in cages. Often a tall woman, an elf maybe, seen through the trees or on the edge of the blaze.' Ginni held up her hand to forestall questions. 'But here's the interesting part. There is always one or two spared to spread the tale. Always, one or two not quite old enough or young enough or sharp enough to be believed.'

'But who can spread the terror like the most subtle poison,' added Roslin.

'And that,' said Tom, 'may be her most potent weapon.' He sat quietly. Finally, with the great respect with which one addresses a powerful mage, he asked Roslin, 'What does she want?'

The Sacred Seven

Amy Stout

NEW ENGLISH LIBRARY
Hodder and Stoughton

First published in Great Britain in paperback in 1996 by
Hodder and Stoughton
A division of Hodder Headline PLC
A New English Library Paperback

10 9 8 7 6 5 4 3 2 1

Stout, Amy
The Sacred Seven
1.American fiction – 20th century
I.Title
813.5′4 [F]

ISBN 0 340 65362 0

Typeset by
Phoenix Typesetting, Ilkley, West Yorkshire

Printed and bound in Great Britain by
Cox & Wyman Ltd., Reading, Berkshire

Hodder and Stoughton
A division of Hodder Headline PLC
338 Euston Road
London NW1 3BH

To generations before, after and concurrent –
my parents, Madalyn and Frank Stout; my children,
Alexandra, Andrea, and Abram Rodgers; and my
husband, Alan Rodgers.

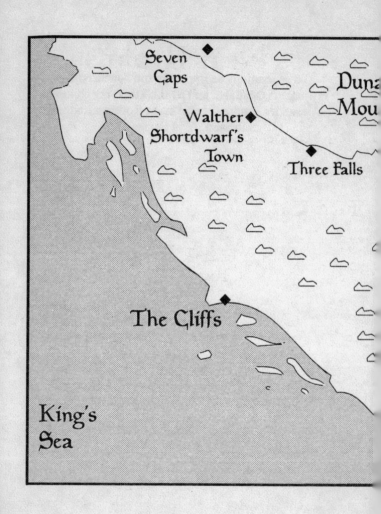

Near Realms
of the One Land

ins

Lyda's home Town

Twin Gates

Queen's River

Elfwitch Stronghold

Tomar's River

Elven River

Acknowledgements

Many people encouraged me – or at least didn't laugh when I suggested writing this book. My three sisters, Lisa, Stacy, and Luci; my brother, Sam; my friends, Liz, Dan, Lois, Becky and Charlie, Margaret and Don, Tracy and Laura, Pete and Bob, Chris, and Jenni, Jamie and Steve, Steve and Laura and my editors and publishers, Carolyn, John, Jennifer, Jennifer B. and Lou. My husband, Alan Rodgers, created the map. Finally, a very special thanks to Kay. I couldn't have done it without you.

From the far end of the hallway, Maarcus the Sixth could make out the short form of the royal magician, chatting it up with the purple plumed guards. When the king's physician reached where the three stood watch outside the patient's room, Abadan broke off his conversation and the sentries snapped back to attention at their posts.

'Anything useful?' Maarcus asked under his breath.

'I don't work that kind of magic,' the sorcerer grumbled. 'I'd wager even the stablehands know the good commanders have all grown lazy, and the new men are as ill-trained as children.' He looked up at the doctor. 'I was only waiting for you. First you're late and now you're stalling. Let's get this over with.' He motioned for his companion to lead.

Maarcus's hand hesitated at the broken brass catch. He hardened his resolve to ignore all but his lifelong friend, then pushed wide the heavy door.

Finely dressed minor nobles and royal offspring packed the bed chamber. They joked and mingled as if attending a celebration rather than a death vigil. The rich tapestries lining the walls in tribute to the king's Great Truce hung this way and that, and added to the drunken, carnival air.

Maarcus the Sixth crossed his arms against his chest to keep himself from straightening the nearest carpet and shook his head. These sponges seemed to think King Tomar's triumph in uniting the One Land was no more than a happy accident of youth. They simply didn't grasp the cost.

The doctor watched his patient in frustration. More than once he had reminded the king that allowing these daily audiences while he lay in such poor health would only slow recovery, but Tomar persisted in rejecting medical advice. He continued to indulge both children and lesser counselors as if the stakes were only a card game.

'Disgraceful river leeches,' Maarcus muttered to the magician at his side.

Abadan stared with a bland expression and didn't answer. His words of more than a year ago echoed in the physician's mind. 'It's too late to put backbone into any of the bumbling fools. The king knows he won't live long enough to see the fruits of the attempt. We must try a riskier route if we expect the One Land to last beyond the smoke on his funeral pyre.'

Weeks had dragged into months before plans reached the current stage. First the doctor had attempted to explain away the signs of his friend's worsening health while the magician tried and rejected his own remedies. Then he stubbornly believed in his medicines and refused Abadan's help. Finally he admitted no amount of serum mixing would cure the patient. Together they had convinced the king.

The rest lay in the palms of the Seven Sisters. Maarcus hated to rely on deities he privately called the Capricious Mothers, but he'd learned he could lean only so far on mortal magic – or human science.

A thin voice rose above the din. 'Please, sire, allow me. You need to keep your strength up.'

The king waved a hand without bothering to see which of his ineffectual children had spoken. 'Not now. I'm resting.'

'The soup is—' The son tripped over a ripple in the carpeting or perhaps a jealous rival intentionally shoved him. Whichever, the boy fell, the porcelain bowl flew out of his hands and splintered against the carved headboard inches above his father's face.

The king opened his eyes. 'The soup is too cold,' he said to the boy.

His five children all hovered, afraid to speak. A few of the seemingly countless advisors began sidling toward the door but instantly halted when he looked in their direction.

No one moved to clean up the mess.

He nodded to the two men standing on the edge of the crowd. The big-boned doctor began elbowing his way to the king's bedside, letting the slighter Abadan follow in his wake.

King Tomar the Great turned back to glare at the roomful of apprehensive faces. He kept his voice at a whisper. 'Go. All of you. Now.'

The clumsy son fell again in his rush to be the first out the door. The others stepped over him as they hurried out.

King Tomar pushed himself up. 'A towel would be useful,' he said, unable to hide a sad, lopsided grin.

Maarcus exchanged a glance with Abadan, whose short headshake reminded him of the more important matters for discussion. He remained tight-lipped as he deftly mopped the soup from the top of the man's head, changed the linen pillowcase, and placed it behind his shoulders.

Abadan checked for stragglers under the bed and behind the draperies, then shoved the cedarwood door closed.

'Report, please.'

By prior agreement, the magician answered for both. 'It's done.'

The ironic half-smile transformed to a rare one of genuine pleasure. 'How long until we are certain all is well?'

Maarcus the Sixth's height and stiff, military bearing made him the natural choice to pass along the bad news. He stood with legs at parade rest and hands clasped behind his back. 'Well, Your Majesty, it's hard to know exactly. This sort of thing has never been attempted in living memory. The spells require upkeep. We had to request the aid of an elf not altogether sympathetic to our cause.'

King Tomar absorbed this. 'The fate of this elf?'

'She'll be well cared for but confined, as have others before her when necessary.'

'And the twins?'

Abadan's hand twitched slightly. The king did not seem to notice as the magician hid it in his flowing robes. 'Your newborn heirs are on the way to their foster parents. The couple knows only that they are to rear the infants as their own. So long as the children thrive, they will enjoy a generous income from an unknown source.'

King Tomar gave his most trusted men a hard look. 'By the Seven Sisters, do you judge these "distant cousins" of mine as sound as our very mothers?'

'They are beyond the age of childbearing but are renowned for their love of several foundlings now grown to adulthood themselves. Maarcus has chosen as best as one might.' Abadan masked the uncommon compliment with a shrug and gave a slight nod to his one-time enemy turned accomplice.

'The children will receive the proper instruction with as much affection as if they'd been brought up in court,' Maarcus added.

'I was hoping for much better than that,' snapped the king. 'The point is precisely the opposite.'

Maarcus the Sixth – physician to King Tomar the Great since before his most celebrated campaign and companion back to their days of wooden swords and scalpels – winced in embarrassment. 'But of course. I realize that. I was merely—'

'You were merely trying to set my mind at ease should this plan fail. You know as well as I do – have indeed repeatedly hinted as much yourself – that the entire kingdom will surely crumble if we don't succeed.' His tone grew morose. 'It's too late for anyone to reassure me I haven't already lost what I built.' He sank back into the pillows and closed his eyes. 'I should have listened to you instead of insisting on personally overseeing my heirs. Who else would have thought I'd be so soft . . .' He waved a hand in dismissal. 'Ach, an old man's lament. Enough for today. You've done what you could. Let me know how it progresses.'

Maarcus felt no victory over Tomar's fresh admission of his one enduring mistake. This turn toward brooding worried him. Outside the royal chamber, he spoke sternly to the captain, 'Call us instantly if His Majesty's rest is interrupted.'

'Yes, sire.'

Halfway down the hall, Abadan shouted over his shoulder in a surprisingly loud voice, 'And should you allow it to happen on your watch, we will personally see you reassigned to the border.' While the palace guards gaped at such a severe threat, he quietly admonished the doctor. 'You didn't tell him about the boy.'

Maarcus took several more slow steps. His hip was bothering him again. The long arguments over priorities, balancing the needs of the nation against those of the children, were still fresh in his mind. Their resolve to disguise the son – and the form that had taken – weighed as heavy as his old memories of battle carnage. 'We'll have to tell him tomorrow.'

'You've waited too long as it is,' Abadan protested. 'Despair can overwhelm the spirit with cancerous speed. It is his right to know what we've done.'

'He will, he will.' As they neared the top of the grand staircase, he added, 'And by the Seven Sisters, I hope he doesn't have our heads cleanly—'

Abadan cut him off by a discreet pinch on the elbow. 'Company.'

The doctor eyed the corner Abadan indicated. An elf, cloaked in black and well hidden in the shadows, removed her hood and slowly shook her head.

'By the Sisters!' Maarcus swore in a whisper.

Anyone else in the castle – and barely a handful saw her at all – would have dismissed the gesture as unimportant, for most of her moves were equally understated. To Maarcus, this news was second only to the impending death of the king.

As always, Abadan needed to voice the obvious. 'She's escaped.'

The elf nodded once and again joined the gloom.

'Sir Maarcus, Master Abadan!' a sentry yelled.

'What now?' Abadan asked Maarcus.

'The king . . . he . . .'

Despite the urgency of the man's voice, the two turned around with the practised timing of feigned calm.

Close up the young soldier looked panicked. He could not catch his breath though he'd run but the short distance they'd just walked.

The physician felt a familiar cold stone in his gut. 'His Majesty needs us?' he prodded the heaving man.

The plumed helm went back and forth. 'No, no. His Majesty doesn't need—' he started without thinking, then stopped. He straightened to full height and said with as much dignity as he possessed, 'Sirs, His Majesty, King Tomar the Great is dead.'

Chapter 1

DISCOVERIES

The girl stank of trouble, showing up at the end of the day and strutting around the store like she owned it. When Lyda caught the shapely thing winking at Willam, and him blushing like a school boy, she figured she'd had enough. Poor Willam wasn't much to look at and his business head was often cloudy, but he was hers.

'I'll tend to this 'un,' she told her husband. 'Why'n't you go polish the—'

'Everyone in town says you collect the most interesting pieces.' She clasped her hands in front of her and smiled in the very picture of innocence.

Lyda glared at her husband and the object of his foolishness. '*I'll* show you our wares while *he* tidies up 'ere. It *is* closin' time you know.'

'That would be very kind of you.' The child picked at her dress with a feigned modesty that no doubt disarmed only barren old grandmothers.

Lyda led her a few steps to a back corner of the cramped

shop where small, ornate but dusty caskets lined one shelf just above eye level. She stood, trying to decide which would most quickly satisfy the likes of this harlot, then reached for one on the end.

'The middle box strikes my eye . . . if it wouldn't be too much trouble?'

The shopkeeper's wife gave an exaggerated sigh to show the girl what she thought of her nonsense, but the painted child simply smiled without comment. 'This 'un's much more interestin' to someone of your – ' she looked her up and down – 'type.'

'Someone of my *type* often has money to spend,' she answered without a hint of shame.

'Hmph,' Lyda grunted, but she brought down the requested box. She rattled and lifted the catch before turning to face the girl with the lid opened. Holding tight, she thrust it toward the customer but didn't let go or offer to put it down.

The girl dug through the tarnished junk, oohing and aahing. There was nothing a classy woman would ever wear here, but the flirty ones rarely had such taste. Lyda shook the box. 'Got work to d—'

The word died on her lips when the girl's hand closed over a charm bracelet. She lifted out the plain silver piece.

'Where did this come from?'

The shopkeeper tightened her grip on the casket. 'Hear tell that belonged to an elf. Couldn't 'magine wearing such ugly jewelry myself.'

'Do you know what became of the elf?'

Panic seized the woman's stomach. She couldn't let her take that piece. 'He died.'

'Oh,' the other said, still clutching the bracelet.

She looked from the girl to the elven jewelry, considering. It had cursed Lyda and Willam from the first. Surely it was another's turn. No one else in all these years had ever paid it the least notice. Perhaps the child was meant to have it.

Maybe she should bargain after all. In a kinder voice that had once regularly spiced her everyday speech, she said, 'It's good luck, y'know.'

'Doesn't sound very lucky if the former owner died.'

'Oh, but he lived long and well. Died of old age, not from some 'orrible wastin' sickness or at the hands of the trolls in the border wars.'

'What do you hear about the border wars so far inland?'

'Nothin' to bother your . . . um.' She bit her tongue and let the insult hang unfinished. 'That'll be ten bars.' Lyda held out her hand before either of them could change their minds.

'As likely to be cursed as blessed. I'll give you five.'

'Five? Why I've paid f – It's yours for seven.'

'Seven it is.' She pulled a small purse from her low-cut bodice while Lyda swallowed a disgusted snort. 'My mother and I both thank you.'

What did the child mean by that? 'Yes, well. Thank you for your . . . business.'

The girl took a side step to scoot by Willam on her way out, lightly touching his arm. 'Thank you for all your help. I do hope I'll see you again.'

'We're closed,' his wife answered for him, pointedly waiting by the door.

The girl gave both shopkeepers a smile that could have been mistaken for genuine. 'My apologies for keeping you.'

Lyda watched the departing sway of the child's hips, pushing away her own misgivings. Finally, with the latch pulled tight, she turned to her lust-addled husband. 'And as for you . . .'

The forest dripped. Clouds, trees, Jilian's clothes. *Every*thing dripped.

The mercenary examined the wood, hoping for a single dry branch. Useless. She'd asphixiate before getting dry from a fire made of this stuff. Jilian let the kindling fall to the ground, where it landed with a quiet splash. For good measure, she gave the pile a hearty kick, scattering pine and birch twigs. 'Well, Mut, that's what we get for trying to race those rain clouds as if they weren't cursed by . . .' The thought trailed away unspoken.

Digging at the brush behind her, a young dragon the size of a large dog snorted.

'All right, that's what *I* get.' The mercenary crouched with her back against a tree for what little comfort it offered. Absentmindedly listening to Mut and a rare night owl, she grudgingly allowed the rain to win this round. She reached inside her pack. No overlooked pieces of hard cheese or forgotten bits of cured mutton. Nothing.

Well, not quite nothing.

Jilian's fingers brushed against cold metal. She took out a medallion and settled crosslegged on the soaked earth. 'Come over here and take a look at this.'

Silence as he paused in his rooting.

'Unless you've found something better.'

The dragon padded over. Damp leaves and scraps of muddy debris clung to his shaggy fur. Ill-formed wings were pulled back tight against his body. He sniffed at her hands.

Jilian quickly jerked it out of nose range. 'Careful!' she shouted, her voice sharper than she'd meant. 'What if this one can't stand up to dragon spit?'

Mut nuzzled her hand, then ducked his head and peered out from beneath his eyebrows.

She wagged a finger at him. 'Please, not the poor puppy look.'

Mut cocked his head and waited. Laughter shined in his eyes.

'Arrogant animal.' She didn't want the distraction of dragon charm. She'd been preoccupied all day with a stray detail her mind chewed around but couldn't fix on. Jilian stared at the thing filling one palm. Her voice softened. 'Sorry, Mut. The rain just makes me so . . . tired.'

Rain was the least of it. They were out of money, out of food, and out of luck. The relay messenger calling her to Rivertown had seemed the solution for her predicament. A minor noble needed her peculiar talents and would pay well for the service. Jilian set off in an instant, Mut at her side. They arrived two days early, expecting to 'skulk and observe' – as her mentor named it – but they found only charred corpses amidst the ruins of the oldest human settlement in the One Land. The mercenary couldn't say the noble's fate, though fleshless faces would fill her dreams many nights yet. Not one honourable death among the corpses. Not one proper burial. She'd gone a week since without speaking to someone who could answer in a language other than barks and yips.

Jilian scratched Mut behind the ears. The dragon snuggled against her and closed his eyes.

With force of will, she refocused her attention on the medallion. Unable to bear a careful examination of any reminder of Rivertown before now, Jilian felt the weight of the inevitable as she rubbed the soot off the partially wrecked engraving of a dragon's head. She brought the medallion closer to see better in the dark. It had once been round, but it was now warped and curled about the edges, as if subjected to a great heat. Knowing the condition of the razed city where she'd found it, Jilian had no doubt that it had withstood much. Given, too, what she knew of her own smaller token, she was surprised that this one had not come through the searing fire intact.

From a pocket inside her shirt, Jilian withdrew a near mate

to the one already in her hand. This one still showed the full figure of a dragon.

The things seemed to accompany death. She had found hers among the embers of burnt and useless scraps of parchment in what had been her mother's keepsake box. Nothing else survived the fire, including her parents. Orphaned at sixteen when other girls were mothers themselves, Jilian took Mut and joined the Wanderers. They had learned to get by.

Jilian never considered selling the coin despite her hardship. It remained intact against all odds. The fact that her mother owned it whispered of secrets she would risk her life to unravel. That it depicted a dragon when her only constant friend was Mut hinted at unknown but undeniable fate. With a teenage girl's single-mindedness, she spent that summer trying to put a hole in the strange medal so she could run a thong through and tie it around her neck. Hot pokers didn't work; sharp blades couldn't even chisel off a piece. She finally settled on sewing leather pockets to the insides of each blouse and pair of pants. As her clothes wore thin, she painstakingly added a small pouch to every new garment. Jilian came to think of it as her special charm though it never brought her what she would call good luck. Eventually she all but forgot about its particulars the way people do with anything familiar and routine. It was a part of her, like Mut or her knife.

Now Jilian studied it carefully, comparing it to the other. Her own looked freshly minted despite years of handling. Words from a language she didn't recognise – though it seemed a cousin to the low script of the One Land – adorned both sides of each. The two had some words in common, but the one was too damaged to know if the inscriptions were identical.

Still deep in concentration, Jilian felt a sound not quite

heard. She patted Mut's flank. The dragon pressed gently against her leg, confirming a presence in the gloom beyond.

Jilian didn't bow to chasing noisy shadows in the dark. The two made a formidable team and it was easier for Mut to guard her back and let the thieves come on. She might yet find some peace after. The dragon paced the clearing. ''Been a long day, Mut. Let's get some rest.' She made the motions of putting the medallions in her pack, then slipped both into her inside pocket as she spread her sleeping roll.

She lay down on her side, fully clothed atop the blankets. The dragon shifted his weight to stretch out next to her, resting his head on his front claws. With Mut so warm and close against her back, Jilian almost didn't miss her old bed and the quieter times.

She stared into the black, waiting. Heavy clouds covered moon and stars. The rain had stopped, but muffled splats would last until the sun burned high. Under such cover, it would have been easy for a professional to surprise an unsuspecting victim.

Jilian was rarely prey for thieves.

He came from behind her, foolishly risking Mut's teeth over her own defenses. The dragon nipped the attacker's knife arm while Jilian rolled to meet him. She chopped his knife hand and the blade flew across the clearing. Mut bounded after it like a puppy chasing a stick but was all business once he reached it. The dragon calmly put one foot squarely on the handle and looked first to Jilian then the intruder.

The man moved to reclaim the knife and met bared dragon's teeth.

'That's twice on the same arm. I wouldn't cross him if I were you. He tends to get cranky when I send him to bed without his supper.'

The man stepped back and offered a wincing smile. 'So I

see,' he said, without adding any of the usual remarks. No 'What kind of dragon is that' . . . 'no one has a pet dragon' . . . and 'they don't have fur!' Jilian always answered the last statement first by asking, 'So you've seen enough live dragons to know what one looks like?' and thereby cutting off other, more probing questions.

This one didn't seem surprised at Mut. Instead of gawking, he ignored the dragon as he held up his hand for inspection. At this close distance, Jilian could make out a fine cut to his sleeve. He was no commonplace thief – though she'd already known that. The highwaymen would not bother to track a mark in this rain when they could find easier work along the roads.

She paid no attention to the man's overplayed injury as she stooped to ruffle Mut's fur and relieve him of the knife. The dragon had yet to do permanent damage without cause. Jilian straightened, and looking the man in the face, she asked, 'What brings you out here on such a fine night?'

The man let his hand drop. He stood at ease. More, his casual stance suggested he thought the Sisters – or at least the current Shoremen king – guarded his back. 'Looking for you. Wanted to enlist your assistance,' he said.

Jilian didn't like it. She'd known since early childhood not to trust the king's men. They were only good for the next tax collection, and those came all too frequent since no ruler lasted more than a twin-year or so. 'Odd way to ask for help. What am I to do, teach survival classes to the royal ruffles?'

The man reflexively pulled at his cuffs. 'Uh, no.' He licked his lips. 'Actually, we need some protection.'

She lifted one eyebrow – an expression practised to look careless for just such hook-and-bait moments as these. 'Oh?'

'My job was to see if you are, uh, as good as your reputation.'

Her second eyebrow joined the first. Why couldn't they

ever spit out the bad news without the tiresome play-acting? 'And?'

'I'm pleased to say you're quite acceptable.'

'But I didn't say I'd accept the job.' She stared into the grey eyes. 'Are you truly the best the Shoremen can boast?'

'One of the finest, not that flattery will raise your wages.'

He wouldn't have come alone. She needed to discover the strength of the force hiding in the woods. Jilian circled while keeping her knife ready. It was too dark to see well, but there couldn't be many. More than a few men would never have been able to remain silent for so long.

'How'd you know I'm a Shoreman?' he asked.

She saw no harm in answering. Jilian pointed and threw the knife at the ground between his feet. Before he could pretend to recover the wits he hadn't really lost, she snatched up the blade by the handle. 'Your boots. They're not meant for this terrain.'

'What's the matter with them?'

'Walk around long enough and you'll find out.' She sighed. She couldn't believe he thought her foolish enough to be taken in with his performance. 'Enough chat. You were saying you needed protection. What kind? How long? How much?'

'I see they don't teach the finer arts of polite negotiation out here in the wild.'

Jilian studied the knife blade, pulled out a stone to sharpen it. 'No, just survival.'

His right hand twitched a time or two before he slid it into his pocket.

Any more of this and she'd walk, no matter how loud her stomach growled. 'The terms?' she prodded.

He spoke precisely, almost as if he wanted her to know he quoted someone else. 'Half now, half when the job is done. Length of service indefinite.'

Jilian looked down at the dragon. 'Some deal, eh, Mut?' The animal snorted in contempt. With his diet so hard to come by he'd be hungrier than she, but he didn't like the act much either. It reminded Jilian of the heavily spiced meals elves gave human prisoners to hide the tainted food. She turned to the man, her face hard. 'Sir Maarcus the Seventh, I am growing very impatient. Yes, I know your name. I'd have to be a fool not to realize you are one of the most trusted men among those attached to this year's Shoremen king.' She continued without giving him a chance to respond. 'Let's just get on with it. I'll give you one month at my usual rates. I'm sure you know what they are. They're well known throughout what some still call the One Land. Since this is obviously more than the ordinary mission, I expect three-quarters before I stir from this clearing.' Abruptly, she sat on her sleeping pack. The dragon hesitated before he moved to wait by her side. He wanted Jilian to know he thought she'd been rash in her bravado, but joined her in making it plain neither would step foot from their camp until they were ready.

Maarcus made no attempt to bargain. 'I'll need to speak with someone.'

Jilian waved him away, cautiously hoping he only bluffed in order to whittle at her confidence and bring down the price. Peering after him, she saw a glint of metal flash among the trees. She placed her hand lightly on the dragon's flank and together they prepared for an ambush.

Maarcus returned leading a lone elf woman dressed in travelling clothes.

The mercenary stiffened. Her fingers dug into the dragon's side. Mut whined quietly and she forced her hand to relax.

Jilian didn't like elves. Few humans did, but elven magic clouded her battle wits and robbed her balance more than most. Never knowing if the elf were a mage who controlled one of the seven powers, she seldom trusted herself in their overwhelming presence. If their last job hadn't . . .

A man's voice brought her back to the clearing. She shakily rose to her feet and the buzzing in her ears dropped to a hum. 'That won't be necessary,' Maarcus said. Whether directed to her or the elf, Jilian couldn't be sure. He inhaled, then spoke with the air of formal decree. 'We're agreed. Here's your payment.' He tossed the leather bag at her feet, narrowly missing the dragon's head.

Mut growled, but he reached to take the pursestring in his teeth, unknotted it, and held up the open bag. It was one of his favorite tricks.

'Thanks, boy.' She answered the dragon's grin with a pat on his head. Jilian felt her strength and focus return with the familiarity of Mut's fur between her fingers.

While she counted the coins, Maarcus went on. 'You're to guard this . . . *per*son.'

Out the corner of her eye, Jilian thought she saw the elf wince at the reference to person – a strictly human term. No self-respecting elf would ever refer to herself that way.

'And to what destination am I to guard this female?'

Maarcus's smile veiled a darkness, maybe even sorrow. 'Wherever her visions tell her she must go.' He raised his hand to forestall questions. 'That's all I know.' He bowed once to each of them. 'Good night, ladies.' Again the repulsed elf responded with a slight shudder.

'Good luck.' This last to Jilian seemed genuine.

'Luck!' She started to give her usual retort – 'luck plays no part in my life' – but stopped short. Though she wanted to ignore his comment as the ordinary salute from one who underestimated her, she found she couldn't. His closing words were a bad omen. Jilian rubbed her ears, trying to kill the dull drone before it rose back to the buzz and robbed all her attention.

Maarcus could have gone as quietly as he came, but he swaggered into the forest with more noise than Jilian would have thought possible given the recent rain. He sang a rousing and bawdy song to himself, though Jilian had no trouble making out the words. She might almost have thought he sang the refrain for her:

Oh, there once was a maiden, I declare
And she had the fullest, most flowing hair
But what she had beneath it there . . .
Well, she sure was a maiden, I do forswear

Jilian felt strangely lonely as his voice faded. She almost called out to him that he had left the knife, but thought better of it. Someone of his caliber would not have forgotten it. Then, too, she never knew when a fine blade would come in handy – and this one was very well made indeed. She allowed herself the satisfaction of cursing, 'By the Sisters, you'll find your double-headed fate.' Then added, 'Unreliable men!'

Mut barked his disapproval.

'Sorry, Mut. You know what I mean. Come on. Let's see what we can find out from the . . .'

But for the dragon, she was alone in the clearing.

The smoke rose above the trees, foul black, deadly. Walther Shortdwarf followed the river awhile just in case the fire turned his way, knowing the whole time it didn't matter. Beneath the stench his home burned.

The closer he got, the more he feared there would be no one to greet him. 'Nonsense, all nonsense,' he repeated again and again. The stories he'd heard in his travels were just tales to frighten children into behaving. The dead had names, but no clans Walther recognized.

Everyone knew it was a drier season than usual. Fire more

28

of a threat than normal. The children needed more warnings to be careful, that's all.

On impulse Walther left the riverbank so that he could enter the village through the welcome arch. He tried to keep to his hiking pace, but in the end couldn't hold back. He was running full out and breathless by the time he reached the tree marking the official village border. Around the last bend in the trail and to the arch—

He thought he was prepared. How could he have been?

He'd seen the smoke, expected some houses burned to kindling. It was a danger with wood in dry years even though his people were always careful. Being woodworkers and fearful of fire, they had chosen the site overlooking the river in his grandparents' grandparents' time. Had developed failsafes, alarms, drills.

This kind of devastation could not happen. Bells would have clanged. Every dwarf old enough to carry water would have run to their station on the riverbank. It was all as unconscious as eating and as solemn as any important ritual from his own childhood.

And the fire would have been drowned and no one would have been burned or killed or . . .

The entire village, gone. Row upon row, dead. Everything lost – home, family. The maple welcome arch, tended and carved year after year, ashes.

He'd been gone only a month, indulging a little wanderlust now that he was finally old enough to be allowed such things. He'd returned on a fine afternoon. The crispness of fall come a few weeks early lightened his step, made him glad to be home. He found himself whistling a light tune.

Whistling, running, crying through a graveyard.

He ran, fell, picked himself up, and continued running. He ran without purpose or pattern. Looking for some sign, some clue, some life.

The town had been levelled. All their possessions thrown into a heap, then burned. Only traces of smoke and ash remained. On the cliff overlooking the river stood rows and rows of crates built from mountain ash trees. Each housed a corpse, emaciated or bloated, misshapen and tortured. Some not dead more than a few days. Insects and vermin flew and crawled across the bodies. The fire had not touched them.

Walther's stomach rolled and he was sure he would be sick. The stories had not been gruesome enough. He stared and took a deep breath of the strangely sweet air. Without meaning to, he began a silent roll call then stopped when he realized what he was doing. He wasn't ready yet. Much later he'd think back to this quick eyeball count, mark that half the townspeople were missing.

Now he set about looking through the refuse once more. He began at the dust and embers of the arch. This time he wanted to know not just who the intruders were but where they'd gone.

Memories seemed to slip away along with the final black wisps as Walther tried to recollect his happier times. He thought he recalled teasing about his height, but that soured like fresh milk left too long in the sun. The joy and good nature of their jests faded as he passed their ruined homes, leaving nothing but the embarrassment and frustration behind. They'd never meant to hurt him, had comforted him when they'd cut too deep. He knew this as well as he'd known the way home. Here though, amidst the rubble, his heart warred with memories and neither could be at peace.

Until he realized he knew no one with a talent for this kind of evil. In their darkest moments, his friends never would have conceived of such gruesome magic. Walther set his confusion aside. Whatever his panicked mind told him about his past, whatever rumors he had heard, this could not have been magic. He could see that. The people had been locked in crates and left to starve, the town set afire later. All of it bore the mark of the crude meanness of the trolls. Walther shuddered. Even hearing the stories and now seeing the destroyed town, he couldn't imagine what the trolls gained by forcing scores of people to such an end.

Sifting through the dust, Walther at last came across the rubble that had served his own clan for generations. The tall dwarf fell in on himself, echoing the collapse of his home. Utterly alone, he put his head in his hands and sobbed.

They could not do this to his people! They would not do this to him. By the Seven Sisters, they would not get away with it! He sat, shaking with grief and rage through the afternoon.

By the time he'd cried himself dry, the sun had nearly set. In the waning orange daylight, he said goodbye, walking among the rows of dead. After a while, the bodies began to seem all the same. Twisted, anguished, scarred. At the end, he still failed to name them all.

To his shame, he could not stomach traditional burials. He covered his beloved, his friends, and his adversaries with kindling and set them alight. At least he could keep them from the further humiliation of becoming prey to the body scavengers he'd heard of in his travels.

All through the night, Walther watched the flames, beating down any which threatened the dwarves' prized maple forest.

At sunrise, he began one, last, dry-eyed and coldly methodical search of the town's refuse. Somewhere there was a clue to this evil and Walther would find it.

The town had been razed, the sturdy buildings burned to cinders. The intricate carvings of the Maveclan destroyed. The fine pottery work of the Ridgeclan nothing but occasional chunks and pieces. Of the weavings of the Roseclan, a few charred swatches were all that survived.

Walther gathered up the remains of his people as best he could. He found a shovel missing its handle and scooped bits into a heap nearly as tall as himself. Though he couldn't pay the clans tribute with proper funerals, he would show due respect for those things which told who they had been.

The dwarf dug a huge grave, the likes of which he hoped never to see again. Gently he laid in the mound of craftworks one shovelful at a time. It was slow and lonely duty, more devastating to him than disposing the bodies had been. He had allowed himself not to think past the shock; he needed only hand and arm to set the funeral pyre alight. But now he forced himself to remember. The endless teasing of his younger sister and her proud, quiet smile when she mastered a difficult project; parents who enjoyed time with each other and their children; the practical jokes of his friends; even the curse of an enemy who seemed now to have fallen prey with the rest.

Lost in his reverie and not really seeing what he was looking at, Walther almost missed it. At the bottom of his original collection and now about to be the top of the new burial mound was a strange metal medallion. His people did not work metal, but rather traded with nearby towns for the necessary utensils, tools, and arms. This was blackened from a fire of high heat, but there was still faint evidence of an unfamiliar script on one side.

Walther felt heavy but filled with a grim sense of direction as he put it in his pocket for later study. He bent once again to complete his chore. He had the lodestone now. He would find them.

Perhaps an hour later, the dwarf straightened and stepped back to survey his work. He was startled to realize that he had flattened the pile without conscious thought. When the snows came, no one but he would be able to find it.

Chapter 2

PROPHECIES

Roslin sat at the writing table and rolled open the scroll. Her fingers smoothed the ancient parchment with the great care of a blind woman finding her way in unfamiliar lands. A scarce smile spread across her sharp-featured face. The peddler had spoken true: the paper *was* more chart than text. Roslin hadn't offered to tell him of her peculiar passion for maps or her obsession to gain this one in particular. Instead she'd accepted his apologies with a grave 'I understand,' and bargained hard over the price.

The door creaked open behind her. Only Ginni or the child's father could walk through the warding spell so effortlessly and both knew better than to expect her to interrupt her work with an unnecessary greeting. The nauseating smell of ale and raucous sounds of an early evening brawl wafted up from the tavern downstairs. 'The carpet only works when the door is closed,' she reminded the girl without looking up. The door thudded shut and the two were cocooned in silence and the scent of mold and dried parchment.

Still deep in studying the magnificent scroll, Roslin said, 'It's after dark. What happened?'

Ginni sighed dramatically and crossed the small room to plop down on the sagging bed next to the mage's chair.

'Oh, same as all the rest. Doesn't really know anything, but he's good for a few shiny bits.'

Roslin turned to stare at the teenaged girl. 'The money was not part of the plan. You're certain you're not taking this too far?'

Ginni removed a shoe and balanced it on her forefinger. 'Oh, I can't say I'm keeping myself for a prince, but they'd be suspicious if they didn't pay at least enough to buy a meal.' She pulled a face. 'I couldn't bear to kiss such men for free.'

'This is more important than your discomfort.'

Ginni's face darkened. 'Not to worry. I've done as you've asked.'

Roslin looked at the girl, trying to think of an answer that wouldn't open another argument.

The child softened first and offered a cautious grin. 'And I wouldn't bother giving it to men who fall asleep so easily.'

Roslin laughed outright. The map had put her in a very good mood. 'It is a useful potion, isn't it? How did this one go?'

Ginni shrugged, reluctant as always. 'He'll wake content and tickled by a stray hair of embarrassment when he can't remember the details. He can swagger all he wants around the men but he won't risk another try with me.'

Roslin stifled the urge to turn back to the scroll. She wanted information – not this, this disgusting . . . 'Any news?'

Ginni shook her head. 'No. I don't know why we even bother anymore.' She studied her mother. 'Why keep this up? Why not *do* something?'

'You know why,' Roslin said, beginning to lose her patience.

'The unpolished twins,' Ginni quoted. 'What does that mean really?'

Roslin stared down at the scroll, fingering its ragged edges for a long moment before looking back to the girl. Wanton Tom's child would never amount to much without time-consuming training – difficult in ordinary times, and these times were anything but. Still, they could not waste the least resource. Her own great power and middling years would not keep the days from running short, and they would all be tested so very soon.

The girl's foot jiggled, shaking the entire bed. Her finger twisted a strand of hair. The mage silently relented. She could afford a few begrudged hours of instruction with this unruly misfit now that she finally held the legendary map of the Seven Realms.

Roslin set aside the lost charts, drawn in the days preceding the world's crumbling into the One Land and its surrounding neighbors. Perhaps if she started gently so as not to overtax the child . . .

'Before you were born; before I was born; before my mother or her mother was born, we saw this time. The current border wars are only the beginning unless we find the twins. Somewhere there are two who will return the balance. Until we do, it will have to be enough to continue the search.' She paused for Ginni's reaction.

The child watched her tutor with that constant unreadable expression. 'And?'

'And?' Roslin echoed.

'And then what happens?'

'This is not a toddler's bedtime fable,' the mage snapped. 'We don't know what will happen once we find them.' Roslin's jaw tightened to check herself from saying more.

Useless. What had made her insist on retrieving the girl from her sneak thief of a father?

Ginni spoke, her voice barely above a whisper. Sometimes the mage thought the girl lacked the nerve to challenge her own shadow. 'But don't the prophecies say what will—'

'The great sister mages are not common fortune tellers, who spout nonsense of perfect husbands, dutiful children, and long lives.' Roslin closed her eyes. The girl was utterly hopeless. 'So tell me how the last three days have gone while I was away.'

Ginni began to recite as if she were a first year apprentice. 'It's the same story everywhere. Giant trolls, led by a beautiful elf-witch. Some say it's an unstoppable plague, others a curse the villagers brought upon themselves. To a man, none expect the tragedy will find their secluded corner of the One Land.'

'What of the constable?'

'How did you know?' Ginni asked, surprised. 'I didn't know myself that I'd be seeing him today until I chanced upon him this afternoon.' When Roslin didn't answer, understanding dawned. 'You set it up,' she accused.

'I did.'

'But Mother!'

'Don't call me that.'

'Mother,' she repeated pointedly. 'Isn't it enough every river stop in the One Land thinks me a harlot without you confirming it – and probably pulling down the price in the bargain?'

Roslin spared the girl nothing. 'If they think you a whore, then they consider me worse as your whoremonger. It doesn't matter. We seek information, not the high opinion of no account peasants.'

The girl's mouth dropped open in astonishment, but no words fell out.

'Now, again, I would like to hear of your encounter.'

'Very well,' she answered stiffly. 'We met under a dying ash tree on the edge of town. He pawed my bodice and pulled off a button in his eagerness to get inside my dress.'

Roslin frowned, but let the girl go on. Ginni knew this was not what the mage wanted to hear and was purposely baiting her with sordid details.

'I tried to draw conversation out of him, but I could have done better squeezing rain from the cloudless sky. His pig-eyes followed his hands and his ears—'

'You should start with more casual talk. The weather, droughts, floods. Work your way into rumors of the borders.'

'He had no interest in the weather,' Ginni said drily. 'Not even to notice if the ground where he intended to bed me was damp. His two audible words, muttered with increased annoyance as I chatted fetchingly, were, "How much". I was only too happy to brush his lips with the kiss of sleep. The high moment came when a snore escaped his open-mouthed smile before I could lower him all the way to the ground. I would have preferred to leave him choking face first in the dirt, but propped him against the tree. He was worse than a coward,' she added, defensive. 'I couldn't resist patting his clothing until I found his coin purse. I took an additional fee and safely stowed it . . . on my person. Then I hurried home to you.'

'You risked much for a few coins,' Roslin admonished.

Ginni began to pace. 'I have been on the road my entire life – first with you, then Wanton Tom, and back to you. Time runs together – days divided by travel and rest; nights separated by rocks in my back and bugs in my sheets. I am entitled to what little I can gather.' She mimicked the voice of a young, wide-eyed boy she had heard in the tavern as she worked the room. 'No humans have the strength to fight trolls. And giant trolls, so much the worse!'

'The elf-witch,' Roslin prompted, hoping to focus the child on her task. 'What of her?'

She went on in the perfectly pitched falsetto. 'It's all utter nonsense, impending doom. Where can the people go? How can they fight it? Everyone knows all the great magic died long ago in the time of our grandfathers' grandfathers.' Her voice rose higher still as she imitated a street urchin. 'My ma says this one's evil has growed in the telling, is all. Trolls are so terrible they don't need a witch to give 'em twisted idears.'

Ginni's face suddenly grew solemn. 'I wish I could tell someone.'

'Don't even think it!' Roslin shouted, then quieted to a hissed whisper. 'You must never even think it. It invites the worst, makes it the inevitable.' She stood, grabbed Ginni as the girl swung by in her circuit of the room. 'Promise me. You must promise me.'

The girl stopped to stare into her mother's eyes. 'I'm sorry. I'll never say it again.'

'No, more than that. Don't even think it. Promise me.'

She did not answer.

Roslin squeezed the child's shoulders. 'The box, daughter. Open the box, place this thought deep within, and lock it up tight. It is forgotten now until the end of our days.' She loosened her grip. 'Done, yes?'

Ginni nodded. 'I promise.' Her voice sounded sincere.

The mage let go. 'Any word of that . . . your father?'

'No, not yet.'

Roslin ignored the anguished longing in her daughter's eyes. 'Very well. I have work to do.' As she settled into the

38

map, she noted and dismissed the gentle opening and closing of a door.

'Don't get excited, Mut. We know the elf is here somewhere. She's probably just . . .'

The tilt of the dragon's head clearly indicated who *he* thought was distressed.

'OK, let's spread out and . . . Right. Dumb idea when there are only two of us. OK, what do you suggest?'

The dragon looked skyward into the treetops.

Jilian considered this for a full second. 'You think she's up there? Whatever for?'

Mut chose that moment to water a tree on the edge of the clearing.

Jilian burst into laughter. 'I'm convinced.' She called out, 'Come on down, whatever your name is. Fun and games are over.'

The elf woman silently appeared in the lower branches and dropped lightly – too lightly – to the ground. Jilian's panic was replaced by a sinking stomach. Maarcus would have been pleased to give over this one's care to someone else. The elf was more than nobility among her kind. She was a witch, and likely a powerful one.

Jilian sobered immediately. Despite her long-standing fascination with the medallion, it had taken her most of the past ten years to make peace with her own repeated brushes with magic. Even now, she was not altogether comfortable with the truce. Pushing aside her delight at Mut's utterly male display, Jilian forced an outer calm into her movements and leaned down to give Mut a casual pat. 'Good work.'

The elf's face gave away nothing, but she must have detected the human's unease. She gave a solemn nod first to the dragon as if she divined some secret there, then to Jilian.

'You don't look like much but you'll do.' She held out a hand to Mut and snapped her fingers.

'How dare you treat Mut like a common – ' Jilian began when the dragon nuzzled his snout into the witch's outstretched hand. 'Housepet,' she finished lamely.

A genuine smile. 'I'm pleased you've grown nearly as strong as your reputation suggested. It makes this so much more interesting for me.' She nodded her head at someone behind Jilian.

Reluctant to take her eyes off the elfwitch, Jilian only barely caught sight of the huge creature moving in her direction. She didn't need to see it to know what it was. The ground vibrated with the troll's heavy footsteps. He stopped beside the human awaiting further instruction.

A terrible foreboding filled Jilian as she looked up at the largest troll she had ever seen. She forced back the memory of the first time she'd encountered them ten, fifteen years ago. She'd been playing fetch with Mut in the field and smelled the smoke with something ugly underneath . . . Jilian reflexively fell into a fighting stance and prepared to battle the elfwitch.

The witch didn't bother to acknowledge Jilian but spoke directly to the troll. 'Hold her until we're gone. After that –' she shrugged – 'let her go. I can always find her when I need her.'

The troll immediately took hold of Jilian's arm. She yanked it back to see if she might catch the troll unprepared and throw him off balance – they were notoriously stupid – but the beast held her with an unbreakable grip.

The elf stood staring into the forest, seeming to wait until she had Jilian's complete attention. 'I am Alvaria. We will meet again.'

'I'll look forward to it.'

Alvaria smiled again, assured of her power and the

inevitable. With great ceremony, she bent to Mut and lowered her voice. Though the dragon stood close to Jilian, she couldn't make out the words. Shouts of 'Get away from my dragon' were ignored.

The elfwitch stood and waved her arms in a wide circle. A fine mist rolled off her fingertips, thickening instantly and filling the clearing.

Jilian redoubled her struggle against the troll but succeeded only in wrenching her arm. She would have had better results pulling against a stockade. Suddenly the troll released her and retreated back into the forest. The fog disappeared in the next breath.

The witch was gone. The troll was gone. Mut was gone. Jilian was alone with her panic.

She couldn't lose Mut. He was more than her pet and companion, more than the dragon she'd known since birth. He was ... Well, she didn't know what he was exactly despite their years together. None of it mattered now. She had to find him.

She circled the clearing, giving vent to her anger and fear while frantically looking for a clue to their whereabouts. She hated magic. It was an untrustworthy thing, wild and unruly as an orphaned child. It had just spirited away the only companion she'd had for all her life and without so much as a whine of protest from the dragon.

Jilian paced, studying the clearing and the trees ringing its edge. Much to her surprise and setting off her suspicion, there was a trail of broken branches leading back into the forest. Too obvious for the witch and too small for a troll, but definite.

She looked into the night wood for a long time, probing her instincts and measuring her feelings. This path would not lead her to Mut directly, but no route would. The witch would keep a rearguard.

The trail seemed to fade as she stared. A quiet voice murmured to leave it be. She could be on her own. The dragon had left willingly, an ungrateful beast. Jilian argued with the whisper. Mut's behavior made no sense. They'd been inseparable all their lives, and now he'd left without hesitation or warning. It was as if his connection to the elfwitch were even stronger than that to Jilian. Jilian shook her head. After all they'd been to each other, it was inconceivable that another could have a stronger hold.

She must follow the trail. It would bring her back to Mut. The trees seemed to close against her. The voice grew more insistent, speaking of what else this choice might bring her.

But power draws power, magic to magic. Her hand brushed her amulet twice for luck. She ignored the dark warnings and entered the forest to rescue Mut.

The shopkeeper was still yelling in the small hours of the morning. His voice had gone hoarse some time around midnight – a good thing since he'd had several visits from sleepless neighbors not long before that. He kept at his wife still, though his croak was fading to a pained moan. 'Lyda, how could you? We promised t' guard it. We promised.'

Lyda sat with her arms stubbornly crossing her chest. 'Like I said all night, Willam, tell 'em it got stole. Tell 'em we was robbed. It's true in a way. She knew just what she wanted.'

'They'll know it wasn't stole. *He'll* know. He can smell a lie like a cook breathin' bad fish.'

'I don't care anymore, Willam. I just . . . I won't. I can't!' Her face was the hardest he'd ever seen it.

Willam stopped his pacing and sat on the edge of the sleeping pallet which had brought him much joy in years gone by – before the stillbirths, before business fell to its hardscrabble state, before the bracelet. Lyda had loved him well then.

'I had enough, Willam. I lost my babies, I lost my looks, and I lost my money. But I still got what's left of my life and I'm gonna live it if it's a day or a year.' Her expression softened and she bent to gently kiss his cheeks. Her own were wet with silent tears. 'Goodbye, Willam. Good luck.'

He hadn't noticed she'd been packing a large traveling kerchief until she hefted it with one strong arm. His wife of fifteen years walked out the door just as the sun's first rays streaked the sky.

Willam opened his mouth to call her back and found that he had no voice at all.

On the fifth or sixth circuit, Jilian finally admitted defeat. Scratched, exhausted, and annoyed at traveling in an irregular but unbreakable orbit around the clearing, she sat against a tree, closed her eyes, and fell asleep.

Her dreams were instantly filled with visions tinged in red, strange flickering lights and mournful howls. Just before dawn, she woke to find the witch standing over her, humming an ugly, unfamiliar tune. Jilian's head felt full of black spider webs and she couldn't quite remember what she'd been doing for the past several days.

Mut crossed in front of Jilian on his way to sniffing out a rabbit in the bushes. He snatched it in powerful jaws and swallowed it in one gulp. Completely out of character, he had not so much as waved it her way. Seeing him made her world shrink to a tiny focus, as if she were a slave wearing blinders. Her past hours of worry over the dragon blocked out her relief that he had survived. For the flicker of an instant, she imagined him part of a magician's shadowy conjuring.

Suddenly her thoughts were full of an unreasoning anger, the likes of which she hadn't felt since her parents died. Each and every one of her mercenary's nerves jangled with the need to get away from the beast before he turned on her. The fact of his lifelong companionship meant only that she was more vulnerable.

Past and future with Mut collapsed in her mind to become only the *now* of needing escape. At exactly that moment, it no longer mattered whether she ever solved the mystery of Mut's origin. It simply stopped being Jilian's concern.

For his part, the dragon paid her no attention as he rooted under a rock near where the troll stood. His neglect only made Jilian angrier. The sight of the hideous troll sent an involuntary shudder down her spine. The witch struck an odd complement to the other two. The entire lot of them was disgusting. Flesh and brain both recoiled. She needed to leave. Now.

Jilian moved to stand. Nothing happened. Leg, arm, back muscles, all felt flabby from disuse. An unseen weight bound her to the tree and kept her from sliding to the ground.

The elf snapped her fingers and Mut walked stiffly to her side. She looked down to address the human. 'The king's man was misinformed. I won't be needing your services after all. I have what I need, but you can keep the money.' She laughed, a sharp unpleasant sound. 'I won't miss it.'

Jilian struggled to clear her head. *King's man, money. The money.* The weight of a pouch tripped a memory of Maarcus, but she couldn't fathom where the witch entered into the transaction. When nothing else came to her, the need for freedom and food won out. What did the job matter if she'd completed it and had the payment in hand?

Again she focused on the witch, who was patting Mut's flank with the familiarity of an old friend. 'Thank you for your excellent services. I'll be happy to recommend you to my associates.'

Another shiver of revulsion, but discipline held. Elves and

trolls and dragons naturally repulsed humans; Jilian often felt the same way about her customers. These were worse than most, but it was only a matter of degree.

The witch turned to the troll, said something in elven too quickly for Jilian's muddled brain to understand. Then in human, 'I am Alvaria. We will meet again when the twin moons are full.'

The name tolled a distant bell. 'Alvaria? Twin moons?' Jilian began to ask, but the witch had already turned to face the opposite edge of the clearing. She ignored the human as she conjured a thick mist. It clung to clothes and smelled of festering wounds. Jilian quickly lost her appetite for questions. She wanted to be away, anywhere else but here.

She tried once more to get up. The muscles tensed beneath her leather pants, but her legs were still too weak to support her. Jilian redoubled her efforts.

By the time she finally succeeded in pulling herself to her feet, the mercenary's face dripped with sweat and her thighs quivered. Her legs held only a moment then collapsed beneath her. As she fell into the nothing of unconsciousness, she realized the mist had cleared.

Jilian came back to herself in full daylight at the foot of a tree – which now seemed to be more than a tree. The elfwitch, her troll and the dragon were hours gone.

She tested her feelings about Mut: found them a jumble of confusion. Her ears buzzed. Relieved at the excuse, she set aside the dilemma of Mut for now.

The mercenary turned about, seeing her surroundings in sunlight for the first time. An odd trail all but beckoned to her and she wondered if this had been the way the Shoremen king's man had gone. Suddenly she knew Maarcus was her link to unraveling the twisted road she'd happened upon. Without hesitation, she plunged into the wood.

She could have sworn the branches softened to allow her passage.

Once the fire had burned down, Walther doused the embers with water from the river then half-heartedly shoveled dirt over the remains.

Whenever he thought back on it, he wondered how he'd managed. From the moment he first saw the destruction, his mind had fallen into a sort of fugue. He did what any of his people would have done, but he'd never be able to recall the details without powerful magic.

Walther had meant to follow his destiny on foot, but found himself staring down at the river. Runoff from all the rain made the river wild and gave a focus to Walther's anger and grief. Though he'd avoided river travel since childhood, water and man seemed newfound soulmates. Not altogether under control himself, he scrambled down to the riverbank carrying the worn pack.

Most of the boats were beyond repair, but a few of the larger ones looked serviceable. He picked the smallest of these and set about tightening this knob and that handle to assure himself she was in fact seaworthy. The dwarf wasn't much of a sailor, but the work felt good after his earlier labors. As sunset closed in, he put down the wrench, examined the boat fore and aft, and pronounced her as sound as she was going to get.

Still Walther couldn't bring himself to leave. His stomach rolled. He paced two steps up, two steps back. The dwarf looked over the side at the roiling water below and suddenly decided to search the other boats for tools and supplies.

Afraid of ending up in the river and being carried away with the raging current, he passed by the vessels which seemed closer to sinking than sailing. He checked a few others, but discovered nothing helpful. All the up and down, on and off rocking decks had his stomach doing strange unsettling things. Walther was beginning to rethink the advantages of simply leaving the way he had come as he stood in front of the last boat tied to the dock.

She was beautiful, much too large for him to work alone, but well-cared for certainly. Even now, the trim seemed to shine from a recent polishing. If there's anywhere I might find something useful, he thought, this is it. So he heaved himself aboard.

And slipped on the freshly waxed deck.

'You should be more careful,' came a high-pitched voice.

Walther moved to sit up and came face to face with a miniature crossbow held by a very short female dwarf. No, not just short. The dwarf was still a child.

He scooted back, but the girl moved closer until his head smacked against the side he'd just climbed over. Eyes on the child, he whispered, 'If you let go of that, who will take care of you?'

She giggled. 'Doing OK so far.'

Walther nodded, carefully, so he wouldn't startle her into letting loose the arrow. 'True enough.' He needed to disarm her, but he didn't want to hurt her – or find himself impaled by accident. 'Doesn't that make your arm tired?'

The girl tried to make her chubby, ash-smeared face look tough. 'My daddy taught me and I been practisin'. No tricky stuff,' she warned.

'Oh, no. No tricky stuff.' Tricky, one of his goddaughter's favorite words. Could she have survived? 'Ceeley? Celia Sailclan, is that you underneath the mud and rags?'

'Rags! This is my birthday dress!' To Walther's relief, she lowered the crossbow to show off her now filthy dress. 'Unc' Walther, that you? Where you been? You missed my six year birthday party. Your sister Rea was there. My mommy and daddy were there. Your mommy and daddy were there.

Everyone was there.' Her round face tightened at a new thought. 'Were you with *them*?'

The way she said 'them' confused him. 'Them? I don't even know who "them" is!'

'What 'bout Shoremen?' she asked. ''Been with any of them?' Her face held more suspicion than he would have considered possible.

He nodded. 'Some, here and there. Not enough to amount to the talk we're having now.' He peered hard at her face, not ready to believe even one dwarf had lived through the massacre. 'Celia Sailclan, that is you, isn't it?'

'Of course it's me,' she said. She slapped an open hand to her chest, proud to be recognized. 'And I'm six! It was my birthday when they . . . We were playing a game.'

'What game? Bucket Brigade? Hide and Peek? Wood Whittle?' he asked quickly, before she had a chance to think about the fate of the others.

There was a long silence interrupted only by the sound of the river against the hull. 'I can't remember,' she answered in a very tiny squeak, but she didn't cry.

'Oh well, doesn't matter,' he told her with forced cheerfulness. He stood, brushed off his trousers. 'Ready to go?'

'Go where?'

'After the villains, of course!' As if a girl her age had any business on such a mission. As if he had any idea how he would find them. But he had to go and he couldn't leave her here all alone.

'I can't.'

'You can't? Well you sure can't stay here. What if they come back?'

Her face went suddenly fierce and she knelt to pick up the crossbow. 'I hope they do.'

Too tired to realize what he was doing, Walther conjured a vision of Ceeley fighting off invading hordes. Distortions gave the picture a comic feel that made them both laugh.

'Hey, how'd you do that?'

The vision disappeared abruptly. 'Can you keep a secret?'

She gave him a six-year-old's look of disdain. One hand on her hip, she said, 'I don't think the rocks or the river will listen to me, do you?'

Walther's voice was serious. 'Never discount nature. It knows more than you think.' He held a breath then let it out very slowly. 'You would have found out soon enough since we'll be traveling together – we *will* be traveling together, won't we?'

She nodded her agreement, probably more to get him to tell her his tale than anything else. Walther didn't care. He desperately needed to talk to a fellow dwarf, even a child.

He fell into a storyteller's voice that seemed to carry the legends of the ages. 'Somewhere, wa-ay back in the family tree, there was an elf. But not just any elf. *This* elf was one of the most respected magicians of his – or any – time.

'It has always been believed that dwarves cannot, um . . .' He considered his young audience and realized she must know something about breeding animals. He continued, 'it's always been believed that elves can't have babies with humans or dwarves, but *some* of us know this is not completely true.

'Every so often, a member of the Shortdwarf clan displays a wi-ild elven talent.' The dwarf waved his arms above his head and Ceeley jumped back, out of his reach. 'It's rarely dangerous,' he assured her. 'But – ' he paused for effect – 'it's very, very possible that the Shortdwarf magician won't be able to control his power.'

He stooped down level with the child. 'After all, who is there to train a dwarf in magic?'

'I know who—'

'We've always kept it a secret.' He held his finger to his lips and shook his head to remind her not to tell anyone.

'But I know who . . .'

'That's really sweet, honey, but—'

'No, really!' she said with all the patience she could muster. 'I know who can teach you magic stuff. He'll be here soon. Honest.'

'How would you know an elf-mage? You've never even left our village, have you?'

Ceeley answered the first question while ignoring the second. 'Oh, he's not a elf, or a mage . . . 'Least, I don't think so. He's all human . . . I think.'

Twice the uncertainty. It worried Walther. Then again, it made him think of the one human town he'd seen in his travels. He'd come across the village on a holiday with everyone dressed in their finest. Not too different from his own childhood, the boys teased and chased the girls. The festive ribbons in the girls' long hair flew behind as they ran away, calling their own taunts. The vivid memory materialized unbidden and quickly faded. 'And how do you happen to know a human?'

'We're, um, friends. Could you bring that back?'

There was an unmistakeable lilt to 'friends'. 'OK, I'll bite. Why is your friend coming here?'

She dug her toe into the boat deck. 'Well, I, uh, asked him to. Could I see the girl with ribbons again? Please? She looked a little like my mom.'

'She wasn't your mother; she was my first sweetheart,' he answered without thinking. Before she could start pumping him on that particular topic, he added, 'No, I won't tell you about her. It was a long time ago. And quit changing the subject. Now about this human, he's coming because you asked him and being the good little human he is . . . ?'

'Silly Uncle Walther. He'll come because he just does.' She shrugged her shoulders and looked toward the forest opposite where the torture cages had been before he set them afire.

This was not getting him anywhere. Celia acted as if she expected him to do as she pleased. Worse, Walther found himself wanting to talk to her as if she were an adult. It wasn't just the episode with the tiny crossbow, though he supposed that must have started the notion she could care for herself. He forgot her age altogether when he saw such maturity and pain lingering in her eyes and on her brow. Ceeley had seen something perhaps even worse than the horror he had come home to. She must have been there, hiding and hoping all the while.

Exasperated with himself and the child, he finally said to her back, 'Look, that boat is ready.' He pointed to the one he had prepared though she didn't turn around to see him do so. 'I'm going to set sail, shove off, *leave*. You're welcome to join me or not.' He made motions to depart and hoped she wouldn't catch him in his bluff. He had no intention of leaving her here. It would be plain out wrong. He simply couldn't do it.

She laughed aloud and his heart sank. Walther had forgotten how easily Ceeley and his sister Rea read him. The best friends never hesitated to let him know they were onto his game. He longed to ask about Rea, but instead said, 'Something funny?'

Celia waved a finger at him. 'One. That boat won't get much past the dock. Rotten wood. I know 'cause it's my other uncle's.' She lowered her voice. 'And my aunt is always yelling at him. He never takes care of anything, 'specially his boat.'

Her middle finger joined the first. 'Two,' she wagged, '*I*

am a much better sailor than you. This boat was my daddy's.' Her face lit with obvious pride in her father. 'He's the best sailor ever.'

'And three,' she said triumphantly, forgetting to shake her finger at him, 'there's Uncle Maarcs!'

Chapter 3

DECEPTIONS

The illusion of welcome faded quickly. A few steps in and Jilian found herself mired in the underbrush, pulling loose from another choke-holly. 'Looks like we've walked hip-deep into another witched-cursed lot, Mut.' She reached down for a reassuring pat on his coarse fur, but spiked leaves reminded her the dragon no longer dogged her heels. She slapped at the holly branch and it sprang back to smack her open palm.

In motion without thought, the mercenary yanked her knife from its leg-sheath . . . only to realize she held an unfamiliar blade over an unarmed bush.

Slowly her confusion of the past hours lifted and she finally understood what her heart had known all along. The elfwitch had clouded more than the clearing when she departed. Jilian's mind had been the true target of the magical mist – and the trolls' own guess what it had done to Mut.

Jilian stood as stiff as a battle-chipped statue in the Shoreman capitol. Her hand still hefted a strange knife, the one belonging to Sir Maarcus. She stowed it, grateful no one had seen her foolish display, and rubbed a hand across her face to focus her thoughts.

Something stunk beneath the prettified air around Sir Maarcus, and she'd bet her boots he produced some of the stench. He had no business brokering with elves, not with the border wars heating up.

To be sure, she would find the witch and free Mut – and she had a hunch a talk first with a certain beruffled human would speed the rescue. Maybe she'd go so far as to convince Maarcus to come along. She could always trade him later to win Mut's release if need be. She tapped the knife strapped to her thigh and grinned. The blade was no more than a downpayment for the trouble he'd caused her.

Jilian studied the forest for a sign of his passage. His thrashing about must have left . . . There, a heel print in the still soft ground. Not much farther, a bit of brown cloth hung from a broken twig at waist height. Jilian had her bearings now.

She moved quietly and ever more quickly toward Maarcus. The trailmarks were tiny, insignificant, spaced so that anyone less stubborn or careful would soon be lost. They never failed to appear whenever she might be tempted to quit. A snapped branch, a piece of rag no bigger than her fingernail, the impression of boot toe, each in its turn a taunt to keep her going.

Jilian fell into his rhythm. She still didn't trust him, but she began to feel stirrings of interest despite herself.

By late afternoon, she topped a rise and heard water rushing below. Green and blue ridged mountains aflame with the colors of autumn stretched in every direction. A sharp breeze hinted at the first snows only weeks away now. She sucked in deep breaths and allowed herself to get lost in the wondrous view, momentarily at peace.

A wisp of smoke tainted with a foul odor arose from across the riverbank. Jilian forced down bile. This was her destination. Maarcus was here.

Celia jumped up and down, waved and shouted, 'Hello, hello! Uncle Maarcs, where've you been?'

Which was, Walther noted, a much more enthusiastic version of the same question she had asked him.

The human's greeting was a fatherly peck on the cheek. Walther almost approved until the man picked up the child and swung her in a wide circle as she squealed with delight. Maarcs planted her back on the plank dock, which in turn swayed sickeningly with their movement. 'Sorry, honey. I had a few unexpected detours.'

Walther didn't like the sound of *that* and he couldn't fathom how the pair had come to be so friendly to begin with. He had to talk to this human after Ceeley went to bed.

'When do I get to meet the elf-person?'

'Don't ever let her hear you call her that, Ceeley,' he admonished gently. 'She doesn't like it.'

'*You* call her that.'

'I have indeed now and then – and it may yet cause me trouble.' Ceeley's smile showed more skepticism than remorse, but the man let it go.

'Where is she? Is she hiding?'

'I don't know about the elf. I think something's . . . changed.' His voice trailed off and a troubled expression flashed across his face.

'But you said she liked dwarves.'

Ignoring Ceeley's puzzled look, Maarcs said, 'But I think a woman with a dragon will be here tomorrow. Sooner if she's as good as her reputation.'

'Tomorrow? A woman? What kind of woman? Does she really have a dragon?'

'A human kind. She had it when I saw her last. Cute little dragon about the size of a really big dog.' He held his hand out to indicate the height. 'A little taller than you, Ceeley, but probably shorter than – ' He turned to Walther, but no one moved to make introductions.

Celia struggled to keep a grown-up face but finally blurted, 'Where are they?'

Walther could just see someone coming through the trees over the rise. 'Is that her?' He pointed.

'Couldn't be . . .' Maarcus started, but twisted around to follow the dwarf's hand. When he faced Walther again, he seemed awfully pleased. 'Quicker than I'd expected, but yes, that's her.'

She picked her way carefully, her nose and face wrinkled with disgust. Once on deck, she made no attempt at a greeting. 'That's the worst smelling cookfire I've ever had the displeasure to witness. You people burn garbage for dinner?'

Walther looked at Maarcs. 'Came in from upwind, didn't you?'

Again the brief worried frown, but he nodded.

The dwarf addressed the newcomer. 'It's worse from downwind, miss . . . ?'

'Jilian. The name is Jilian.' She folded her arms across her chest. Her face dared him to call her anything else.

He spoke with mock graciousness as he introduced the group. 'Pleased to meet you, Jilian. This is Celia Sailclan. I am named Walther Shortdwarf and you apparently know this . . . person. That awful smell is my friends and family.' He paused. 'Recently murdered.'

The horror on Jilian's face instantly gave way to understanding. 'So they've been here too,' she said under her breath.

'You've seen this before!' Walther and Ceeley shouted.

'Upriver from here. Before I met up with him – ' her voice

made it clear how low she considered the other human – 'and his elf stole my dragon.'

'Uncle Maarcs, why'd the elf-person take the lady's dragon?' Ceeley asked.

The man sighed. He suddenly looked very tired and rather ill. 'It's a long story and it's not stolen . . . I hope.'

'Where are they then?' Jilian demanded.

'I'm not sure, but I have a few guesses.' He tipped his head toward Ceeley and said with false cheerfulness, 'Why don't we all get going? We can talk once we're underway. Everything stowed aboard?'

'No,' answered Walther and Jilian in unison.

'No? Then let's get ready.' His voice, though still bright, held a note of polite steel, making it clear he was accustomed to obedience.

'Why such a hurry?' said Jilian.

'You came alone? No witch? No dragon?' he asked her.

Jilian's head bobbed once, curt, angry. Her fists were curled tight. 'So?'

'So it's a longer story than I wish to tell here. We'll be more comfortable away from this.' When no one moved, he added, 'I'm sure we'd all prefer to hear the tale *up*stream.'

'Let's go!' Ceeley shouted. 'I want to hear a story! Come on everybody.' She took up position at the wheel and waited for the rest to find their places.

Walther didn't trust this Maarcs. He must be using Ceeley as a cover for another purpose. Then too, the man's dealings with the human woman left the dwarf feeling as unsettled as his discomfort over the rocking dock.

Just the same, Walther was eager to leave the nightmare behind and he hoped it couldn't hurt to obey the human in just one thing. 'I guess I'll go get my things,' the dwarf said to no one in particular.

'I'll help! You'll get done sooner.' Celia jumped up again. Walther nodded without speaking and waved to the child to join him.

Jilian watched the dwarves leave, feeling Maarcus's presence heavy beside her. Out of the corner of her eye, she could see that his posture was easy and relaxed. His mouth twitched as he tried to hold back a smile. Jilian waited in an oddly companionable silence until she caught herself. Appalled at her willingness to like this man, she exploded. 'What could possibly be funny? We're standing here watching two strangers walk away into unknown dangers while we all inhale the remains of . . . of an entire town!' She turned to look at him full on, her face hardened with accusation. 'I followed you through the weirdest trail I've ever seen and you, *you* helped that, that *witch* steal my dragon!' She let loose and kicked his shin with enough force to knock over most men—

And immediately regretted it. Without knowing Maarcus's sympathies, she risked unnecessarily angering an enemy – or alienating a powerful ally. The elfwitch had chosen Mut, in particular, and getting him back would not be easy. Maarcus wasn't just a convenience; she needed his help. She loathed the thought, had refused to consider it before now, but the truth glinted like sun in her eye. She seldom allowed herself to lose control and she would not do it again with this man.

Maarcus relaxed his fighting stance once he saw that her assault had been spent. He bent to examine his leg. His fingers probed briefly as if to assure himself that the injury was no more than a likely bruise. When he straightened, his face had lost all of its earlier humor. 'You will never do that again.'

He said no more. He didn't have to. His eyes, his mouth, his complete being told her that the next time she crossed him one of them would die.

The mercenary who had fought many and killed not a few tried to hold his gaze, but couldn't. 'I'm sorry,' she mumbled. 'I got carried away.'

He shrugged. His forgiveness was easy and apparently genuine. 'Under the circumstances, it's almost expected.' She burned with the humiliation of his dismissal until he added, 'Even for you.'

They stood, studying each other. For the first time, Jilian really looked at Maarcus. She'd known from the beginning that he was more than he appeared. Now it seemed there was yet another layer of disguise beneath that other. Jilian's interest moved up a notch. He was proving to be much more of a puzzle than she'd anticipated.

His voice broke into her thoughts. 'That was quite a difficult trail.'

Jilian returned his smile with a proud one of her own. 'I know.'

He held out his hand. 'Truce?'

She clasped his hand in her own and shook it once. 'Truce,' she answered sincerely. It was only after she spoke that she wondered what exactly she had agreed to and who owed fealty to whom.

Ceeley skipped along the dock, pulling and hurrying Walther. 'Come on, Uncle Walther. Come *on*! We're going t'miss the story.'

Walther smiled to himself at Ceeley's energy. 'Oh, I don't think he'd start without us, do you?'

Celia stopped short to consider. 'Well he might. We don't want to take the chance, do we?'

The kid had a point there. He nodded. 'OK, race you!' He set off at a slow run.

The giggling dwarf ran beside him until they reached the boat owned by Ceeley's lazy uncle. At the last moment, he slowed to let her pass him and jump aboard.

'I win! I win!'

'You win! You win!'

She collapsed in a laughing heap.

He told Ceeley, 'My things are in the cabin. Be right out.' He left the child to catch her breath while he gathered his spare belongings. That chore quickly done, he picked up his ragged pack, but he still didn't feel ready to leave. Thinking he was forgetting something useful, or perhaps just stalling the inevitable river travel, Walther gave the room a last onceover.

It was on the floor in the corner, a medallion similar to the one he'd found in the town's wreckage. The dwarf stood, listening to the blood pounding in his ears. This had not been here before, had it? Could he have missed it?

Behind him, Ceeley called, 'Come on, Unc. What's taking you so long?' She came running and bounc'ed into the back of his legs. 'Uncle, you OK? Uncle?' When Walther still didn't answer she came around to see what held him. At the edge of his vision, he watched her follow his line of sight to the coin.

'They were here! They were here. They came back. You brought them back!'

Her voice was filled with hate. 'It's your fault. You went away and then they came.'

'Ceeley, honey . . .'

'Stay away from me!' She took two steps backward and slipped. Her rump hit the floor first, then her head. Hard. Her body went limp.

Walther panicked. 'Celia? Celia! Oh, not you too. Celia!'

He bent to help, but she came to at his touch on her arm. Her child's big eyes went wider.

'You were there. I know it.'

'No, honey, I wasn't. I was . . .' What could he say? I was out being irresponsible while everyone I've ever known and loved was being tortured and killed? No, he couldn't, but maybe he should have.

'You were there. You saw the trolls. Horrible, huge and hateful.' Her voice took on a strange rhythm, as if reciting a clan legend. Her eyes fixed on the medallion beyond Walther. 'You saw the elfwitch in the distance waving her arms, laughing when we cried. You saw everyone running, screaming, hiding. You saw the trolls find us all. You saw the trolls send us all to the river where the cages waited. You heard us scream, terrible, terrible screams. You counted the minutes, minutes only and we were . . . We were dead.' She turned away from him, curled into herself, and began to sob.

Walther spoke softly, trying to soothe and calm. 'But honey, you're here. It'll be OK. I promise. I'll protect you. Celia?' He reached out to smooth her hair.

She flinched. 'Don't ever touch me!' With that, she got up and ran past him and off the boat. 'Uncle Maarcs! Uncle Maarcs! He's trying to kill me. *Un-cle Maarcs*!'

Her voice echoed in Walther's heart, each cry of 'Uncle' pounding guilt deeper. Under his hand lay the hated coin. Repulsed but unable to ignore a growing pattern, he picked it up.

It was almost too hot to hold and very heavy. He imagined the weight of all the village forged into the metal. The dwarf wrapped it in a kerchief and dropped it into his pocket. He pulled himself to his feet, hefted the pack onto his shoulder, and climbed over the rocking side to the swaying dock.

Ahead Celia reached the two humans. She waved her arms wildly but the wind carried her words away from him. She looked like a mechanical doll gone out of control.

The dock stretched before him, barren and lonely. Walther took a shaky step forward.

Wanton Tom filled the doorway of the dingy pub. The gloom blinded him after the bright mid-day sun, so he waited – blocking the only exit – until his eyes adjusted. Notoriety had its drawbacks and this tiresome display was one of them.

After his face had begun to appear on posters now and again, foolish challengers started seeping from the nooks and crannies of every place like this. It finally got so bad, he couldn't enjoy a lousy mug without cracking a chair over the heads of a couple of the get-rich-quick cowards who hung in the tavern rafters. Weary of paying for broken furniture – and the locals always charged Tom – he devised the scheme of barring the way out in plain view of all. When the dragonbait moved in on him, they would find the former soldier armed and not as taken by surprise as they had hoped. He could easily finish the uneven scuffles outside if it came to it. Eventually word had spread. Few risked their necks anymore.

Tom scanned the room that was twin to plenty of others. Rough wooden tables stood amidst rough wooden benches. A handful of scraggly humans crouched over their drinks.

(Other times it was dwarves or elves, but seldom an easy mix of the three. On second glance, make that no *scraggly* elves. Even down on their luck, elves always put in a refined appearance.)

The keg housing the tavern's best ale would be watered to the point he'd almost rather drink his own piss. Almost.

Tom found a solitary three-legged stool in the corner. Leaning against the wall, he surveyed the crowd through half-lidded eyes. No one special. A couple of farmers escaping their wives. A traveller in mud-covered cloak. He'd come from high country then. They'd been cursed with a summer of floods while the rest of the One Land shriveled and burned.

A tall boy lay draped over a table. The barmaid came to swipe at the dried food and mug rings. She poked at the snoring boy and whispered something in his ear which made him smile without opening his eyes.

Tom grinned to himself at the imagined tryst and waited for the wench to come see to his needs, but she went back to arranging dishware. Instead the boy got up, stretched, and swaggered to the nearest table.

'Sweetheart, a mug of your finest for my new friend.'

The barmaid paid him no attention.

Tom sighed, bored. The mercenary had long since grown used to all manner of people trying to grease the road to his good graces in contrast to those trying to capture him for the king – though they were not uncommonly one and the same. 'I pay for my own. Go away.'

'It'll be some time before you get any service from that girl.' He laughed, then said to Tom in a conspiratorial whisper, 'I hear you're looking for someone.'

'Were it the case, I assure you that you would be useless in finding this someone.'

'Don't judge so quickly. Many surprises come from modest circumstances.' The boy lit a small flame that flickered in his palm then died.

Tom placed the stool back on all threes and leaned in close. 'What do you want?'

'Just a moment of your time, Sir Wanton Tom.' The boy's eyes sparkled with a familiar intensity.

Tom gave a short nod. Not even the most observant would have caught the signal. 'Very well, but make it quick. This barmaid's so slow I haven't had the chance to douse my thirst.'

'I've got much better where we're going.'

'Do you now? And how did you come by it? One of your mother's tricks, no doubt.' Even here, Wanton Tom couldn't keep the disdain out of his voice on the word 'mother'.

'My mother is quite talented, it's true. But no, I came by this on my own. After you, Sir Wanton.' The boy stepped back to allow Tom to preceed him through the door. Outside, he slapped the outlaw on the back with a great show of hearty cheer then linked his arm in the other's. 'This way,' he said leading him in a drunken stumble around a corner and up a flight of back stairs.

Once inside, Tom closed the door tight behind them. The boy leaned against the wall and laughed silently. When he could not contain the noise, he bit a knuckle and slid to the floor still quietly laughing.

Wanton Tom looked from the boy who was in truth a girl to the woman sitting at a table covered with a map and the magical tools of her trade. 'I suppose you put her up to this.' It was the most cordial words he could summon. These days, Tom never bothered to greet the woman who had borne his daughter.

'Of course not,' Roslin answered. 'I don't have time for such creative nonsense. I've got work to do.'

Tom mock bowed. 'Pardon me. I mistook you for a woman with a sense of humor. Must have been someone else I knew once.'

Roslin let him see her wince. In a very quiet voice, she answered, 'That was before the war, Tom.'

'That was before a lot of things.' He regretted the words instantly, but Wanton Tom was too proud to take them back. Better to change the subject. 'You're right. There's a lot to do. What can you tell me?'

'I've stayed inside mostly and let Gin do the leg work.'

'You're letting our daughter – !' he exploded.

'Tom . . .'

'Mister Wanton Tom, sir. It's the only way, sir,' came the sure and quiet voice, teasing him again, from across the tiny room.

Tom turned to Ginni. She had transformed herself back into a girl in the brief time he had been speaking with her mother. Ginni curtsied, graceful and perfect. 'Father, I know what I'm doing.' Her face, hands, posture, all her being showed strength, power, a sense of purpose.

The two had agreed years past that she would call him 'Uncle'. It let others believe what they would with fewer complications. To this day she only used 'Father' when the situation was of utmost seriousness. And when Ginni took on the tone she used now, she would not be denied.

Tom felt disgusted at himself. His daughter turned him to bread dough in an instant. Her intelligence and looks were no comfort. The talented ones just got into deeper trouble. Just like her mother.

He sat on the edge of the bed. 'All right. What have you heard?'

Ginni came to sit next to him. With the excitement only the young can find in such work, she launched into her story.

'We've been traveling, watching, asking a question here and there. I've been at this pub every day for a week.' Before he could interrupt, she added, 'Fretting doesn't become you, Uncle Tom. I'm not always the boy. Twice I was a barmaid. The owner doesn't care as long as the ale is served. He abuses all equally.' He opened his mouth to ask about this abuser, but she hurried on. 'The regular girl thinks me odd, but she doesn't mind the free hours. And I give her most of my tips.'

His scowl deepened.

'Don't be such an old man. She wouldn't trust me if I didn't keep some. Anyway, it's more than she makes all day. She's too lazy by half, as you may have noticed. She never did ask your pleasure or bring you a pint.'

'And she didn't know the boy was you?' he asked in disbelief.

Ginni answered him matter of factly. 'You didn't know it was me at first. Why should she? Can I get on with my story now?'

Wanton Tom knew when he'd been beaten. His willful daughter had given him plenty of practice. He nodded. Maybe he was getting old.

'It's the same always. Huge trolls run rampant and unstoppable, village destroyed by fire, bloated corpses in cages. Often a tall woman, an elf maybe, seen through the trees or on the edge of the blaze.' She held up her hand to forestall questions. 'But here's the interesting part. There is always one or two spared to spread the tale. Always, one or two not quite old enough or young enough or sharp enough to be believed.'

'But who can spread the terror like the most subtle poison,' added Roslin.

'And that,' said Tom, 'may be her most potent weapon.' He sat quietly. Finally, with the great respect with which one addresses a powerful mage, he asked Roslin, 'What does she want?'

Roslin, feared magician in her own right, mother of his child, stared above his head at the door and did not answer.

Walther took the last steps to the boat with trepidation. He'd lost her, the one survivor linking him to the tragedy. His desire for revenge suddenly seemed pointless and impossible to carry out.

He could hear Ceeley gasping and sobbing between

stuttered words as she told the humans what they'd found. Maarcs' deep voice made soothing sounds, promising over and over that it wasn't a dwarf's doing, while Jilian 'there there'd' in her higher pitch. Together the two formed a surprising and unusual harmony that even Walther's unmusical ear could detect. He let the sounds wash over him.

The rushing river drew his attention and drowned them out. He'd thought he might be able to manage water travel on his own by resting through the worst bouts and letting the boat drift. After he found Ceeley, he remained the adult leading the charge. His adopted niece would not have questioned him – or at least would not have humiliated him. But he'd never be able to hide it from the humans. They would expect his help. They would surely be watching him and the truth would come out. He already felt sick from watching the white-capped water hurling past.

They'll throw me over the side rather than keep such a useless wretch on board, he thought glumly. And then, where will Ceeley be? he answered himself. Ceeley, who hated him, abandoned to strangers.

Jilian looked up at him over the top of Maarcs's head, as the man bent to comfort Celia. She stood motionless, waiting for Walther to return her gaze, then she turned back to the child.

The human woman had done no more than acknowledge him, but Walther felt a challenge. The evil thing in his pocket weighed in a taunt of its own. Ceeley's crying, calmed to sniffles at last, held its own accusation.

He ignored the river and steeled himself. Whether pride, stubborness, or the need to protect his own moved him forward, he couldn't have said. One foot aboard, he said, 'I tried to explain to her, but—'

Maarcs waved him to silence. 'The child's exhausted

herself. We can talk after I've put her to bed.' He picked up the sleeping girl and gently carried her inside the cabin.

Walther looked to Jilian, but she had gone to the opposite side railing. Her back to him and head down, she seemed withdrawn, troubled.

The wind suddenly gusted with enough force to bow the trees along the riverbank. With it came the stench of the devastated town, burning his eyes and nose. The dwarf felt his stomach roll with the boat. Walther closed his eyes to gather his strength and waited for it to pass.

'Evil wind . . . Twice-cursed tempest . . .'

'Jilian?' Walther asked, focusing once more on the woman. She stood as before, closed in. He thought he saw her waving her arms in small circles in front of her, but couldn't be sure. 'Jilian, did you say—'

'She's as safe as a newborn tight in her mother's arms.' Maarcus returned, grimacing at the smell. He pulled a fine handkerchief from his pocket, then changed his mind and put it back. The human woman turned and he motioned her over. 'I was going to suggest we discuss this discovery of Walther's while Ceeley's asleep, but I think we'd do better to get her away from the reminders.'

Jilian started to protest – 'That witch still has my dragon . . .' – but trailed off. She seemed to change her mind and nodded agreement. Her abruptness left the dwarf ill at ease, though it satisfied Maarcs.

'We're agreed, then. Jilian, you . . .'

Another gust rocked the boat and the dwarf saw the world dissolve to gray-white. He tried to find a focus to smother the queasiness. OK, Walther admitted to himself. Destiny was not back there in the ashes. Destiny was . . . shouting at him in the voice of a human male.

'Walther! Shortdwarf!'

'Oh, uh, Maarcs . . .'

'You all right?'

'Well, uh . . .'

'Never mind. I don't want to know right now. Just give Jilian a hand, won't you. By the way, the name is Maarc*us*, Maarcus the Seventh of the Shoreman King's Own.'

When had he promised to take orders from this pompous human even if the man did seem to have a plan? How could he protect Celia from him? Walther shook his head. He'd settle it later as soon as he got hold of his river fear.

Jilian was weighing anchor – or was that when one threw it overboard? She was definitely reeling it in. He began to offer to untie the ropes binding the boat to the dock and found the last of them had been undone already. Then they were free and floating.

Wind fought with current. The main mast bucked and a sharp crack split the air. Maarcus and Jilian hurried to check the damage.

Walther barely noted any of it. He stood, instantly and violently ill from the moment he saw the boat untethered.

One of the humans swore. To Walther, it seemed code for movement. He ran to the side and spilled the bile of his empty stomach into the river. He leaned, gathering what was left of his strength and watching the mess swirl away on the current. The sickly patterns only made him feel worse. Better to distract himself by looking upriver.

Though he'd lived here all his life, he so seldom traveled by boat that it was like seeing his land for the first time. He briefly wished he weren't too ill to appreciate the view, then his gaze fell on the water directly below and his stomach heaved again.

The impulse to seek out a boat had been so strong that he'd known it a good one. He'd convinced himself he would be fine. But now? He forgot all about Maarcus, Jilian, Celia, his town turned to wasteland, and concentrated on a calm place where he could gain control. He gathered the strength to tell the others, 'I'm going below,' and went down without waiting for a response. From far off, he thought he heard a snort of disgust.

Walther claimed the hammock next to Ceeley's and listened to the water slap against the hull. The entire episode was embarrassing. It didn't help that his illness had nothing to do with the motion of the boat. He wasn't seasick. He could have tolerated that. The simple fact was Walther could not bear to be away from land – even when it was close enough to touch. His stomach roiled at the thought and he willed the nausea away. He would not give himself over to the phobia.

The boat lurched and bucked. Walther curled into a tight ball and let the world become a quiet spot in his mind. He would survive this – for Ceeley who lived, for the others who did not.

Chapter 4

FLIGHT

Hours after his wife left, Willam sat as stunned as if the Great Sisters themselves had spirited her away. Her mother had been right: he didn't deserve Lyda.

And now, by the Sisters, she was gone. Truly, dreadfully gone.

An unseasonably harsh sun glared through the half-open door and he thought without humor, *Well, at least she can see where she's goin'.*

He considered the remains of their ragtag lives – a sleeping pallet stuffed with brittle, years' old straw; a change of clothes (or two if he counted the pants that hung too loose); the holiday jacket his once high-spirited wife had sewn for him. The years spent struggling to get the shop going while her dowry dwindled away . . . Lyda had allowed for that, and more.

But not the stillborn.

Willam's chest ached whenever he thought about it. They'd held their hope until the late weeks, and finally dared to believe that the child would make it after so many false starts . . .

They did not try again. Willam never told her what he'd promised the witch to work such useless magic.

He took the thin jacket down from its hook and ran his fingers across the faded pattern. He'd never asked Lyda to mend it for fear she'd refuse him, but instead kept his tongue and restored the torn stitching himself. It had lasted through all their time together only because he looked after it the way another shopkeeper might have cared for a fine chokeberry wardrobe, the kind inlaid with gems imported from the far off lands beyond the Dunavian Hills.

Willam's mouth soured. He'd had his lifetime fill of the Dunavs. *His* elves, as Lyda called them, never said straight out, but he'd wager a year's earnings those same mountains spat out the three who found him. They charged him with watching over a silver bracelet like it was a slow-witted toddler. 'Never let it too far from your sight,' they said, 'but beware all the more when you think it safe. Trust no one, especially those you feel closest to.'

Always and again, the elf bracelet. It ruled Willam as surely as the Great King's memory gripped the land – twenty-some years dead, but still more powerful than all the pairs of highwaymen claiming the throne since. The cursed jewelry had been with Willam two-thirds that long and had more bearing on his day by day toil even now.

He had to find it.

Reluctantly, he returned the quilted coat to its hook. Hoping against hope that Lyda had not really sold the elves' precious trinket, he began at the top shelf, looking in this pot and that box. He worked his way to the bottom, turned and went up yet again. He checked every dusty canister and spider-webbed corner.

No elf bracelet.

Lyda had truly done it. Knowing the cost to them both, she'd gone and broken their promise. No, *his* promise, as she'd taken to reminding him with growing bad humor. No matter whose promise. *He* would not have the bracelet when they came to reclaim it.

The place was a shambles. Sneezing from dust and feeling as ill-used as a tavern barmaid, Willam made his decision. He slid out an ornate, wood and metal-bound chest and lifted its begrimed lid. Coins lay among the scraps of mouse-eaten cloth.

The shopkeeper shook his head and tsked sadly at the last of the elf payment. He'd planned to surprise Lyda with a trip to see her family come next summer and here he was squandering the money to go chasing after her. He knew it was a fool's errand. He'd never catch up to her – didn't have the grain of an idea where to start looking – but he couldn't imagine a different course. Going after a runaway wife seemed to hold more sense than facing his old age without her, let alone waiting through the endless hours until the elves returned.

He took the casket into the back room, set it on the floor and began gathering the things he couldn't bear to leave behind.

The store had been his home and means for more years than he wanted to count. He soon discovered the heap growing around the elf chest was well more than he could carry. He packed and unpacked a full hand's worth of times before he understood why his wife had taken so little. Whether he ever saw her again or no, he would need to travel as she did. Though valuable, the heavy casket would stay; his worn coat would go.

It was late in the day when Willam felt ready to depart. He hefted the kerchief onto his shoulders and shifted it to make the weight passable. Two things happened. First, the cloth tore apart, spilling the goods; and second, a woman's voice called to him from the front of the shop.

'Elves and dwarves and Seven Sisters, go 'way!' he swore under his breath, and bent to pick up the mess.

'Hello, anyone home?' she said again, her footsteps picking their way toward him. 'The door was open and . . . She – your wife? – she sold me a bracelet yesterday.'

'Please come back t'morrow,' he hollered from his place on the floor in his polite shopkeeper tones. 'The wife is . . . the wife . . .' His voice broke. He swallowed and tried again. 'The wife is ill.'

'I'm so sorry. She's a good woman.'

This last seemed spoken with a sincerity that sent a chill down Willam's spine. 'Yeah, yeah, she is at that.'

'I hope she'll be up and about soon.'

'I've no doubt of it,' he answered without emotion.

She stopped outside the curtain-hung archway separating store from home. Her voice quieter, she said, 'The bracelet? It's . . . I wondered . . . Is there another? Or a necklace to match?'

She's the one, Willam thought. That silky voice slides right in between your ribs. 'You bought the elf bracelet?'

'Yes, and I really can't thank you enough. It's very special.'

Willam studied his scattered belongings, thinking, *I should kill 'er*. He shook his head. He wasn't much of a fighting man, and well far from being a murderer. The elves hadn't asked him to kill. They'd counted him a coward from the first, assuming his fear of them would make sure he did their bidding. And of course, Lyda knew. She loved him anyway – but she never forgot it.

The girl pulled back the thin curtain. 'Oh, uh . . .'

Willam looked up into her face, familiar from yesterday but still so beautiful that his fingers itched to touch the smooth skin. "Pologies, miss. Had a bit of trouble, I did.'

'Robbers?' Her brow tightened in concern.

Willam choked back a laugh or a sob. 'Might say that, yes.'

'Can I help you? Clean up, I mean? – ' She lifted a tattered shirt and uncovered the wood casket.

'No. No!'

The girl halted, her young form at eye level, her fingers dropping the cloth. Willam understood why Lyda'd sold the bracelet: his own fault for strutting for this child. Yet he ached to take her hands in his even now.

He considered trying to buy back the bracelet, but knew it was too late. She would not sell it to him and he was not a sneak thief. They would come for him, sure as sure. He'd broken his word even if Lyda'd done it for him.

He stared hard at the girl's face, memorizing every feature should he ever need to describe her. Feeling old and spiteful, he found he'd lost his voice again. It came out in a whisper. 'Please go 'way. I do not 'ave what you want. Shop's closed.' He turned his back on her, not caring what she stole on her way out. Let the child traipse down her own road of folly. Willam would not be here to watch.

'It'll never support the sail,' Jilian told Maarcus. 'It's cracked at the base.'

Maarcus nodded, but didn't answer.

'You'd almost think someone didn't want us to leave.' She spoke without thinking and instantly regretted it. In the habit of traveling with Mut and saying whatever came to her, Jilian knew better than to confuse this man, any man, with a dragon. Whatever talents Maarcus might have, Mut walked closer to the unseen forces. Jilian relied on him to sense what mortals did not. With him gone she was lost.

She clenched a fist and prepared to hit Maarcus if he

laughed at her superstition, then quickly shoved the hand into her pocket. So soon after their truce wasn't the time to take him on. Jilian steeled herself against the biting remark she would have made.

Instead he surprised her by ignoring the comment. 'Not good. Definitely not good.' He frowned.

Maybe he hadn't heard? Well, Jilian didn't see a need to repeat her error.

The two stood together, eyeing the broken mast. Suddenly the mercenary wanted to lie down and sleep for twenty years. Just once, she wished trouble would not always trail after her as close as a child's favorite blanket.

She was getting too soft. She fretted for Ceeley, for herself, but for Mut most of all. The animal had a delicate, even unstable nature. She couldn't say how exactly, but she'd known it from her earliest days. Whatever his essence, the witch could do him terrible harm. She shuddered. No use in continuing that thought.

She needed to heed what her friend called the Free Man's Prayer. 'No worries to weigh down my arm and dull my knife. Plenty of anger to raise my fist and sharpen my sword. With no enemy at hand, laughter cuts the time well enough.'

'Beer.'

'What?'

'Beer. You were whispering the soldiers' motto. It's "beer cuts the time well enough."'

'I was? I thought it was . . . One follows the other, no?' She'd done it again. Voicing her thoughts to strangers could get her killed. And then where would Mut be?

'Lifting a mug keeps the sword arm tight.'

'Yes, well,' Jilian said primly. Time to change the subject, she decided. 'At least we're away from—'

'Floating downstream on an undermanned boat with a cracked main mast.'

'Definitely a man of cheer, Sir Maarcus.'

'At your service.' He gave her a small mock bow.

'Nothing we can do about it before daylight.' She needed an excuse to go below before her mouth volunteered something important. 'I'm going to check on our charges.'

Maarcus raised an eyebrow at 'our charges' but waved her on with a free hand.

With the king's man out of sight, Jilian loosened her shoulders while she let her eyes adjust to the dark. Every moment she spent with Maarcus reminded her how much she missed Mut.

Ceeley slept sprawled on her back. Her face held an incongruously thoughtful expression. Jilian kissed her on the cheek and wished her the blessing of the Seven Sisters. The child smiled and rolled onto her side.

The other dwarf had folded in as small as he could make himself. His face was covered with sweat.

She gently touched his shoulder. 'Sick, Walther?'

'Yes,' he moaned, too ill to be anything but truthful.

She put her hand to his forehead, but felt the usual warmth for a dwarf. Maybe exhaustion had finally overtaken him. She watched him for a while to see if this might be the cause, but her instincts denied it. Some unknown dwarf disease? No, she couldn't think of one that combined the sweats with a normal temperature.

An outlandish idea struck her. She'd never quite believed anyone could suffer merely by leaving the shore, but she'd listened now and again to tales of the symptoms and treatment of a similar sort of affliction in elves. Maybe the two races had more in common than overlapping land. It was worth a try.

'I think I can help you,' she whispered to him, 'but it'll have to wait until tomorrow night.'

The dwarf managed to sit up. In this state, he seemed too

77

small and fine-boned to withstand untested medicines. She considered an unintended effect of the expected cure and decided the risk was slight.

His voice was weak but his eyes were clear. 'Please don't put yourself out. I've tried everything including an old family remedy of leaves under the pillow.'

Jilian stifled a laugh. 'You almost had it right. Have you tried dirt in your pocket?'

'Of course not!' The dwarf answered, indignant. 'I'm no fool who believes such nonsense.'

'Some say such nonsense has saved many an el – many a life.' She put a finger to her lips, glanced to the sleeping girl and back to Walther. 'Don't worry. It'll be our secret.'

The dwarf moaned again and lay back. As Jilian opened the cabin hatch, he grumbled, 'The family secret wasn't this well-known when the entire family was alive.'

What exactly did his clan hide? She shrugged and left the dwarves to rest, suddenly feeling less tired herself. There would be time aplenty to riddle out the dwarf and here was a chance to gain a true liege man. She and Maarcus were allies who could work together – for the present. In the end, though, they would choose different paths. Each had well-cloaked secrets, which would never be revealed to the other.

But Walther, here was a dwarf who wore his heart like a pendant. With an occasional well-phrased anecdote of Jilian's own life, she could gain Walther's enduring loyalty. Controlling his seasickness would put him in her debt – and keep him there so long as she didn't give away a crucial detail. The mercenary nodded to herself. Yes, Walther could be trained to be just what she needed to free Mut.

Back on deck she reported to Maarcus, 'Sleeping like babies.'

'Both of them?'

'Yes, both.' She paused, then said, 'Give the dwarf a little rope. He's just lost his entire family.'

'He's not the first to suffer tragedy. We could use his help.'

Jilian looked hard at Maarcus, but his closed face did not invite questions. 'No, he's not and yes, we could,' she agreed at last.

The two grew quiet then, mirroring the silent forest on both banks. Only the water lapping against the hull made any sound at all. Maarcus rose and went to inspect the mast once more, as if hoping the damage might yet be a trick of the eyes. She turned to cover his place at the wheel then changed her mind and joined him. 'You've done what you could. I'll take the first watch.'

He stiffened. 'I don't need your sympathy' came through tight lips.

She backed away. 'Not to worry, Sir Maarcus. I am never sympathetic with royalty. Just the same, it's time to rest. Anchor overboard.' She turned a crank and the anchor splashed into the river.

Mut never learned a dragon's dignity. He couldn't help it. He'd been with Jilian from the first, a hatchling found among the newborn girl's swaddling clothes. He had a shadowy sense he'd been charged with protecting her, but he was as likely to cause trouble as spare her from danger.

Getting kidnapped by elves and trolls, for instance. Soon after leaving Jilian behind, the elfwitch had dropped him in the trolls' care. The trolls were so very, very stupid, and Mut was so very, very bored.

They trudged endlessly onward. They didn't stop to rest, never bothered to eat. When Mut lagged behind to tease a squirrel, the nearest troll carelessly snatched him up and tucked him under its arm. After a touch of the ooze seeping through the troll's skin, the dragon kept pace to avoid the rancid goo on his fur as much as the creature's bruising grip.

His crippled wings itched to catch an updraft just for a moment, but the witch had warned him to stay firmly on the ground. Beyond the elf's threats against Jilian, Mut felt the tugs and twinges of magic hamstringing his steps. With each move, he searched out a means to break the unseen bonds.

On the second day, he set up a game of harassment as much to amuse himself as to test the witch's power over the trolls. He ran between their legs, he jumped on their chests, he dodged in the way of their lumbering steps. The beasts reacted slowly – with surprise on their faces as they bent down to catch him – but their footfalls were heavy and their grip could crack bones. After one landed on his tail, he learned to move faster and keep clear of the huge feet.

By the third day, Mut felt annoyance settle on him like a family of flees. He wanted food. Now.

Sure he could go a week or two without a meal (and half that without drink) when necessary. But he'd started this forced march with a grumbling stomach and it was getting hard to think around the complaints. He considered chasing down a bird or a rabbit and decided small prey would barely brush the problem. Besides, Mut didn't like his food raw.

The witch be damned, he needed to eat. Time to escape.

Knowing the creatures must have a weakness, Mut watched them closely all during the morning. He was past patience with their tireless motion when one got caught in the underbrush. Some continued on, but a few trolls stopped to untangle a vine wrapped around the leg of their fellow. They seemed to hold real affection for each other, offering assuring grunts as they yanked at the plant and worked to free their companion.

Mut hesitated for the long space of a dragon's breath at exploiting the only scrap of virtue he'd seen in the trolls, but slowly dismissed his concern. War seldom leaves room for an overactive conscience and nothing better had come to him. This was his chance. With a little luck, it would do.

He spent the remaining time before sunset resisting temptations to bait and vex the trolls while he studied the terrain they traveled through. He was hoping for an exact blend of light, shadow, and trecherous footing.

Finally, the sun rode low enough to blind his captors' unshaded eyes. The trolls kept hiking just as they had from the beginning. The dragon searched the forest. There up ahead was just what he needed – a good-sized ravine. Mut waited. Five of the total seven neared the gorge. Suddenly the dragon dashed between their feet.

The first troll stumbled and fell to the ground. The second tripped over him. Flailing to catch his balance, he grabbed hold of the arm of a third. All three went tumbling over the edge and down the side to splash into the creek below. The largest lay on his back, waving arms and legs like a turtle rocking on its shell unable to right itself. The others rushed to pull him up.

Mut watched, stunned at how well his plan had worked, until a grunt returned him to his goal. One of the beasts was reaching out to grab him. Time to go before the noise brought the other three. The dragon dodged the troll, circled around to get a running start and jumped the ravine.

Mut paddled air. He'd overestimated his spellbound wings, hanging limp, adding drag and distraction. He was falling.

He desperately urged his wings to stretch and flap just once. A gust caught the half-extended wings and lifted him up, only to slam him against the soft dirt of the cliff. Dazed, he started to slide down. His foreclaws snagged on a tree root. He clung, gasping for breath, then scrabbled up over the side. The air went winter cold, but Mut didn't stop to puzzle on it. Once across the ravine, he ran with all his dwindling strength.

A sudden wind carried agonized cries from behind. Thunder rumbled overhead. The ground quaked. Mut slowed his steps against his better instincts.

The forest echoed with a great boom, as if mountains crashed together. The shouting cut off abruptly.

Mut's stomach lurched as he pictured the trolls caught in the ravine when the elfwitch slammed it closed. A quiet voice whispered in his ear, 'Not to worry, my strange friend. I have better plans for you. This is my land. Nothing escapes me. Not even you.'

The dragon ran on, his hunger almost overwhelming but his appetite crushed like so many brittle bones. When exhaustion took him, he slept in the open under the stars with no one to guard his back.

Roslin did not allow Ginni to dream under the cover of sleep. Each night Ginni mumbled words a stranger might mistake for prayers to keep her imagined box of mental keepsakes safely locked. Each morning she altered the spell so that she could go about her day with a clear head but still allow her mind to stray now and then on a sort of wandering rest.

So when she woke well before first light having dreamt for the second night, her every organ seemed to vibrate. Her head ached. The shock quickly gave way to wonder and overwhelming relief. By the Seven Sisters, she missed her dreams.

She lay still and tried to conjure up the details. Most were lost – or taken from her. Ginni remembered only a battle between elves. In its aftermath, the truce-makers fashioned bracelets to serve as a memento to the terrible war. Her own bracelet was obviously one of these, but she felt the hole of a small but important *something* missing. She sat up from her pallet on the floor.

Her mother slept trancelike on the bed. Her father had left shortly after their meeting and never returned. It was becoming clearer that these brief brushes were too hard on her parents. Only Ginni actually enjoyed them; found herself anticipating the next before the current one ended.

She lay down and tried to go back to sleep. She shifted position again and again. The floor seemed as uncomfortable as the rockiest terrain. Sunrise was a relief.

The just waking town gave little vent to her frustration. She couldn't speak plainly with these people. Her mind was all a jumble. When the hour was decent, her feet once again led her down the alley to the shop where she'd bought the bracelet. The building was deserted. She could feel the human life gone. When she'd visited before, the poor man had obviously been up all night and had no interest in business. Just as certain, his absent wife had already embarked on her own journey, one much longer than to the privy or the well.

She kicked at the loose dirt in disgust. She'd been walking in circles for hours with nothing new to show for it. A younger Ginni might have returned the bracelet yesterday, but this one was already hardened to the necessity of allowing the few to suffer while she worked to protect them all. Still it left her restless. She decided to return home and try to entice her mother to study the elven trinket.

Although Roslin's magic permitted only Tom and Ginni to enter the seemingly unlocked door, Ginni opened it slowly so as not to disturb her mother. As was all too often these days, Ginni realized her effort was wasted. A herd of wild horses would not have caught the woman's attention.

The girl controlled her voice, letting only a little excitement tinge the seriousness of her discovery. 'Mother, I f—'

Roslin's hand cut her off before she could explain. Without bothering to look up from her scrying, she said, 'You are as loud and cumbersome as a family of elephants, daughter. You can see that I'm working and mustn't be interrupted. Go outside and find something useful to do.'

'But I have—'

'Now.'

The dismissal stung, but Ginni would not be bowed by the great Roslin. She straightened her slumped shoulders, changed clothes to dress as the boy, and went downstairs without wasting breath to explain her intentions to a disinterested mother.

She searched all over town for Wanton Tom, but he'd gone off on an untraceable mission of his own. In late afternoon she listlessly entered the pub, the main source of news and gossip in any village. There was no one to listen to but a neighbor who'd been kept awake the night before last due to the row between the shopkeeper and his wife. Ginni felt sorry and a little responsible for her role in the anguished couple's argument. Still, by the third telling, all she could think was how she'd like to drown the sleepless bore in the nearest keg.

She thought about flirting with the barmaid rather than hear a fourth drunken rendition and dismissed it for not being worth the trouble. She considered playing barmaid for the evening but ultimately didn't want to be indoors.

Ginni was too much like her father. Her restlessness couldn't be cured by anything the town offered. Her patience was edged with the need to travel, the desire to seek someone who knew the true origins of the bracelet.

In a flash of insight, Ginni knew Roslin wouldn't leave the inn now. These frequent meetings with Wanton Tom after so many years of avoiding him affected her in a way none of them had expected. She acted tired, deep down in her bones tired. She was becoming more and more distant, withdrawing further and further into her magic. Roslin might come around in time, but Ginni couldn't sit about waiting. She had to act.

Time to find someone who could tell her about the bracelet. And she wasn't going to find them in this weak excuse for civilization.

The shopkeeper and his wife had already fled. She needed to convince her parents to follow – or go alone if they wouldn't budge from their comfortable surroundings.

Jilian woke thinking of Mut and feeling oddly relieved. She was sure danger still loomed, but the slowly descending axe had been lifted higher for the moment. It gave her hope as she climbed overboard to splash fresh river water on her face and clean the grime from her arms.

She studied the dense foliage. At home the trees were in full greenery while here the leaves were a tart furled brown. Perfume from fringe trees flowering out of season hung heavy in the air.

The elves were said to hoard a bin stocked with service-berry whenever they broke camp. It would preserve Walther's dirt, keep it fresh and damp long past when it normally would have dried to dust. She'd have to keep an eye on the bank today so that she could find it after dark.

'Aunt Jilly. Aunt Jilly! Maarcus has a trick to show us. Come see!' Ceeley shouted from the front deck.

Jilian waved and smiled. 'I'll be right there.'

His trick was no more than easy sleight of hand, but it held the child for some while.

Walther stayed below deck the entire day as the boat continued its course downstream. His face was greyer and more pinched each time Jilian checked on him, and she went topside to rejoin Maarcus and Ceeley with relief.

Towards nightfall the dwarf's moaning took on a new

pitch. Jilian's stomach churned whenever the sound pierced Ceeley's patter. Maarcus's lips formed a tight line, which only now and again twisted into a smile at Ceeley's antics as she pranced about the deck and talked to imaginary friends on shore.

'Celia!' he called sternly, a touch of panic tinting his voice. 'Come away from there!'

Celia stepped away from the rail and stamped one booted foot. 'Ah, Uncle Maarcs, when did you become such an old troll?'

'Just since it got dark.' He lowered his voice to a conspiratorial whisper. 'I'm afraid of the dark, you know.'

She put her hands on her hips, incredulous. 'You are not.'

'I am, it's true. Isn't it, Jilian?'

'Absolutely. What's more he can't swim – ' Maarcus's eyebrows twitched. Not surprising, few learned to swim in country crossed by rivers with such strong currents – 'which means *I* will have to fish you out of the river. And Ceeley, I really detest taking cold baths at night. Don't you?'

Celia laughed as she joined them. 'I don't mind,' she said. 'Dada always lets me play in the sand to make it more fun.' Her face suddenly sobered and tears filled her eyes.

The night had settled to full dark. The air felt dense with the taste of the unknown.

Maarcus picked her up. 'Did he now? Well, I guess we'll just have to throw you in and see how you like it. Jilian, you grab her feet. I'll keep the end with teeth.'

Jilian snatched the squiggling child's ankles while he slid his grip to her wrists. She nodded a mock salute. 'Ready, captain.'

'Ready. A one, and a two and a three!' They swung the giggling girl back and forth until all three were out of breath.

Back on her feet, Celia said, 'I'm hungry.'

Jilian felt her own stomach growl in answer. Supplies were low to start and she'd added nothing to their stores. 'Tomorrow—'

'Tomorrow we feast!' Maarcus interrupted with an over-abundance of enthusiasm. 'But tonight – ' he raised his arm in courtly fashion. The lace sleeve showed at the edge of his jacket cuff. 'Tonight we have a delightful evening snack. I'll be right back with a charming starlit two-course dinner.' He danced a few graceful steps and disappeared below.

Celia put her chubby hand into Jilian's. 'Isn't Uncle Maarcs the best, Aunt Jilly?'

The woman put her free hand on the back of the child's head, stroked and smoothed the curls which sprang up when let loose again. 'Yeah, he's certainly something.' I just wish I knew what, she finished to herself.

Maarcus returned carrying two sizeable hunks of hard bread and smaller bits of jerky, and held them out. Jilian hesitated, then decided both pride and fear of poison were foolish.

Ceeley was already chewing the dried meat. 'Are you going to eat, Uncle Maarcs?'

'Don't worry about me, honey. I ate a while ago.'

Jilian paused with the bread dissolving on her tongue. Maybe she'd assumed too much. 'You need to keep your strength up. Why don't you have mine?' She offered the jerky, her challenge unspoken.

He blinked, his face quickly masking hurt, and nodded. 'Just a little. Though I did eat already.'

She watched him bite a small but respectable amount, chew it carefully and swallow. 'It's tastier on the other end, but Celia's is delicious through and through,' he joked.

Jilian felt a pang of guilt when he returned her food. She realized that he wasn't eating due to their shortage but hadn't wanted them to know. If she insisted he share their meal now, it would likely do no more than risk upsetting the child.

She bit off some jerky. 'Love that black humor of yours.'

'What's bla-goomer?' Ceeley asked around her food.

'Something grown-ups do at night when you're asleep.' The smile returned to Maarcus's face. 'Don't talk with your mouth full, munchkin.'

'I'm not a munchkin and my mouth's not full. It's gone. See?' She opened her mouth wide for them to inspect.

'I think I see some stuck to your teeth.'

'Can I watch?' asked Celia, with a child's single-mindedness.

'Watch what?'

'Aunt Jilly! We were talking about the bla-goomer.'

'Sorry, no bla-goomer tonight.' Jilian grinned.

'But you just said—'

'I know, but I was teasing Uncle Maarcs. Right Unk?'

'Oh absolutely, no more bla-goomer tonight. Finish your food, Ceeley.'

'But I already did. And I want to see a bla—'

'Here, you can have mine. I'm full.' And she gave what was left of her meal to the child.

Ceeley studied the food. 'You sure?'

Jilian nodded.

She bit her lip, apparently hoping to figure what the adults were up to and finally deciding she was too hungry to care. 'Thanks.' She took the food and waltzed it across the deck before finishing it with all the enjoyment of a holiday meal.

Jilian watched the child but her thoughts returned to Walther – and she couldn't do a thing about him until later. Trying to get her mind off him, she asked, 'How'd you come to know Celia, anyway?'

The hint of smile disappeared. 'Long story.'

'Can't be that long. The child's only six,' she teased, ignoring his obvious discomfort.

'I knew her father.' Another tight-lipped answer.

Jilian's curiosity took over. His reaction made it clear this was a tale a mercenary ought to know. 'A man of your stature travels far and wide. I guess you might befriend a dwarf or two.'

'What of it?'

'Would I be judging you?' She slapped her hand to her chest. 'I who normally stalk the hills accompanied by a dragon?'

It was the wrong thing to say. Just the mention of Mut brought back yesterday's tension. Jilian worried over Mut more than she did herself. She blamed Maarcus for the dragon's predicament and the man knew it.

'Ceeley, time for bed, honey,' Maarcus said. His voice made it clear the other conversation was finished.

'Ah, I'm not sleepy,' she protested, even as she failed to stifle a yawn.

Jilian giggled at the child. 'Me, I always yawn when I'm wide awake. You too, Maarcus?' She looked at him as she spoke, hoping he would hear her apology. His face was closed to her. She swore silently and gave it up to steer the child toward the cabin.

Ceeley slipped around behind Maarcus. 'But I can't go in there!'

'Why not?' the adults asked in unison.

She turned to Jilian, her mouth tightened in fear. 'He's in there!'

'Well, yes, but—'

'And he's too noisy,' she added with false bravado while keeping as far from the cabin as she could.

Jilian didn't miss a beat. 'Well, I guess we'll just have to lie awake out here and yawn. Come on.' She sat down near the side and patted the floor boards.

'Ah, Aunt Jilian . . .' Celia made a final grumbling stand then curled up against Jilian on the deck. Her eyes fell closed. The child's breathing evened out and the mercenary's along with her, though neither meant it to.

Chapter 5

VISIONS

A hard knot of anger lay heavy in Lyda's stomach and pushed her over the packed dirt roads. Dust puffed around her feet, rising thin and gritty to cover everything – buildings, animals, clothing, skin. She coughed, the dry hack itself another reminder of a drought none of the people of the Seven Caps ever expected to suffer.

The town had always been green. People paid no more attention to water than the sky or the trees or the mountains. Regular rain and snow filled the wells and fed the Queen's River a half day's walk east. Flowers bloomed in hundreds of windowboxes come every spring. Lyda herself couldn't resist a small, ornamental garden next to the store; for her trouble this last season she had watched with her arms crossed as a constable roughly plucked stem after stem from the ground.

The shortage was official. Shortage – a strange, nearly forgotten word used to name the uncommonly light winter snows, to describe no spring rains to speak of. None of the old-timers could recall a summer so stifling that leaves withered on the branches. No one could remember a time when paint peeled from storefronts and the owners wouldn't bother to add a fresh coat.

Farmers dug deeper and deeper wells, but relief eluded them there too. Finally, they converted the great beer caskets to water barrels and began relays to and from the waning river. Too late. The harvest season already upon them would yield no more than soured fruits and shriveled vegetables.

A scent of something worse than drought lingered on the arid wind. The townspeople quashed their panic and waited.

Lyda left the Caps behind and entered the fields just outside the wall. Despite the water runs, signs of scarcity lay everywhere. Brittle, yellow-tinged leaves, normally a rich, unfurled green, littered the baked ground. Wheatstalks faired no better than the beans and millet.

Seeing the paltry crops, Lyda fully understood the depth of the miserly, pinching mood infecting the town. As the farmers worried and kept more for their own, the rest fought over the leavings. Willam would bear the bitter winter alone, a winter certain to be much crueler than she'd realized when she left.

But still she did not turn back to accept her comeuppance and help him face the elves' wrath. Instead she left the main path to avoid any who knew her and might pass on her whereabouts to those who didn't.

The woodland west of the river was barren and rocky. A generation ago, the land was lush with forest that stretched from the tilled farms to the river, and the undergrowth sheltered great stores of game. The town was a rich place where every man could prosper, not least a shopkeeper and his new bride. Lyda sighed.

The Caps – these days more often called the Cups for the many breweries and taverns – had grown. Newcomers needed trees for timber. Goats and sheep overgrazed the newly cleared meadows. The drought had taken its toll as well.

Lyda stumbled and landed hard on one knee. Tired and dispirited, she shut her eyes. She emptied her mind but for half-remembered childhood rhymes and let the pain wash over and away. Her legs ached from hiking the rough terrain. Her hands and knees were bruised from the fall. Her parched throat closed in on itself until she scarcely breathed. The sun's warmth, once so welcome in this cold, adopted land, seemed to add to her sorrow.

The wind gusted and the air cooled around her. Lyda opened her eyes. The wood called from ten steps ahead. Slowly she stood. Her limbs moved as if entranced and she entered the edge of the forest near what had been its heart in a time before memory.

The turmoil in her mind eased beneath the shade and quiet. In the early days of Willam's courtship, they had come here often. After the wedding, the edges of newness wore into the smoothness of the familiar, and the shop consumed their days. She didn't begrudge the work then, for they shared it side by side, but now she saw how much she missed the woodland's salve. There was the tree where he'd carved their initials. Here was where they'd joined that first time. She let her feet take her where they wished and stopped by a clearing next to a pool formed by a bend in a sidestream.

She pulled off shoes and socks and waded into the cool water. It eddied around her, ticklish and tempting.

Willam had never meant to harm her. He'd simply always found himself on the wrong end of a bad bargain. More than once she'd walked into a sale at the last breath and saved him from giving away goods clearly valuable to the buyer – if not to the seller. She set things aright often enough to keep them afloat, but never would they prosper. The elves were just another short stick Willam had pulled, unknowing, from the bundle.

She watched the flow, clear to the bottom. Festival fish with colors brighter than her own coming-out clothes swam through the reeds. Water lilies waved in the current. A frog croaked from his broad leaf.

The tension slipped out of her, as palpable as milk from a mother's breast. The shopkeeper's wife inhaled deep and slow. Let it out. Again. Years of stiff bearing and shouldered burdens unknotted. Back and leg muscles barely held her upright.

She shuffled along the river's edge until she reached a rock shelf, then gently lowered onto it. Lyda rested her head against the bank. Water lapped at her chin.

The currents blew heavy with magic. Her eyes watered at the cloying scent of fringe flowers out of season. She wiped at the tears but a haze remained.

She'd always assumed she'd be too frightened to beg for her life when they came for her. Here the moment hung and she felt no fear, only an unusual calm. They would swing the elven axe or they would not. As if in a waking dream, she saw herself from above. The air rippled strangely over the pool and the half-sleeping Lyda didn't turn, didn't move.

'They've found you! Get up! Run! Hide!' she shouted to herself; but the fool woman rested, watching the elves and letting the water glide by.

Living in a town butt up against their land as she did for so many years, she'd seen plenty of elves. These were not part of any tribe she recognized.

Partly hidden by a mist sure to be of their own making, the three stood where the bank met the river, seemingly not on the one, nor in the other. They appeared all of a height, tall and stretched thin in the face. Their brilliant robes swelled their flowing movements and distracted her from staring too long into the strange purple-yellow eyes.

She splashed water into her own eyes to wash away the teary film. The spectre of the three remained, indistinct but constant.

They spoke softly, soothingly, hunters to the rabbit they might shoot and might yet take in as an exotic pet. 'We foresaw this day. We have always known you just as we have always known your husband. So we put a great geas upon the bracelet. Only the proper seeker could discover it. Even in your anger, you have done well. We require from you no more than the name of the one who purchased the trinket.'

Struck dumb, motionless, Lyda remained as she was. Could it be so easy?

'What do they call the one who bought the bracelet?' the three repeated.

Her brows tightened in concentration. 'Name? Name.' She shook her head. 'I don't know 'er name. She was a trav-eller, a 'ore per'aps. A *flirt* no question.' She shrugged a wet shoulder as if to say the girl was beneath notice. Her voice grew harsh. 'I 'ope she—'

'Do not wish evil on your enemies,' they whispered to her as one voice. 'Else it will come back to you and your own sevenfold.'

Their warning struck harder than the expected blow would have. She nodded, suddenly beginning to understand. Her envy of the fair and the lucky weighed on her like so many rocks thrown into a sack and carried across her back wherever she went. She pictured loosening the string which bound the bag. A pile of poorly cut gems floated around the bend and away.

Lyda began again. 'The girl was young, pretty.' She checked a reflexive frown. 'Blonde, I think, but maybe brunette. Something 'bout her looks, though.' She stopped, thinking back. 'Made you notice her 'ole, not the particulars. Knew just where to go for the bracelet too.' She paused again as her surprise built toward awe, both at the girl and her own insight. 'That child had some sort of talent. Yes, she did.'

The elves smiled. 'As do we all.' They nodded together. 'Thank you. Journey forward in peace.' They spread their arms wide and quietly backed into the enveloping mist. Murmurs of 'peace' echoed in their wake.

Lyda examined herself, poking, prodding, still unable to believe they had not set a hand upon her. She soon found instead the elves had left her more than complete. They had restored her wish to see truly for the first time since she'd come to this foreign land. Lyda was new, scrubbed clean of the little bits of anger that she'd parceled out day by day to Willam and his string of flirting girls. She was lighter than the stray leaves and flotsam swirling downstream.

She longed for Willam, but she could not go back to huddling in tiny rooms. She had always seen into her patrons' hearts – the better to jiggle loose their money – but the one-time shopkeeper's wife saw her talent turning down a different road. She would not deny the destiny the elves had shown her.

Lyda rose from the eddy, her dusty world-weary clothes dripping a trail of bright festival colors behind her. When they dried, they would be more splendid than her coming-out skirts.

'So you're leaving in the middle of the night, no matter my advice?' The chair scraped the floor as Roslin stood.

Her only child, fruit of forbidden union, looked at her with the expression of all rebellious daughters since the birth of the world. The girl's hand rested on her outthrust hip. 'But Rosl – ' She paused, then began again. Her speech was colored by the placating tones she normally used to calm informants. 'Mother, this is the first completely new discovery I've come across since we began our travels. It means something. I'm sure of it. We can't ignore it.'

Roslin's jaw was so tense her entire face ached. She tried to keep the contempt out of her voice, but doubted she succeeded. 'Of course it means something. But we must have a plan, a method. We can't just go running across the countryside every time one of you unearths an interesting bauble, and thereby risk all we've done.'

Ginni turned to her father for support.

'Ros, we're not getting anywhere this way.' He spoke in his gentle, lover's voice, which peeved her all the more.

'I'm not some fragile flower who must be coddled,' she snapped. 'Lest you forget, I see things neither of you do. This is a diversion. It will take us further from our goal.'

'But what's the goal? To remain safely gathering scraps of rumors, hoping we trip over the twins?' Wanton Tom, sometime mercenary, man of action always, shook his head. 'You know me better than that, Ros.'

Tom seemed to be purposely baiting her, probing the wound he must realize would never heal. For him she had risked her very ability to perform magic. But he'd left her anyway, snuck out under cover of dark like a common thief. Even then she'd known the damage was done, the child already quickened in her womb.

'You never wait until morning.' The sarcasm didn't altogether mask her hurt.

Tom concentrated on the door and would not meet her eyes, while Ginni's face showed surprise and maybe a hint of insight. Her mouth opened but Roslin forestalled her with a raised hand.

Her voice was barely a whisper. 'I can't stop you. I never could. Do what you want, both of you, but remember you were warned.' Roslin tried to wish them luck and found her jaw tightening another notch as she bit back spiteful words.

Her temple throbbed with the beginnings of one of her headaches. She closed her eyes. Her hand massaged her temple in futile comfort.

In the blur of her pain, Roslin barely felt Ginni's brief hug, Tom's mumbled goodbye. She opened her eyes at the soft thud of the closing door.

She supposed they'd chosen to take her silence as a begrudged blessing. They could not pretend she agreed. But still, Roslin thought, even though she'd never told anyone of her weakness, an observant mage's daughter should have seen the signs of her mother's anguish.

Alone, always and again alone.

The mage sat down at the table which held her potions. Looking past the bottles and through the wall beyond, the vision came unbidden as they often did. Elves at the dawn of time held her with a bond unlike any in the world of human flesh.

The stoop-shouldered elf sat surrounded by children. The female's thin, unkempt white hair hung about the weathered face in ragged lines.

Not much to look at, thought Roslin, even as she recognized the scene from her own childhood and knew it to be repeated among all the races time and again.

Storytellers were the most respected persons in the clan, for they told the legends and lessons of their people. Attended by young and old, here was one who needed no magic, only voice and body, to weave the tales of the world and its creatures.

Another child joined the circle and sat. Abruptly, Roslin's view shifted and she found herself looking up into the wrinkled old face.

'There was once an elderly elf couple, who had travelled

the River all of their lives. They walked up and down and up and down until they knew every speck of mud along the shore.' The storyteller trotted back and forth, leaning on an unseen cane. 'This way of life was as natural to them as sleeping is to a newborn. They had lived a good life, a proud life. They had borne and reared many children, who had in turn borne and reared their own. They had set and broken many camps, leaving always a thing of beauty to thank the Great Sisters for guiding them in their journeys.

'One night, the elf mother had a dream.' The storyteller rested her head on clasped hands and closed her eyes. 'In this dream, she came to realize the land was beautiful because she, her husband and children had done much to make it so. They had worked hard all their lives and now it was time to settle and live in ease.

'She awoke renewed and vigorous. First she woke her husband. Then she called her people to join them.' The old storyteller opened her eyes and jumped up. She mimed waking others and gathering them together.

'She spoke to the crowd in a large booming voice. "We are the First People, the Favored Ones. As long as our people can remember, we have traveled the River. We have moved up and down its length so often that every child of ten or twenty can find last year's encampment.

' "We are a great people, for we are the wandering artists who beautify ourselves, our homes, the world. We do not collect goods for the sake of owning. We do not trade for indelicate handiwork simply to possess the tool. It has always been the elfin way and we are proud of it.

' "Our lives have been full, have they not, as year unto year we have adorned the river banks. But" – she met the eyes of each in her clan – "it is time for the First People to be at peace, to settle upon the river bank, to repel those who forced us into this nomadic life. There is no longer any need for us to skulk along like thieves and beggars, for the Great Sisters will thank us by protecting us and supporting our needs." The woman jabbed her pointed walking stick into the ground. "On this day, we stake this land and claim it for our own." The group cheered.'

The storyteller nodded solemnly. 'And so they chose this place. We have worked hard for generations so that you, our children, can know a comfortable existence.'

The children clapped and hoorayed. Roslin jumped and cheered with the others. Filled with delight, she turned to share her joy with those behind her. In the back sat a thoughtful boy. While the others applauded, his hands remained still in his lap. While they cheered, he offered only a cautious smile.

The storyteller waved the unruly children back into her circle. 'So it is decreed unto the ends of our days.' Her voice grew serious. 'A warning to you all: There are those who will try to take what you have, but know that it is yours to keep as you please. There are those among our own people who dare to suggest we are challenging the Great Sisters to reject other bends in the River for this one.'

She pulled a long face and shook her head back and forth. The children became restless and stirred in their places on the ground. The storyteller's smile returned. 'But surely this is not so. We would not risk our precious children thus. We are led by a great and wise seer. All is as it should be. We remain here while those who wish to continue the weary road are encouraged to depart. Their children will remain among us to learn the true ways of our people.' The storyteller gave a knowing nod to the quiet boy. 'We will care for all.'

The scene washed away to leave Roslin puzzled. Her readings had never suggested that the elves' migrations had been forced upon them. It was simply part of the elven nature, just as the sedentary humans could not resist building bigger and bigger cities.

And yet, her visions had always spoken true.

'Ginni! Hand me the—' She turned to face the empty room. 'By the Sisters,' Roslin swore, 'that girl is never around when I need her.' She rose to get the scroll herself.

'One day soon she will learn the value of patience.' The mage shook her head. 'I only hope I'll be free to rescue her when she does.' But her face held the preoccupied lines of a woman too busy to tolerate interruptions – or to remember where her only child had gone.

The house burned. A small child ran and ran. Screaming, 'Mommy! Daddy! Mommy! Daddy!' but getting no answer. The fields behind were on fire. The fresh pretty, corn stalks blackened and curled and fell to ashes. The air smelled awful.

Still the girl ran. She looked and looked. They had to be somewhere. She got tired, so tired. And scared, so very, very frightened. She went to her favorite secret hiding place – the place where she played with the baby dragon. She waited. They would come to her and she would be safe. She slept.

And woke.

They never came. Oh, they never came. There was only a small girl and her pet dragon in all the big world. Even he had burned his feet.

They went back to the ashes. Her parents, her parents . . .

Jilian awoke in a sweat. She was always much younger in the dream than she had been in life, and she never could bring herself to remember what she had seen when she found her parents.

The boat rocked gently on the river swells. The mercenary lay still and listened. Ceeley's breath blew warm and even on Jilian's cheek. Maarcus sat propped against the side near the cabin, his mouth hanging open slightly and his chest rising and falling in sleep. Walther too seemed to have found rest. The cabin was quiet but for regularly spaced snores. There would never be a better time to search for the serviceberry plant.

Feeling both reluctant to abandon the child and disgust with herself for allowing such an attachment to anyone other than Mut, she lay cuddled against Ceeley a while longer. Finally she gathered her resolve and slipped out from under the girl's draped arm.

A little shaky from the dream and acutely aware of being alone, she made sure of her reflexes and her knives before she hefted her pack. The mercenary glanced a last time at Ceeley, resisting then giving in to an impulse to kiss her goodbye. I'm making too much of this, Jilian thought. The child won't even know I was gone. All business now, she climbed over the side and slowly lowered herself into the water.

As the mercenary waded ashore, she kept alert to danger. Her movements blended into the normal night sounds; her splashing barely amplified the lap of waves on the bank. She reached the water's edge and moved inland, carefully picking her way to avoid snapping twigs or tripping over a button-bush root hidden in the shifting shadows.

Jilian came across a likely spot not far from the boat and spent a moment weighing her exposure and means of escape against the possibility of a better place nearby. Satisfied this would serve her well, she was soon completely engrossed in looking for the rare blue serviceberries in the scant moonlight. She found a small patch of blackberries and bent closer to pluck out a palmful of the blues. They were said to grow only among the more common black serviceberries, where color was a matter of shading and the casual eye could not tell them apart. A sure sign of the blueberries was that they always fruited in twos while the blackberries bunched in threes or more – that and the effect. Blackberries could be fatal.

A loud crack broke the night quiet, followed by what seemed a herd of heavy, lumbering footsteps shaking the ground. Jilian's curiosity won over a brief battle with her fear and she quickly scaled a tree noted earlier for just such a purpose. Flattened against the trunk, she watched as three trolls thundered into the clearing. Each was as huge as the brute who had attended the elfwitch.

One carried a human or perhaps an elf thrown over its shoulder. The person moaned and rolled in the troll's grasp. The creature lost his grip and dropped the man face first in the dirt. The creature kicked him and he curled into a ball and lay still. The troll nodded as if to say 'so there'. He picked up the body and held it out to his fellows. The other two shook their heads 'no' and crossed their arms against their chests, refusing to accept the body. The first threw it at his mate and so on as they argued over who would carry the unfortunate man.

The captive must have been drugged. Clearly he wasn't dead yet. Besides, trolls would never bother to carry around a corpse. Then again, she couldn't think of one who troubled to hold onto anything but food. Were they becoming cannibals?

Moreover, where were these giant beasts coming from? She'd never seen any taller than small dwarves before this. It had never been their size but their ill-tempers and single-mindedness that made them dangerous. Most times, everyone simply avoided them in their native woods. Only a crazed troll would enter a town, where it would be instantly brought down by the sheer number of villagers.

These mammoth creatures, though, were both impossible to fight – as Jilian had discovered – and increasingly difficult to avoid. Something had shifted among the powers of the One Land. Jilian bit her lip. Change seldom meant peace.

She watched from her perch as the three outsize trolls continued their stubborn quarrel, shoving the poor man back and forth and dropping him now and again. Temperament had not improved with height.

She debated trying to rescue the victim before he succumbed to fatal clumsiness, but common sense ruled. Her own experience told her she could not overcome one, never mind a trio. The mercenary considered the odds on whether following their trail might lead her to Mut, but then she remembered her companions on the boat and the reason she happened to be in this grove in the first place. 'Those orphans mean nothing to me,' she told herself.

A dragon whuffed quietly and nuzzled her hand. Jilian reached out to calm the animal. But no, there was no dragon. No Mut in a tree.

Jilian's vision blurred and her ears buzzed. She tightened her grip on the trunk.

Had Mut been missing her so badly that he'd sent her a message? Had the elfwitch found a way to track her? No, it wasn't the elfwitch. Jilian sensed no apprehension accompanying the ringing ears. Somehow Mut had been able to work a most comforting kind of magic. Jilian smiled. 'I'll find you,' she promised.

The largest troll whapped another atop the head and pushed the body into the other's arms. He bowed and took his time wrapping the limp form around his neck like a stole. The three tromped on and away.

'Sisters, watch over him,' Jilian whispered for the man as she climbed down from the tree and returned to her berries.

He came to as a man, leaning on a shovel. On either side stood more men swinging picks and shovels. In front of them stretched a long narrow ditch. Loose dirt piled high at their feet. A troll was issuing orders.

'You there, Mut, get moving! It's not big enough yet. Come over here next.' He pointed toward the far end of the ditch.

Trolls? Orders? Something seemed wrong, but hadn't it always been this way?

Mut shrugged and went to stand where he'd been told, dragging the shovel along behind him. Arguing logic with trolls made less sense than trying to teach manners to a dragon. Still trying to recall what he'd done before he became a digger, he picked up the spade to finish the trench around the tree. His masters were single-minded about getting the job done and the diggers each had bruises to prove it.

The trolls watched them work with a strange intensity as the sun rose then fell. The routine never varied. Awaken to an unfriendly boot in the side and one or another of the trolls pointing to a shovel. Dig a trench no wider than an average man's stride but deeper than a tall elf's stretch. Go on to the next. At dusk they called a halt for a brief supper break of bread dipped in a thin and flavorless broth. The digging went on until deepdark only to start anew each morning without ever crossing the previous day's chore.

Mut thought the ditches formed a pattern together, but he couldn't make it out. They made an unsolvable puzzle for he had no idea of the whole or when it would be completed. Yet sometimes, against his better judgment, on days like today when every bone and muscle ached for rest, he wasted energy idly trying to decipher its shape and purpose.

It was barely noon, but his limbs hung heavy with more than the weight of the shovel of black earth. He continued to make digging motions without actually moving dirt, hoping to fool the trolls. Even this came to be more than he could bear. Mut suddenly felt light enough to float even as he realized he must be falling.

He awoke face-down with the taste of dirt in his mouth. Slowly he rolled over, expecting a kick to his gut. A female elf stood a few paces away and the trolls waited further back. Several hours must have passed for the sun was now low in the sky. A faint memory of the elf called to him but all his mind could manage was curiosity at her strange garment.

'Arr . . .' She was saying something he couldn't understand.

She raised her voice and addressed Mut directly. 'I can see you're no good for human labor. I'll have to find something more suitable.'

'Mm . . . uh.' His mouth seemed unable to form words. When he tried to get up, his limbs didn't respond. He had to stand. They would beat him severely if he didn't. He inhaled long and deep, then shakily rose to his feet.

A small piece of him was surprised to find the shovel still in his hand, but he didn't hesitate to lean on it for support.

'Well, get to work,' said a troll. 'You've rested long enough.'

The diggers' corpses stood in the trenches, placed feet first. Everywhere all around. He spun about looking for . . . someone, and breathed relief when he didn't recognize . . . her.

There was the face of one he knew, though – a troll who'd fallen into a ravine and been left to die. But that was a troll not a human digger. He turned toward his masters, confused.

The elf threw back her head and laughed.

Mut tossed his shovel at the ditch and ran.

The dragon woke, running, his legs circling uselessly. The elfwitch's laughter still echoed in his ears, and the horrifying sight of the troll he'd killed, buried amidst the others in his dream, left his heart pounding. As he rose to four legs, he found himself groggily wondering what it would be like to stand on two.

Mut snorted. What an unworthy thought – he had never wanted to be human. Even with limited flight from his damaged wings, any dragon could hold sway over puny humans. Neither the elfwitch's desires nor remorse over a creature's death could rule one as powerful as he.

The dragon stretched his wings and glided low a short distance. The elfwitch was becoming a nuisance. He would have to do something about her. He landed and set off at a good pace.

It was time to find Jilian.

Chapter 6

DECISIONS

The elves caught up with Willam just before sunrise.

An odd, moldering dankness settled deep into his sleep and jerked him awake. He sat bolt upright on the hard ground, not altogether sure where he was.

The remains of a horrible dream about Lyda and the bracelet clung to him like ill-sewn nightclothes. Willam rubbed a hand across his face and tried to dredge up what had brought him to this patch of dead land. His memory cleared as he looked out on the overgrazed hillside and he slowly came to accept that the nightmare was true. Lyda was gone and he was here, cold and stiff from a bad night's rest after a worse day's run. Fully awake now, he couldn't shake the shadowy misgivings of troubled sleep. In the eerie predawn quiet not a single morning bird called to its mate. Willam shrugged. There was nothing to do, but get on with things. The shopkeeper put his feet under him to stand . . . but a voice commanded otherwise.

'I wouldn't recommend that.'

Utterly surprised, he fell back on his rear with his legs splayed before him like a child at play. Out of nowhere, a strange elf suddenly towered over him so close that his black cloak dusted Willam's shoes. They always did fancy a grand entrance, the shopkeeper thought.

The soldierly bearing of this one denied any hint of friendly intent as he said, 'Our brothers found your wife.'

Willam's stomach clenched. He pulled close the kerchief he'd been using as a pillow and held onto it with both hands so that he wouldn't be tempted to swing a punch at the elf, at least not yet. 'And?' he asked, not really wanting to hear.

The elf spoke at right angles, toneless and blank-faced. 'Anger consumes. Lyda the shopkeeper's wife has come to understand this. So will you.'

Poor Lyda. They've done 'er in, he thought. And now they'll do me. He struggled to keep calm. He had to live to avenge his Lyda.

'Fear can sap a man's strength,' said the elf, mistaking William's silence. 'Mark me. Do not fail us again. *You* will find the bracelet. *I* will know when you do.' Each word tolled like the pronouncement of doom.

'And what'll I do with it when I 'ave?' he asked in a hoarse whisper.

'You will know when the time comes.'

'But, 'ow – ' he challenged.

The elf raised an arm and beckoned. Two large trolls appeared from behind a giant boulder. Willam braced himself to ward off the killing blow, but the pair remained where they stood.

'You will know,' he repeated. A tiny smile teased at the corners of his mouth and chilled Willam to the core. 'Remember all that I have said,' the elf warned in the same dead-flat tone. He returned to his bodyguards. The leader seemed to float just above the rocks and debris, gliding away towards the farthest mountain peaks, while the trolls lumbered behind, pebbles clattering and dust rising in their wake. Willam watched them go, their silhouettes dissolving into the horizon.

They'd given him a second chance – maybe – but oh, poor Lyda. Her death lay at their feet just as he'd feared it would from the very first time he saw the cursed bracelet. They'd lied when they promised to protect him and his.

Did they truly think him such a cowardly idiot that he wouldn't have the gut to protest the loss of his own wife? Willam the storekeeper was several things – among them, oversoft in his bargaining with pretty girls and perhaps slight in his attentions to Lyda in recent years – but he was not a fool to be dismissed.

As the birds woke at last to welcome the dawn, Willam made up his mind. 'I'll know what to do, all right. By the Sisters, I will.'

He couldn't wait to show the soulless beasts just how well he understood the job he had to do and the exacting care he could take to see it done.

Herb pouch only half-full with the serviceberries, Jilian reluctantly headed back toward the boat. She'd meant to slip on board before daylight, but the incident with the trolls had stolen her time and sapped her strength. The sun would crest the hills soon and someone would know she'd been gone. The mercenary needed to come up with a reasonable story for leaving under cover of dark without warning.

As she picked her way under the brightening sky, Jilian considered a few unlikely ideas that even Ceeley would doubt before the obvious came to her. She'd tell them she'd heard a sound on shore. Knowing better but still hoping it was Mut, she'd hurried to investigate. She could describe the trolls and the man and by-pass her vision of Mut – or whatever that was. The facts were terrifying enough that they might distract Maarcus from his original question if she got lucky. She'd have no trouble feigning her reaction. Her hands still shook whenever she thought about the fate of the prisoner.

Back at the spot where she'd come ashore, she could see Maarcus pacing the deck. Jilian gave a hearty wave and called out, 'I'm home, Dad! Don't wear out the wood on my account.' She waded into the rushing river.

He went to the side and frowned down at her. Her remark must have been closer than a pickpocket to a victim's purse because he didn't speak at first. His furrowed brow said it all. But then he said, 'Glad you're back, but it's not you.'

No? 'Ceeley!' she shouted. 'She followed me and got captured by the trolls!' She'd never forgive herself if . . .

Maarcus shook his head. 'Trolls?'

A moan loud enough for Jilian to hear rose up from the cabin.

'No, it's Walther. Something's happened. He's much worse.'

She didn't argue. The anguished cries had taken on a new mournful pitch. She hurried the rest of the way to the boat. 'Where's Ceeley?'

'Hiding in the corner beneath my cloak.' He pointed over his shoulder. 'She says it's Walther's fault their village was attacked. If he hadn't left . . .' Maarcus threw a knotted rope over the side. 'Here, toss me your pack.'

She instinctively clutched her bag to be sure it hung securely. 'No problem, I've got it.' Jilian began to pull herself up hand over hand. Bringing the subject back to the dwarves before Maarcus could have time to be insulted about her possessiveness, she asked, 'You don't believe Walther had anything to do with it, do you?'

'No, but it's plain to see why Ceeley does. She's been

abandoned by nearly everyone she's ever known. Through no choice of their own, true, but she needs an explanation, someone to blame. Better she accuse a favorite uncle than make the next most likely conclusion that it's somehow her fault they died or that she deserved to be left behind.'

The mercenary reached the top. 'But that's ridiculous. She didn't . . .'

Maarcus offered his hand. 'Of course it is, but how did you feel when your parents died and you lived?'

Suddenly Jilian didn't want Maarcus to feel her trembling. She heaved herself onto the deck and he let his arm drop.

'She's no more the cause than Walther is.' Another groan came from the cabin. Close up, the sound was devastating. Jilian winced. 'No surprise Ceeley's so frightened. He could be dying in there. We've got to help him.'

'Agreed,' Maarcus said, 'but how?'

'Have you talked to him?'

'Can't get near him. Ceeley carried on so when I opened the hatch that I was afraid she was going to hurt herself.'

Jilian looked over at the lump under the royal cloak. 'Why don't you stay here and I'll go check on him.'

'No!' yelled Ceeley, throwing off the cape. 'You won't be my friend if you help him, that . . . that clan killer! I hope whatever it is gets him the way he got my family.' Her high-pitched voice echoed with more anger than Jilian would have guessed possible.

The woman stooped and held her arms open to hug the child, but the girl backed out of reach. 'Honey, we can't let him suffer like this.'

'He hurt my mommy and daddy. And Rea, his own sister!'

'No, Ceeley, he didn't.'

The child crossed her arms and stared at Jilian.

Another moan was followed by dry heaves, but the girl didn't flinch.

The woman spoke gently as she stood. 'We have to help him, honey. *I* have to help him if I can. It's a promise I made myself.' Where had that come from? Jilian wondered, but nevertheless admitted it was true. 'You'll understand someday,' she assured the unyielding child. 'All yours,' she said to Maarcus. 'Good luck.'

'Yeah, you too.'

Jilian steeled herself for an unknown much worse than an angry confrontation with a traumatized child. She entered the cabin and went to the dwarf's side. He was bathed in sweat, but his face was pasty white rather than fever red. The color of the dead, Jilian thought. Frantically, she pulled out the herb pouch and extracted one of the blue serviceberries. She hesitated, suddenly afraid it was the common blackberry after all. The light was poor, but she leaned toward the gleam shining through the crack in the hatch. The problem was without one of each berry side by side, it was impossible to be completely certain.

Jilian closed her eyes, thought of Mut, thought of all she'd learned, thought of a man probably dying inches away. He was a dwarf, but still a man. A wet nose tickled her hand, calming her. When she opened her eyes, she no longer doubted herself. She took the blueberry and squeezed a drop across his lips.

Walther tossed and turned and wiped it off as if it were just another bead of sweat.

'All right, Walther, we do this the hard way.' She pinned his shoulder with one arm, nearly lying on top of him to do so. With the other hand, she pressed on his jaw joints to force open his mouth. Quickly she dropped in the berry she'd tucked between her palm and small fingers. Next Jilian shoved his jaw closed and waited until the berry juice began to do its work.

Soon Walther stopped his thrashing and she let up slightly

on her grip. Slowly Jilian worked his jaw up and down, trying to chew his food for him. All this because she hadn't had time to brew the tea said to be the proper treatment for riversickness.

When he had swallowed the last of the berry, she mopped his brow and sat on the three-legged stool to watch. Walther grew very still, but his sweat dried and some color returned to his skin. After a time, he opened his eyes.

'Who . . . you?' he asked.

'Jilian.' It seemed inadequate though it was the only name she'd ever had. She smiled and added, 'A friend.'

'Help . . . me?'

'We're trying.'

'We?'

Jilian nodded. 'You have two more friends outside.'

'Sleep . . . now,' the dwarf said, closing his eyes.

'Walther, I must tell the others how to help you.'

No answer.

'Walther? They need to know about the riversickness and the berries.'

A contented sigh escaped his lips. Was that her answer? Unlikely. He was alive and resting more easily for now. It would have to do. 'I'll be right out there,' she whispered in case he might be listening.

'He's doing better,' Jilian reported above deck.

'So, I hear,' Maarcus said. 'He is still breathing, isn't he?'

Jilian couldn't decide if the man were joking, trying to insult her, or simply too tired to be aware of his rudeness. Opting for the latter, she said, 'Check on him yourself if you like.'

'No!' Ceeley shouted from under the cloak. 'Please, Uncle Maarcs, don't!'

'Status quo out here I take it,' the mercenary said.

'She came out for a while and we were singing.'

'Anything I know?'

Maarcus blushed. 'Probably not. I think I'll pass on Walther for now,' he added, changing back to the original subject.

'Later?' Jilian mouthed.

He tipped his head in a short nod. 'Later,' he whispered. 'What'd you do to him anyway?' he asked.

'There's a herb I know of that calms seasickness.'

'That's the worst case I've ever seen. Are you sure it's not something else?'

Jilian paused before answering. Should she tell him what she knew and ruin Walther's trust in her? Still, it could mean the dwarf's life if she weren't around to help him. She decided not to leave again until he recovered and gave her permission to disclose his secret. 'Well, no, I'm not,' she told Maarcus, 'but at least he's resting more comfortably until we can find out what it is.'

'That man needs a physician.'

'Too bad your grandfather doesn't get out and about much these days.'

Maarcus gave her a strange look. 'Yes, isn't it.' He looked over to Ceeley. The lump under the cloak had gone still.

Jilian's heart raced. 'Oh, no. I hope she's all right.'

Maarcus lifted the cape and put a hand to his mouth to stifle his laughter. 'Sleeping,' he whispered. 'Walther woke her pretty early.' He pointed to a spot away from both child and cabin. 'Shall we?'

Jilian nodded and followed.

'How did you come to know about herbs?' he asked once they were settled across the deck.

The mercenary drew her knees to her chest, then slowly straightened her legs. What could she say that wouldn't betray Walther? 'I've found in my profession that knowledge of certain plants is very helpful.' She answered him honestly, while avoiding the particulars of the dwarf's likely condition. 'A bodyguard gets more work if she can protect against more than one type of assassin – and the intended victims live long enough to pay for my services, too.'

She was tempted to make a show of pulling out her own so-called assassin's knife for an unneccesary task such as cleaning her boots perhaps, but discarded the idea. They had travelled through so much in the short time since they'd met that Maarcus would likely laugh at such an exaggerated display. It certainly wouldn't have her usual desired effect of intimidating the competition.

Maarcus didn't answer, but his thoughtful expression suggested he understood Jilian's position first-hand.

The two sat a while in comfortable silence. Finally, Jilian asked, 'How did you come to be in your line of work?'

'Everyone knows my grandfather was – and still is – *someone*, a man with ideas and the power to carry them out. Few knew about me and that was the way he liked it. I was raised by elves, fostered to a friendly clan.' He shifted position, fidgeting with something in his pocket.

'I hated always being the odd one. They were friendly but foreign in nearly all they did. Even as a child, I knew I was not like them, did not think like them.

'I couldn't even *grow* like them. Our shorter lives are painfully obvious to a kid whose friends change every year. I'd get bored with them and they'd come to think of me as a strange older brother or even an uncle. The easiest taunt was "human". Even some adults used it when they got exasperated.'

Jilian let him talk, knowing it all. Knowing you didn't have to be raised by elves to be different and ridiculed for it. Suspecting too that their lives were connected not just by their isolation, but that there was a greater force pulling their threads together. 'Do you still have friends among them?'

Maarcus jumped, her voice reminding him he had an audience. 'Some,' he admitted, 'though not so many as Grandfather was hoping.'

'What happened?'

'The war mostly. It hasn't just divided elf from dwarf and dwarf from human. It's come between clans and families too.'

'What was it like?' Jilian asked, finding herself genuinely curious.

'What was what like?'

'You know what I mean. Growing up in the capital, living with the elves.'

'I was horribly homesick out in the woods with the elves. I'd been a pampered boy in the court. Everyone doted on me even though the ruling king changed constantly. Rumor held that my grandfather had done something ominous with the aid of the Magician.' He stopped and looked at her. 'Funny, even after all these years there's only one man referred to as "the Magician".'

'Well, did they do something ominous?'

Maarcus shrugged. 'They were always up to something. Can't say that I knew of any one thing back then. So anyway, no one would touch me. To go from that to being less than ordinary, an oddity, was hard, very hard. And the elves aren't known for soft hearts.'

True, Jilian thought.

'The first time I came back to the capital, I didn't think they'd be able to tear me away again. I revelled in the glorious palace where I had my own set of rooms. That I was a child didn't matter. I was important enough to go where I pleased when I pleased. It only dawned on me later that in truth the adults were all too busy with their own plans to worry about a boy of eight or ten who wasn't in the direct line of succession. I was often forgotten and ignored, and I loved it.

'Now and then, Grandfather would sit me down and deliver dry speeches on the politics of court or the perils of this king or that. I sat still as long as I could but forgot it all the minute he released me. Grandfather was right, though. I should have paid attention. I'd have a much easier time determining my enemies now if I had.'

'Maarcus, are you in danger?'

'Me?' he asked, surprised. 'No more than I've ever been. Anyone as close as I am to Grandfather runs a risk by association. Fortunately, the old man has always kept me out of sight.'

'And your parents?' Jilian asked.

'Not so lucky.' He cleared his throat. 'But I was telling you about the palace.'

'Tell me, tell me, Uncle Maarcs.' Ceeley stood with her cloak wrapped around her and pooling at her feet.

'Come sit in my lap. We'll listen together,' Jilian said.

But the child ignored her. She dragged the cloak behind her and settled under the man's arm instead.

Feeling foolish for caring, the mercenary pushed away her disappointment and concentrated on Maarcus.

'The palace had a hundred rooms and big, wide staircases. It stood on a hill that overlooked the whole town. The dining hall seated three hundred – and then there was the private dining room. The kings were forever throwing banquets in vain attempts to solidify power.

'Candelabra fashioned by elves, out of silver the dwarves had mined, lit every room. The finest jeweled tapestries elves could weave adorned the walls. Woodwork, intricate and beautiful, carved by the Maveclan—'

'Hey, they lived in my village!' interrupted Celia.

He smiled. 'That they did. And their work decorated every banister, every picture frame, every bedpost.' His voice trailed away. His face clearly showed how much he still missed the rich luxuries of his childhood.

'Don't stop now,' the child urged.

'The elves live so plainly. Their needlework is beyond compare, but they don't go out of their way to carry around comfortable furniture. I longed for my big canopied bed, the very desire for which made them think me spoiled and pampered . . . Not that they were wrong,' he admitted. 'It was one reason my grandfather sent me away. And he wanted me . . .' He looked down at Ceeley, gave her a one-armed hug. 'He wanted me safe with people he could trust. I didn't realize how serious he was until word came that my parents had been poisoned while dining with friends. Grandfather's letter told me to think of the elves as my second family. I was more than simply a young ambassador now. I was a son of elves as well as humans. He hoped the bonds I made would be lifelong. He said we'd need them now that the Great King—'

'Is the elfwitch your friend?' Ceeley asked.

At the same time, Jilian put the question more harshly. 'So what were you doing with that elfwitch?'

Maarcus spoke quietly. 'It's another very long story.'

'Oh boy, oh boy. Another long story.' Ceeley jumped up and danced a short jig in anticipation before settling down to snuggle against Maarcus once more.

'That's not quite what I meant, honey, It's—'

'We've got plenty of time,' Jilian reminded him. 'It'll still be a while before he can travel. Besides, I can't help having a "childlike" curiosity about her.'

'Well,' Maarcus began, 'it started when I went home for a holiday visit. As I grew up, I came to realize that it was all coming apart. Skirmishes in the outlands were nothing compared to the number dying daily under assassins' knives. The entire One Land was erupting in battle and the seed of it was my beloved city. After that I was grateful to the elves. I could escape from watching the destruction for weeks at a time.

'As I got older, I knew I'd have to go back. I couldn't hide forever. And when I finally did, it was rubble – hardly a building stood that had not been damaged. But the people go on, fighting their petty fights. They'll go on until nothing is left.' He couldn't mask the hurt or the disgust.

'I reached my majority. It was time to claim my allegiances and take up my trade.'

'Which is?' Jilian asked, unable to wait to hear his self-described answer even though she knew she'd ultimately get more information out of him if she let him tell it in his own way.

His face took on a sour expression as if he'd swallowed rotten meat that was just this side of diseased. 'It seems I'd been groomed to be a spy.'

'Wow!' exclaimed Ceeley. 'I know a real live human magician-spy!'

'Not quite. I'm really no good at it.' He shrugged a shoulder. 'Oh, I can skulk about, but I've got no stomach for the scheming, even less for the death. I might as well have stayed in the palace.'

'If you'd lived to adulthood,' Jilian said without thinking.

Celia jumped to his defense. 'He would have lived, Aunt Jilly. He's tricky like me.'

Jilian nodded to the child, reluctant to reach out further for fear Ceeley would withdraw again. 'That he is,' she agreed.

'I'd just come back to the elf camp, charged with my newest mission, and found that they'd moved on.'

'Oh, no!' Ceeley's eyes were big. 'What then?'

Maarcus looked sheepish, perhaps feeling guilty for frightening Celia. 'It happened now and again. Normally, I simply followed the river up or down, whichever direction they'd last been migrating. But this time – ' he paused for dramatic effect despite himself. 'This time, a few of the clan were waiting for me. They told me they'd been asked to protect the elfqueen, who had in turn requested *me* to guide her through human lands. "Me? Why me?" I asked. It seems she sought an audience with the new king in the capital and wanted me to take her there.' He faced Jilian. 'It didn't make sense really – even now that road is reasonably well travelled and safe if precautions are taken – but I owed these people a great deal. I agreed to take her wherever she wished.'

'So what happened once you got to town?'

'We never got there. We found you instead.'

'Me and Mut.'

'I'm really sorry about the dragon.'

Jilian studied him. He seemed sincere. 'What happened to your grandfather and the Magician?'

'They're around somewhere,' Maarcus said vaguely.

Jilian couldn't tell if he didn't know or just didn't want her to know. 'How do we get Mut back?'

'I've got a few ideas.'

'So do I,' Ceeley chimed in.

'I'm with you,' said a shaky voice from behind them.

Ceeley screamed as all three turned to see Walther coming toward them.

Jilian gasped. 'By the Sisters, he's aged twenty years in the past hour.'

Chapter 7

JOURNEYS

Wanton Tom couldn't be happier. With the town and Roslin an hour behind him, he'd outshouted Ginni's protests and called a halt. He woke fresh from a working man's sleep under the stars and couldn't wait to get moving. As they broke cold camp and cleared away any obvious signs of their stay, he couldn't help but smile.

'And what's got you in such fine humor?' Ginni grumbled. 'We could have been halfway to—'

''That so?' he asked. 'And feeling 'specially foolish when we stumbled right past your storekeeper in the dark.' He flapped his blanket to shake loose the dry sand. 'We're professionals, Ginni. We'll find him.'

The girl snorted. 'Professionals indeed. You sound like Roslin.'

Tom arched an eyebrow and clamped his mouth shut. No point in sidling into that conversation. 'What's the matter,' he asked innocently. 'Lose your taste for mornings?'

Walking toward Tom with hands on hips, Ginni said, 'Me? Why I can outdo anybody, even you, any time. Morning, noon, or midnight.' She punctuated each of the last words with three gentle stabs to his chest.

Not truly awake enough himself for a quick comeback, Tom let Grosik beat him to the punch. In as sweet a voice as he'd ever heard the dragon use, he said, 'Your humble servant awaits the chance to ferry his two illustrious human passengers.' The two stood still in not altogether feigned shock. 'So move it!' the dragon roared.

'Ah, that's more like it,' the man said. Giggling like schoolchildren, he and Ginni hurried to climb aboard.

Grosik took them as high as he dared then headed down at a steep dive. A couple more loops and dips later, the two were holding on for life.

'Don't ruffle the scales.'

'Don't ruffle the scales? How about, don't kill the riders?'

The dragon sniffed. 'I needed to stretch after such an unreasonable day's long wait while you galavanted around town.'

'Galavanting in that dustbin? Fine. Next time you face Roslin. The dragonlady's more your type anyway.'

Ginni stiffened against him. 'Sorry, Gin. It's an old joke that goes back to before you were born.'

'I understand.' More quietly, she said, 'I just never realized how, uh, uncomfortable you two are around each other.'

'That's because we've been avoiding each other for years. Would've been hard for you to notice what we're like together.'

'Yeah, I guess so. But how did you ever agree to work on a common purpose, as worthy as it may be?'

'Kind of a fun tale, actually. I'm saving it for a bedtime story.'

'I'm too old for those.'

Tom laughed. 'You're never too old for *my* bedtime stories.'

'Well, OK,' she agreed. 'As long as you promise to tell me the grown-up version. No leaving out the bloody bits.'

'This one's a clean tale, just a little poison.' He made a gagging noise.

'Fair enough,' Ginni giggled. 'Until then . . .'

She let the subject drop and Tom settled back to enjoy the ride. For a while the three were silent. Grosik eased off his flying theatrics to allow them a chance to study the ground. The terrain was rocky here. Above the tree line, nothing much grew. Still only the dragon's eyes were sharp enough to discern much detail on the ground. Grosik had never seen the shopkeeper, but he could move in closer if he spotted anything looking human-shaped.

The witch's raids had cut down the ritual dwarven wanderings in the last weeks and elves tended to travel in groups, but humans had a stubborn streak that pushed them on. They couldn't keep from hiking their beloved mountains. It was bred into them as much as shepherding was bred into dogs. Alone or accompanied, humans would insist on freedom of movement.

As Grosik flew in great circles looking for Willam, Tom and Ginni's talk eventually took on the banter of two old friends out to waste an afternoon.

'What has two hands and two feet, twenty fingers, and no toes at all?' Wanton Tom asked in an uncharacteristic display of utter silliness.

Ginni feigned deep thought followed by a wide grin. 'A letch!'

Shocked by her answer and embarrassed at his shock, he spoke stiffly in an attempt to mask his feelings. 'I would never tell my daughter such an off-color joke.'

She gently punched his shoulder. 'It's me, Ginni. Remember?'

'That's what I'm worried about.' He let out an exaggerated moan.

'OK, not a letch.' Tom grunted his disapproval. 'Um, how about a pickpocket?'

'Closer.'

'The tax man?'

'Got it. Your turn.'

'What's big and ugly and has three fingers on each hand?'

'A bad pickpocket?'

Ginni laughed. 'I'll keep that one for next time. Try again.'

Tom was quiet, having had to resort to genuinely considering the question.

'Give up?'

'Umf.'

'Can I take that as a "yes"?'

'Umf.'

'Sounds more like "yes" than "no",' Ginni said with the air of authority. 'OK, I'll tell you. A troll.'

'Troll! That's utter nonsense. Trolls are built essentially the same as humans, elves, dwarves, what have you. "Ten fingers, ten toes, two eyes, one nose."' He chanted a childhood counting rhyme.

'Ah, but the troll doesn't know that because he can only count to three.' Ginni burst into laughter.

'I see,' he said, choking down his own urge to snicker. 'My turn. This one will have to be something special.' He leaned forward and whispered into Grosik's ear. The beast let out a hideous, ear-shattering, high-pitched wail that only those closest to dragons would know for a laugh. 'What stands upright but bends with every breeze, changes colors with the seasons, but has claws sharper than a fishing spear?'

'Oh, that's easy,' Ginni answered.

'Give in?'

'The king.'

'How did you know?'

'You forget. I've been traveling with Roslin these last months. I've had more than my share of royal politics.'

The air suddenly seemed cooler. At first Tom thought he imagined it as the result of yet another mention of the mage, until Grosik abruptly dived. Quick as thought, black roiling clouds replaced the high thin wisps. Tom and Ginni hung on tight and didn't complain at the dragon's breakneck flying. Rain didn't bother them, but they knew better than to ride exposed in a storm raised from nowhere – witch-made weather no question, but neither spoke it aloud. The three needed cover and if they could find a dry place to wait it out, all the better.

Ginni spotted the cave first. She tapped Tom's shoulder and pointed at a dark spot against the mountainside. He nodded and leaned forward to tell Grosik. Between the sudden sheets of water, the cave looked like a stain against rockface. Tom hoped it was empty. He was in no mood for battling trolls, three-fingered or ten.

I'm becoming an old lady, the mercenary thought. Since when have I minded a fight or worried that a full grown dragon wouldn't settle a minor territorial scuffle? I could use a good dirty fight after all this sneaking around. Tom set his jaw with the determined grin he wore into battle, but he knew it was Ginni he was truly concerned for.

Grosik landed hard and skidded into the cave. The air seemed to deflate a little when they found nothing to challenge them. A rodent ran squeaking out into the rain rather than risk becoming a dragon snack. Tom and Ginni climbed down, laughing.

'There's one beast who knows which side of the firepit he's on,' said Ginni.

'Should have been mine,' the dragon grumbled and the two humans laughed again.

'Hungry and wet just like old times, huh Uncle?' Ginni said, but the joke settled like a soaked and rotting log, leaving the flat taste of mold in their mouths.

In the early days, none of them had cared about more than catching a good updraft or cooking a meal after a day's battle. Times were meaner now and the elfwitch was much stronger than she had been.

Tom stood at the cave mouth watching the rain while Grosik found a nook big enough to hold him and immediately curled into sleep.

'I do envy him that,' the girl said to Tom's back. He didn't respond. Out of the corner of his eye, he saw Ginni shrug. She closed her eyes and concentrated a moment. A small flame appeared in the palm of her left hand. She balled the hand into a fist and turned it sideways. The flame sprouted through the curve made by thumb and fingers and rode just above so that she seemed to be holding a tiny torch. Indeed, if the company had been different, she likely would have clenched a stout stick to further the illusion.

'Mind your step, child. There's—'

'Snakes and trolls and witches about,' she finished the warning for him. 'Don't worry I'll be careful.' This last said with only a touch of irony.

Tom sighed. He had inherited her care after she'd already learned to walk. A woman friend claimed this was why he'd never really gotten used to the idea that sometimes she got bruised but remained whole. Better an overbearing mother hen than Roslin's constant frowning disapproval, he argued with himself, yet his worry could put them both in danger if he didn't find a way to rein it in.

He counted to ten, then twenty. He lost count while staring at the flash storm and trying to clear his mind.

Finally, he gave in to his fretting and followed Ginni to the back of the cave. It was deeper than he'd expected given the thin echoes of their speech and footfalls. The dragon's snores bounced among the rocks and returned strangely off-pitch.

As the light from outside dimmed, Tom had to rely on the flicker of the magical flame ahead. He slowed his steps and reached out to let the walls help guide him. They were oddly smooth and reflected the scant mageglow as if buffed for many long hours with a polishing cloth, but lacked the bright streaks of mineral deposits. Intent on studying the unnaturalness of the walls, he almost tripped over Ginni, who had bent over a pile of bones spilling out of a small knee-high nook. 'Sorry.'

'It's all right,' she mumbled, focused on her discovery.

'Nothing happening outside in that downpour. Thought I might as well see what you've got yourself into this time.'

Ginni turned to give him a knowing smile then crouched down to get a closer look. She spoke a word and the flame grew strong enough to cast long shadows into the seemingly endless cave depths.

Tom bent over the scattered bones without touching them. Like the walls, they were rubbed smooth. All scraps of meat and tendon had been cleaned away, though some were notched and tattooed with symbols he didn't recognize.

'The elfwitch was here.' Ginni echoed his own thoughts. 'What do you make of it?'

He shook his head. 'The language is foreign, but these must be elven runes. Roslin would know. Too bad she stayed behind in the Caps.'

'No, she didn't. She left there not long after we did.'

'Generous of you to mention it.'

Ginni turned from the remains. 'I didn't know I knew until now.'

Silence hung. The dragon's snores abruptly stopped.

'Who interrupted my well-deserved nap?' he bellowed. 'Does someone wish to be my afternoon snack?'

'Just us, Grosik.'

'Just dinner, you mean.'

'I don't think he's joking,' Ginni whispered.

'Sure he is. Aren't you, old friend? Come and take a look at this.'

'Better be worth . . .' The mercenary could hear the dragon's bulk scratching the wall as he rose to his feet. 'What is that smell?' His voice got louder and angrier as he grew close. 'What're you cooking?'

'There isn't enough left on these old bones to make soup broth,' Ginni said.

'Never underestimate a dragon's appetite,' Wanton Tom and Grosik answered at the same time.

The roof was so low that it made a tight fit for the dragon, but he sat upright as he stretched his long neck around the two humans to look over their discovery. 'This is it? You woke me for these paltry offerings?' He snorted. 'I'm going—'

'Grosik, we didn't wake you.'

He put his face right in front of Tom's so that he could easily snap off the man's head with one sharp bite. The mercenary controlled an involuntary shiver. He'd never get used to the dragon's idea of expressing annoyance even among friends.

'He means, not intentionally,' Ginni amended quickly. 'But since you're here, you'll obviously notice these bones have been through some sort of ritual. Look at the markings.'

'Elven transformation,' said the dragon without hesitation. 'Man bones, elf bones. Never together otherwise.'

'Transformed into what?' Ginni asked.

'From what?' said Wanton Tom.

'How does it work?'

The dragon shook his huge head back and forth. 'Am I an elf-mage?' The beast stepped backward and twisted about. As he walked away, he recited an incantation Tom had never heard before. 'A stupid dragon eats whatever he finds regardless of circumstance. A smart dragon can identify his prey from the bone slivers he uses to pick his teeth. But the smartest dragon knows when to leave them as they lie lest the spell be sent to plague him for the rest of his many years.' His voice faded as he neared the cave entrance. 'Rain's stopped. Time to go.'

'Guess the Big Beast is right. Let's go.'

Ginni didn't move. 'I knew he wasn't overly fond of magic, but isn't this strange?'

'How so?'

'I mean, did you ever see him in such a hurry to leave a place perfectly suited to dragon naps?'

The mercenary shook his head. 'Grosik has a few odd habits even for one of his kind, but you're right. This *is* unusual.' He looked down at the pile of bones and raised a foot to spread them out. He stopped in mid-swing. ''Course this is the first time I've seen him call anything a transformation spell. Even a dragon might be sobered by such power.'

'So we're going to walk away as if we didn't know what we'd found?'

'We've already disturbed them. I for one, incautious though I may be – ' a lopsided grin broke the seriousness of his words – 'am mighty reluctant to ignore a dragon's warning.'

'But—'

'They're not timid animals,' he reminded her.

'All right,' she agreed, too readily.

'Let's go find that runaway store owner.' He rose to follow

Grosik. 'And, Ginni, no keepsakes. You know we always travel light. That's to avoid unnecessary trouble as much as it is to spare the dragon's back.'

Ginni stood, staring down at the mysterious heap.

'We'll find the cave again if we need it,' he told her gently. And we've enough grief as it is, he finished silently.

'All right.' She carefully replaced the two small bones she'd palmed. 'I know it's important, but I don't have the skill to force it to reveal itself now.' She whispered a quick prayer or incantation he didn't quite catch. 'Ready.'

He waited for Ginni to pass him to be sure she wouldn't change her mind.

'You know,' she said as they joined Grosik at the ledge, 'they felt so cold, as if death itself resided within.'

'It did,' rumbled the dragon. 'It did.'

The sky still looked grey and unsettled as the three took off once more.

Mut lay in the shade, listening to the growls of his empty stomach. He needed food, but every time he tried to eat, a vision of the troll's corpse killed his appetite. It made no sense: dragons were not haunted by simple death. Yet here he was too preoccupied with a dead troll to think straight.

And he was lost. Mut never got lost. Time after time, he had guided Jilian across mountains and valleys with the sparsest instructions and vaguest descriptions. Even so, when he came upon a copse of trees he was sure he'd passed earlier, the dragon had to admit it was no use. He was traveling in circles.

Mut plopped down in the high grass and rested his head on his forepaws. What was the best move? On the one claw, the hills and ravines looked overfamiliar; and on the other, the natural woodland clues he'd expected seemed completely strange. On top of it all, his tongue felt dry and swollen. He was getting overheated and dizzy.

Water would help. Water! That was it. If he could find the Queen's River, he could get his bearings, quiet his hunger pangs, and clear his thoughts all in one!

The dragon rose to his feet, excited by his new plan. He stood alert, concentrating wholly on rooting out the river and the way home. He caught the faint sound of splashing close enough that he wondered he had not noticed it before. Hoping to rejoin Jilian soon, he let the burbling serve as a makeshift compass and lure him forward.

The shallow feeder stream ran fast and deep, though it was too small to be the river he sought. Still, it was a start. Mut waded in and drank his fill. The coolness soothed his parched mouth and sore feet but did little to lift his spirits or calm his worries. He followed the creek downstream, sure that it had to empty ultimately into the Queen's River.

The dragon had no heart for his usual play of batting at fish. Even the lizard sunning itself on a rock didn't take his half-hearted pounce seriously. It flicked its tail and closed its eyes before Mut's shadow had passed safely by. The dragon growled in disgust, deep in his throat. He must look as sickly as he felt that so small a creature could afford to ignore him.

The irony was the sight of the thing made his gut rumble. He couldn't digest a lizard no matter how loudly his stomach protested, good health or poor, and vomiting would not help his vertigo. He resigned himself to padding along the water's edge trying to keep his feet under him and his thoughts on Jilian.

Suddenly he found himself face-down in the creek without remembering how he got there. A tiny rainbow fish had lodged in his snout. He snorted and blew out the surprised fish. Not half as surprised as I am, Mut thought. I must have passed out.

Utterly soaked and more despondent than ever, the

dragon decided it would be safer to wait out the dizziness dozing by the bank. He climbed to dry land and shook off the water head to toe, then he picked a place among the tall reeds where the shade would help hide him. Mut curled his tail around him and fell asleep in an instant, dreaming of Jilian in the carefree days before the fire.

Walther leaned against the cabin door, breathing deeply. His limbs felt weak, but he couldn't bear to stay closed in the cabin any longer. Unlike most of his people, his own family had always needed to be outside, feeling the wind. The entire Shortdwarf clan held an eccentric affection for open places. They built their houses with wide windows leading onto wraparound porches and balconies. This to the amusement of their neighbours and friends, who teased, Why go to so much trouble when they had all the One Land to travel whenever they wished?

He looked around and could only barely recall the woman and the man. Ceeley, his niece, he remembered. He tried a smile on her, which sent her skittering to hide behind the woman's legs.

'Feeling better, Walther?' the human woman asked him.

'Some. Thanks,' his mouth answered, while his mind struggled to focus. What is her name? he asked himself, but he couldn't pull it up. Something's wrong. Could this be watershock? He'd never spent this much time on a boat before.

The woman was speaking again. 'Walther? Walther? Do you need to sit down?'

'That's a good idea,' he tried to say, but his tongue felt numb and heavy. The woman looked at the man. Both had worried expressions.

'Maybe you should *lie* down,' suggested the man.

Walther gave up trying to talk. Instead, he nodded. The

movement destroyed the dwarf's precarious balance and his vision dimmed to grey-black. He took a few wobbly steps, but his feet rang strangely on the deck as if the planks were made of china. The violent sound of glass shattering filled his ears. Walther's boot landed on nothing and he pitched forward into the dark.

Walther came to with a wet cloth on his forehead and the humans bending over him. 'It doesn't look like your herbs quite work,' the man commented.

Herbs?

'No, it doesn't, does it?' she answered. 'What now?'

Behind them, Ceeley screamed, 'He's a traitor! Throw him overboard. He's just faking so we won't get rid of him!'

Her fear cut. It was enough to make him wish he stayed out.

'Hush, now, Ceeley. He's still very sick.'

'Good.' The child stomped the deck so hard that Walther felt the vibration.

The woman looked at the man, who said, 'Come over here to your Uncle Maarcs.' The child crossed her arms and shook her head.

'Come on, Ceeley. He won't bite.'

'That's what you say.'

Finally, Maarcs – was that his true name? – went to her. He squatted to her eye level and put an arm around her shoulders.

The motion seemed somehow more intimate than Walther had expected. He turned away, closed his eyes, and listened.

'Look at this poor dwarf. He lost his whole family.'

'So did I. So did lotsa dwarves. We don't make visions and carry witch coins.'

So that was it. He faced the two again in time to see the man masking his surprise. To his credit, he didn't let Celia distract him from his original purpose.

'Yes, you did lose your folks, and it made you sad. Just like it makes Uncle Walther sad that his are gone.'

Ceeley pulled free of Maarcus. 'He's *not* my uncle.'

He dropped his arms and sighed audibly while Walther echoed him inwardly. 'He is at least as much your uncle as I am and he loves you as much as I do.'

'No, he doesn't.'

'And you know what else, Celia Sailclan?' he asked, ignoring her denials.

The child answered formally. 'What, Uncle Maarcs the Seventh?'

'He feels very badly because he didn't come home in time to help. And I bet you know how it feels when you can't help.'

The child burst into tears.

Walther's stomach wrenched. He sat up too quickly and nearly fell forward. 'What did you remind her for? No kid should have to remember something that horrible!'

'No kid should ever see something that horrible either, but she did. And she needs to understand you are not her enemy. You're kin and she needs all the kin she can gather.' He gently addressed the child. 'You see, Ceeley, sometimes we have to make new families. I had to do it when my parents died and so did Jilian. Now you and Walther have to, too. What do you say, curly top?'

Ceeley bit her lip. She stared at the man a long moment. Slowly she shifted to study the woman, who had been quiet all the while, then finally Walther. When her gaze returned to Maarcus, her face seemed to have lost some of its tension. She gave him a small nod. 'OK, Uncle Maarcs.'

'There's a good girl. Now, go show Uncle Walther you're not mad at him anymore.'

The dwarf child walked over to the still seated Walther.

She curtsied stiffly, as if greeting royalty and Walther nodded solemnly in response.

'Truce, Celia of the Sailclan?' he asked.

She hesitated, then answered properly, 'Truce, Walther of the Shortdwarfs.'

Willam put one foot in front of the other, step upon aimless step. His vision felt clouded, as if the Sisters cloaked the world in a heavy fog that faded leaves, rocks, and the path ahead to grey. Despite the haze, the air was uncommon warm and the sun burned hot on his back.

He couldn't remember how far he'd walked or name his goal. He couldn't say if he ate or slept. Without Lyda he was nothing more than an aging shopkeeper, alone, lost.

He'd let go of his own kin string by string, the way men do. Lyda and their future had been enough. But then there'd been no family of their own. And now no future. Not for Lyda and maybe not for him.

'Avenge her death,' he muttered. Left . . . right . . . 'They won't get away.' Left . . . right . . . 'Avenge,' left 'her,' right 'death,' left, *pause*, right.

The words turned into a marching chant, guiding him through the eerie dry mist.

The world was made new for Lyda and her vision seemed to swirl with color. She wandered the forest along the river, examining leaves and stopping to pick up twigs for closer study. Her eyes on the branches above, she didn't see the large pebble that tripped her and threw her down on one knee. Instead of cursing the rock, she scooped it up to look at it as if it were a live thing.

She turned it over and over, brushing off the dirt and revealing the sparkle of quartz crystals beneath. The pebble was smooth and egg-shaped, perfectly formed to fit in the palm of her hand as if it belonged there. She closed her fingers around it, hefted its weight, and sat quietly where she'd fallen on the woodland floor. Lyda contemplated the rock. She considered the stream that had carried the pebble far from its original mountain as was proper for rocks and all the Sisters' creations.

Yet women never truly leave home. This too was the Sisters' way. And it was time for Lyda to return. Then she would see what lay ahead for her.

Chapter 8

NIGHTMARES

Tom and the girl were gone again, and Roslin felt an unexpected sense of loss. She woke that same night, dressed quickly, and rushed down the predawn streets before stopping dead still. Great magicians did not go chasing after apprentices, let alone untrustworthy lovers. *She* did not engage in such complete foolishness. With head high and queenly stride, Roslin returned to her room.

She closed her door on the world and expanded the wards against intrusion to include Ginni and Tom. When they came back empty-handed – and she had warned them that inevitably they would – the girl and the man must offer more than inventive stories and pretty smiles to appease her. She had more important matters at hand.

Roslin had never before felt so alone and isolated as she set about preparing for the morning's work. In the early days after Tom had left her, and over the following ten years, she was still studying furiously. She would often become so preoccupied with her magic that she forgot to eat. Roslin would come back to herself to discover the child had fed them both by foraging food from their cupboards and coaxing milk from their neighbor – or more likely directly from the old crone's goat itself. A plate of half-eaten bread and cheese sat in the only clear space on the table just where Ginni had gently placed the original fresh one, and others before it.

Roslin had felt inordinate pride at her clever daughter, who required just the lightest finger-touch of attention. How well the child could fend for herself – and how she delighted in the counting and word games they played in the moments between studies. The girl learned quickly, too, for a handful of mistakes would send Roslin back to her research.

On this day, the mage chose carefully among her scrying potions. This time Roslin would reach beyond the forbidden limits of her order. They had rejected her, dismissed her farsighted warnings of the coming terror as frightened imaginings of a novice. Soon they would not simply come to agree with her. They would come *to* her, desperate for help when the elfwitch dropped her curtain of pain all around the borders then began to cinch it tight. And she would graciously lead her sister magicians into battle.

Roslin settled before the wide bowl. Blood pounded in her head and hands with the eagerness of a student's first seeing test. She measured the portions exactly, poured in spoonsful of liquids common enough to form soup stock, dripped in three drops, five or seven of the rarer, powerful ingredients. Smoke rose off the mixture and she breathed in its strong aroma. From long practice she knew it was this as much as anything in the bowl which would guide her visions. With one last, daring move, Roslin, the unacknowledged mightiest of her Order, added one perfectly round drop of the taboo sap of the elfin serviceplant.

A thick, black cloud floated above the bowl. Again she

inhaled, but this time the vapor settled into her nose and chest with a cloying scent that nearly made her gag. The mage swallowed bile. She placed one damp palm on each side of the scrying basin and looked in. An unfamiliar film slid across the fluid to strike the inside rim with a high-pitched ring, then circled the bowl's edge before moving in to cover the entire surface.

The witch smiled, triumphant. Nothing in anyone's experience could compare.

Roslin began to chant. The rhymes and rhythms of past, present, and future danced and became one smooth flow of events. She controlled the course. The mage chose the forbidden touchstone of the near hours, prohibited for its dangers to the innocents still living. She sought the great and loathesome dragon Grosik, who was ever the vehicle of human separation. She found Tom and Ginni joking as if the world were a gamesground for children. She saw Ginni's exploration of the bones and tightened her own focus on the runes.

Roslin's hands grew hotter and hotter. Steam seemed to squeeze from the pores until the flesh itself must be melting. Still she ignored the agony and stared into the vision. She would not succumb to the false pain intended to ward off cowards.

She heard the dragon talk of spells of transformation and knew he spoke true. The ciphers squirmed under her gaze and reformed as the ancient language she had believed extinct. Her hands moved of their own will, scrawling out the words on the tabletop, spilling out precious oils in their haste to record what she could not translate.

Unbidden, the vision fell backward in time and she could not control it. She saw the world solidify from molten rock – though all who cared knew it had always existed as it did now. She saw great and powerful creatures emerge from the boiling oceans and learn to stand erect on its shores. She saw the thinking species of man, elf, and dwarf as one clan, short and tall, stout and thin. The family grew overlarge, separated to climb the mountains and travel the inland rivers. Each new family chose their shamans who led their steps and called a halt when they reached fruitful land. She saw trade thrive – goods, trinkets, daughters, sons. She saw terrible winters which froze the streams and isolated the clans. She saw the torrents of rain which flooded the crops and starved the weak. She watched the many sacrilegious burials, for there was not enough dry wood to build the proper funeral pyres and those remaining were too sickly to fight off the wolves. Entranced, she frowned in disgust and disapproval.

Then time moved forward, as she expected. But the landscape of the One Land was barren of forest. Seedlings struggled mightily to break through rock and dust only to strangle in the poisonous grease-clogged air. Roots dug deep to reach yellowed water barely trickling over ledges that had once supported waterfalls splashing down the height of two hundred men. Roslin looked hard into the future and screamed.

Mut's dreams had taken a strange turn. He was half man, half beast. It felt oddly familiar even as it frightened him. A female whispered, 'You were meant to be human,' but the man-thing shook his head, 'no' over and over. He remembered his earliest days – his painful birthing; his despair at lost wombmates; his mother's struggle to survive and her final gasp of air; the spoon feedings; his relief at meeting Jilian.

The dragon woke, shivering in the late afternoon chill. He rose on wobbly legs and shook from ears to tail, trying to throw off the image the way he'd shed water earlier.

Still he felt groggy and confused. He looked around trying

to get his bearings. The sight of rushing water reminded him he'd nearly drowned, but didn't tell him where he was. His best route home was to follow the stream, though, so he made sure to stay high on the bank as he walked into the setting sun.

An hour later, the creek emptied into a basin where the water pooled before moving on to drain out the other end. The world ahead was a blaze of orange and red and Mut was fast losing strength.

On the opposite bank beautifully ornamented tents formed a sizeable camp. He collapsed in the grass and took it all in. The skin tents were decorated with silver and precious stones. Elves hurried about, men and women alike wearing gems and finely hammered jewelry to accent their embroidered clothing.

Was this a festival or everyday dress? The encampment was like nothing Mut had ever seen. He'd worked with elves often enough and thought he knew them, but he realized now he'd never escorted them through their own land. Watching them this way, he wondered why Jilian had never found work with such extraordinary beings – or was it that traditional elves never hired outside their own?

Curiosity overcame exhaustion and drew him in. Despite old habits urging caution, Mut had to move closer. The dragon crouched low, all but slithering through the grass as he sought a better view. He was so intent on what lay before him that he completely missed the boy.

The child came running, waving his arms and shouting gibberish. Mut cocked his head and struggled to decipher the words. At last Mut recognized the dialect of elven just as the boy took aim with a slingshot and a good size rock. 'Get away from my sheep, beast. Back or you'll get it. I won't miss.'

Mut sat back on his haunches and stiffened his shoulders

in his hautiest pose – a trick he'd learned from an older dragon. The posture was meant to freeze a would-be attacker in terror. In Mut's case, he looked as frightening as a curious and friendly dog – or so Jilian said.

At least it disarmed the boy. Staring, he lowered his slingshot and took a step forward. He shook his head in a tiny, hunch shouldered motion as if he expected someone to chastise him for it. 'I know all the animals along this river and you are not one of them. Now what would you be?' The child walked nearer still and held out his hand for Mut to sniff, as if instinctively knowing the dragon wouldn't bite.

Mut didn't need to smell the boy at licking distance; from where he stood, he reeked of goat. The dragon looked at the outstretched hand and the timid smile. The kid could use a pat on the head, he decided. Mut snorted to get the goat out of his nose then held his breath while he politely 'sniffed' at the child.

The boy smiled. 'By the Water, wait until I tell – ' He thought better of it instantly and gave another strangled head shake. 'They don't understand. You don't mind staying out here with the goats, do you? That's a good boy,' he answered himself without waiting for a sign from Mut.

Above all, Mut needed to rest. He *did* mind the goats, but something about the child reminded the dragon of Jilian fifteen years ago. A boy and an elf, true, but still an outcast among his people. Mut closed his eyes and . . .

The boy was speaking. '. . . goats are really very nice, much better than some *elves* I know . . .'

The dragon's knees were buckling. The boy's voice was fading into a happy patter where the words lost meaning, just like Jilian talking him to sleep.

Roslin came to on the floor. She felt rough cloth against her cheek and immediately recognized her warding rug. The witch let her mind trace back to her most recent need of the carpet and decided she was still in the rented room above the inn. Only then did she open her eyes and sit up to confirm her assumption.

The door remained locked and unmolested. The unmade bed stood against the wall. The straightbacked chair was neatly placed under the table as if she had not fallen from it. Scattered around the legs of both chair and table were her jars and vials, leaking their precious contents into the rug and floorboards. She quickly set about righting each of these.

The last bottle on the floor had an odd shape, as if melted then cooled. An unfamiliar pungency wafted from it and made her stomach roll. She stoppered it with her hand and rose to find a proper cap.

Roslin's knees collapsed beneath her. She had to set the bottle on the table edge to pull herself up. She pushed back the chair with a loud scrape of wood on wood and sat heavily in the seat. The mage felt age-old as she braced herself with swollen, unresponsive hands on the edge. Her vision spiralled to black and white as she slid forward to cradle her head in crossed arms.

In the quiet, something was wrong, something missing. Roslin lifted her head suddenly and nearly fell again from a new wave of dizziness. She stared, all her attention concentrating on the desk before her. It was a duplicate of the floor, bottles askew, powders and fluids pooling on the top. Her lips tightened in unconscious disapproval – so unlike her to cause such a mess. Even so . . .

Her scrying bowl!

She had left it on the table, but it was not there. Her hands now rested in its place. She lifted each one and turned it palm up, as if the bowl remained hidden in the lines of her skin. Fighting blackout, she searched the room. Across, under, over. Bed, warding rug, table. Nothing. Gone. Impossibly gone. And now the vertigo was overpowering.

She reached the bed just before the axehandle of darkness struck and the dreams began anew.

A small voice protested – her own. She had seen the past and the future. She had seen the present, forbidden to lesser talents. What more could there be to know?

There is always more, came the silent answer, tinged with the harsh coldness of a stranger who invited no friends.

Roslin nodded, almost humble in her agreement, thinking that this too must be part of the scrying trance and that she had not really awakened and found so much of her valuable magicks squandered on the beechwood floor.

Her seeing had been dark and now grew all the darker. Over and again, she saw the Talented feared, abused, and ejected from their people. Each time, her hawk's-eye view flew in to discover the name of the outcast and each time her own face – younger, older, tear-streaked, or defiant, but always swearing vengeance – stared back at her.

All replayed before her in an endless march. The minor incidents – childhood laughter at her early scrying attempts; exile to the convent when her ignorant parents chose to ignore the talented but unruly girl; the punishment at the hands of jealous hags. The major affronts – the Order's rejection upon discovering her pregnancy; villagers armed with clubs and knives chasing her from her town of refuge when they grew impatient with Ginni's small displays of talent; and finally, finally, Tom and Ginni's own dismissal of her counsel. Damn them!

The world grew cold. Water iced into frozen pools. New green shoots grew brittle from frozen sap, snapped off with loud cracks, and were crushed underfoot. Great beasts fought one another for survival on sparse flat plains Roslin did not recognize. Creatures learned to fly and transformed into dragons, as if only molting a second skin, then flew into the mountains and were lost.

Onto the plains came the three races draped in rough animal skins. Men battled dwarves, dwarves battled elves, elves battled men. Shivering and starving but still they fought. Praying and chanting, they too finally followed the winged dragons one by one.

And the highlands grew miraculously warm, warmer than today. The races flourished, each among her kind, and the Seven Sisters blessed them all with abundance.

Why had the Great King united the One Land? The races had been separate for generation upon generation and were meant to remain separate. His true accomplishment had been to give the humans rest and respite to gather the energy to fight again.

But focusing on the Great King brought her an unexpected scene, a moment of violence and birth. The King himself had fathered the twins she had sought her entire life! And now it was time the twins faced their destiny as rulers of their world. The Mage, Roslin, would see that all was put right.

She awoke thinking of twins, twins and a human male – the one who had kept the bracelet for the hated elves.

Talking seemed to comfort the boy, his constant voice winding in and around Mut's dreams. The words poured out as if he'd never had a friend. Mut grew used to the strange accent and listened as hungrily as if he himself had lost his last friend.

'You know, dragon, all the elven tribes used to travel. Always. The young ones didn't mind, but sometimes the elders grew tired. Still, we've always made camp and rested when we needed. It's not a forced march; something in our blood keeps us moving.' He sounded quite sure on this point and the groggy dragon had to remind himself that elves age much more slowly than humans. The boy had probably been guarding goats since before Jilian was born.

The elf's speech suddenly dropped to a mumble and Mut instinctively strained to hear. 'The One is wrong. We don't need to settle.'

The One? Mut opened his eyes.

The boy was looking out over the meadow. 'How will I feed my goats once they've grazed out the pasture if we claim a single place? Already the supplies grow short and the unfavored go hungry. Already the births of infants are dwindling. We are not farmers. We do not know how to nurture food from the land for all that we may coax it towards beauty.

'The One says we must claim the lands to protect Her river valley. She says the dwarves and humans forced us down the weary road of travel so long ago that not even the elders remember. But now we have become hoarders of goods which crowd our tents and our fields. Everyday joys grow lost among the clutter. And the One speaks only of the shame of overburdened elders.' He wagged his head sadly. 'It will come to no good, no good at all.'

The dragon cocked his head. He didn't know much about shepherding, but he thought there must be a way for the old to find rest without starving the young. This One was wrong but so too the boy.

'They say She'll be back soon.' The boy sighed. 'I don't like her much,' he confided. 'Everyone runs around bowing low and begging Her gracious forgiveness for imagined slights. Nothing is adequate. Elders yell at anyone younger and they come to taunt me. My parents, usually too blessed embarrassed to claim me, suddenly want to know where I'm going and why I haven't combed my hair and how I got my britches torn.' He picked at the frayed edge of an old rip on his knee. 'There's no use in reminding them I'm wearing another's left-behinds. Who knows how they got this way?'

Mut nuzzled the boy's hand in commiseration.

'Powerful ones are a curse and a nuisance. I don't ever want power.'

Mut quietly whoofed his agreement, even as he knew the perversity of the Seven Sisters would place this poor unwanted child directly in the crossfire. It would start as soon as she saw the boy had befriended a deformed dragon, for surely she was allied with the elfwitch – if she weren't the witch herself.

The elf pitched something at the line of trees off to his left. The goats looked up at the sudden movement then went back to their continual eating. Unlike the dull, smelly beasts Mut ignored, he had to fight the urge to bound after and retrieve whatever it was.

Laughter floated up from the pond not far away. 'And when he steps in . . .'

'But it was all Goatboy's fault,' a second voice said in feigned innocence.

The dragon sank into the grass. The elf stood and swore. 'I'd better see what they've done. Most of the others have finally grown bored with such tedium, but those two will die before they give it up.'

The elf casually checked on his goats on his way to confront the others. His swagger tore at Mut. It was the same front Jilian put up when she was desperate and outnumbered.

Jilian. Now Mut was all the more intent on getting back to her. He knew if the elfwitch caught him again, she would not let him go.

When Roslin awoke, stiff from the hard chair, it was dark in the room. She didn't know if it was day or night, or how much time had passed. She didn't care. Her body hummed with the strength of magic beyond her most ambitious hopes.

The mage did not waste time wondering to what she owed the power. Clearly the Sisters had meant it for her because she had studied long years and endured much. She deserved it and she intended to put it to good use.

She rose and once again set about putting away her magicks. Her scrying bowl was just where she left it and the ancient writing was nowhere to be seen. She shrugged her shoulders and went on. It must have been part of the vision. As she worked, the one image which held in her mind, though, was not of death and destruction, of wars across time, or of Ginni and Tom. Rather, the common merchant, Willam, filled her thoughts.

Like her, he was a man who had met great disappointment without buckling. His soul had been scraped clean of all generosity and good will. His driving force was to find the ones who had done him evil in order to take his proper revenge . . . or die trying. This very impetus had caused the wars and could be channelled to her needs. Then too, instead of repulsion, Roslin felt a kinship she had not known possible. Here was a man who had tried and tried to do right only to have it thrown back in his face. Roslin couldn't wait to meet him.

And she knew just where to find him.

Mut was beginning to hate sleep. He'd dreamt he'd been Jilian's true companion, a two-legged, two-armed boy. He'd been a child who skipped stones, laughed, and talked. He held a knife and threw it at his enemy's heart.

Mut shook himself awake and lay breathing hard in the deep night. Even at this hour, elves were stirring at camp, preparing for the One.

He needed to leave *now* before She arrived. He didn't owe anything to the young elf. The entire lot of them had never done him any good. But even as he thought it, he knew the lie of it. The boy befriended him. The least Mut could do was leave by daylight instead of sneaking out like a thief.

For a long while, the dragon listened to the sounds of elves quietly calling to each other as they cooked. As their rhythms lulled him back to sleep, he promised himself he would go in the morning.

The kid must have known in his heart what the dragon planned because he brought a breakfast of hard cheese, bread and water at daybreak. He gently nudged Mut awake. 'Hungry, Dragon?'

Mut licked his lips without meaning to.

'Ah, thought so.' He set the food in front of the dragon's snout. 'Sorry I couldn't do better, but the One will be here today. The elders are watching over the cook pots as if She herself will test it for poison.' He shrugged. 'And perhaps she will.' He pushed the water bowl closer. 'Come, drink up!'

Mut sniffed for toxins. He trusted the boy, but didn't expect him to know that small traces of elements safe to his own kind could prove hazardous to the dragon. Satisfied, he lapped at the water.

The elf held out a palm covered with cheese and bread bits. 'Dragon?'

The boy's tone set Mut on the alert. He sat back without eating and cocked his head to let the elf know he was listening.

'Dragon, I was hoping you might stay until she leaves . . .'

Mut backed up a step.

'No one knows you're here and I won't tell them,' he said hurriedly. 'You'll be safe with me.'

The dragon tossed his head in a violent no gesture.

'I knew you were smarter than the goats,' the boy said to himself. 'I hate to ask this, I do, but their torment . . .' The boy trailed off, unable or unwilling to finish.

Mut looked at the elf, judging him for trickery. No, he couldn't believe it of him . . . Still, his own freedom . . . And if the witch were less than a day's travel . . . But with her so close, he might do just as well to wait until she were occupied with the feast and then escape.

The dragon made up his mind. Hoping he wouldn't regret his softness, Mut moved forward and nosed the cheese from the boy's hand.

A woman called out, 'Goatboy!'

The elf winced but didn't answer. Instead he continued to feed Mut.

The woman hollered again, sterner. 'Goatboy! Come this instant! I want my brooch.'

Without a backward glance to the dragon, the elf ran to join the others. 'Sorry, Mother, I was looking for—'

Mut's stomach rolled. Even the child's own mother called him the hideous name. Surely this was not his own flesh. Surely 'Mother' was a term of respect for an elder – though he had not heard the child refer to any adult with such deference before now.

'Don't bother me with your nonsense, Goatboy.' The woman spoke loud enough to be heard throughout the camp. 'No one cares what games you play. Go into our tent and get my brooch. The One will be here within the hour and I want Her to know of my standing.'

'But Mother, the goats need – ' A sharp slap cut him off.

'One of these days, you will learn never to discuss those disgusting animals in my presence. Further, you are to obey me without question. Now go fetch.'

'Yes, Mother,' the child answered quietly. His voice did

not choke and Mut knew this was not the first time he had suffered such harshness.

I'm becoming as foolish as a pampered lapdog, the dragon told himself as he settled on the edge of the forest and waited for the celebration to begin. He was sure the shepherd would rest amidst his goats when the elves went to sleep tonight. Mut would still be here to join him when he did.

Chapter 9

GHOST-TOWNS

Hours passed, days, maybe weeks. Willam held conversations with himself, trying to find the exact minute where he had gone wrong, where life had led him astray. He dug through memories, now muddied with death, and found only blood.

His shoes went threadbare, but he ignored it. There was no one to repair shoes and he had no money to pay them. The soles wore away until he walked unprotected on the cold rocky ground, but his feet kept moving.

He must have been climbing into the highlands because snow was falling. It settled on his shoulders and in his hair. He pulled on the cap Lyda had knitted for one of her beloved holidays. His fingers grew numb from brushing away the snow, so he stopped bothering after a while and began to consider it a companion. His head felt too heavy for his neck and his back reformed into a hunch.

He attended all bodily needs with the same inattention to particulars. He ate frozen berries and slow swimming fish he speared with a walking stick. He chased animals from their burrows and crawled in to warm himself for a time before going on. He relieved himself against snowbanks that did not melt when the hot urine streamed against it.

Somehow he had lost his way. He could not find the right valley. His home, the entire town, seemed veiled by a fog which hid the familiar landmarks and reshaped the mountains into taller, craggier peaks of a younger range.

'Have you considered your actions?' repeated a woman's voice.

Who's this nag? he thought, not ready to challenge her aloud. 'as she nothin' better to do 'an dog my steps?

And still the harpy kept prodding. 'Will you not join me when I can save you from this misery?'

And still he ignored her.

It took no more than tripping on a sharp rock. He fell and landed hard on his right hand. Tiny bones snapped.

'Now,' said the witch, 'now will you come with me and let me help you?'

He looked into her face, harsher than his surroundings but surely of them. He looked at the bleak treeless landscape, the filth clogged river running nearby, the snow yellowed in dirty patches that mirrored her eyes. 'You – ' His voice cracked with pain. 'You and your kind 'ave caused my "misery", as you call it. I tell you I've 'ad enough of mages for my all days, now and when I rest in the cradled arms o' the Sisters.'

The witch's face grew colder, sharper. She seemed to swell and tower over him as he sat where he'd fallen, nursing the broken hand. She could crush him with a thought, but he didn't flinch. He'd lost his fear when he'd lost Lyda.

The witch raised her arms, then stopped. 'You are not worth my magic. But know this. I never forget a slight – or those who dare to do so.'

The ground under Willam churned and rumbled. He

bounced and tumbled on the rocky path and found himself grabbing hold of a tree that had not been there before. Snow roared past in violent sheets but left him unscathed. When the earth quieted, she was gone.

Willam took a breath. 'Mages and their magic casting,' he muttered. 'They can't join the Sisters soon enough for me!' He spat into snow and watched the steam rise. He needed to break free not of the uncommon weather, but of the unseen eyes, eyes that belonged to yet another arrogant witch.

As Willam used the remains of his kerchief to fix a sling, he discovered his arm wasn't as badly hurt as he'd thought. He tapped and poked at bones and flesh. A bruise, no more.

Suddenly he knew just where to go. He would head down the mountain and travel to the Shoreman capital. There he would find the means to avenge Lyda. There he would find peace from the witches.

The dwarf manning the rudder must have been the only one watching the shore, for he interrupted in a quiet voice. 'There's smoke ahead.'

The other three silenced their chatter as they all turned in the direction of Walther's outstretched arm.

The ugly black smoke drifted out from the deserted dock and carried with it an awful, overpowering smell.

Jilian's stomach lurched with the thought of another town destroyed. Fighting the urge to float past and keep on floating, she spoke almost as softly as Walther had. 'We have to help.'

Ceeley panicked. 'No, no! We have to get far, far away from here, as far as we can!' She ran to hide in the cabin, still shrieking. 'No, no, no! I won't go back ! I won't go back!'

Walther watched the child flee and shook his head. 'Celia, I couldn't help our people. Maybe I can help these.'

'It's too late,' Ceeley yelled from inside the cabin. 'If you can smell it, it's too late!'

'But we have to try, don't we?' Maarcus soothed.

'No, no, no. It's too late, way too late!'

'Maybe one of us should stay with her,' Jilian suggested.

The three adults looked to the others in mute agreement, each wanting to protect Ceeley and at the same time help any survivors who could be rescued.

Jilian couldn't stand the silence. 'I'll keep her company. Just don't take too long.'

'You're sure?' asked Maarcus.

She nodded with more confidence than she felt. She did not say, Walther can't do it because his presence won't calm the child or you obviously need to investigate as part of your mission, whatever that is. I can face my demons another day. She said only, 'I'm sure. We'll be fine.'

Maarcus called through the louvered slats in the cabin door. 'Ceeley, we'll be right back.'

'No, please don't go, Uncle Maarcs.'

He turned to Jilian, clearly torn, then back to the door. 'Jilian's right out here if you need her.'

The girl didn't answer but her heartfelt sobs were plain enough.

As the boat drifted up against the dock, Jilian threw a rope around the nearest piling and knotted it. She waved the two men away. They jumped ashore without another word and were swallowed by the thick, foul smoke.

She tried to open the cabin door but it didn't budge. The child must have jammed something against it. 'Ceeley, are you all right?'

No answer.

'Honey, can I come in?'

'Go 'way.'

It was going to be a long wait. The mercenary took to

pacing the deck. Her feet wore a pattern that led her mind away from Ceeley, away from the boat.

Jilian numbly sifted through wreckage. There was nothing left but charred remains. House, pottery, brick. All nothing but stinking, black refuse. She had no idea what she was looking for, but something pulled her forward. No one could have survived. No one had survived. She was a fool for coming here. Thinking she might save someone if she'd only arrived sooner. Trying to save her parents again and again.

Her gaze fixed on an arm severed from its body. The palm was up as if the corpse might yet have something to offer. Curse the trolls, she thought. Curse their evil, oversized bodies and undersized brains. And still she stared, thinking of another arm beseeching to no avail.

She prodded the arm with her toe. It crumbled as if it had only been made of skin without bone and muscle to support it. Underneath the ash was a tiny metal dragon the likes of which she'd never seen. It was not the work of any family she knew, whether dwarven or human. The elves seemed even more unlikely though she couldn't say why. She pocketed it knowing she was meant to find it.

'They are not here. Your parents were never here. Your questions cannot be answered in the mountains. You must go to the sea.'

At first Jilian thought she imagined the voices. She shook her head as if to rid her ears of water.

An hysterical Ceeley was pounding on Jilian. 'I told you. I told you. It's too late. They were here.'

'Did you see anyone?' Jilian asked, still dazed.

'She was here! She was here!' The child's screams grew even louder.

'All right, Ceeley, it's all right.' She gathered the flailing girl into her arms and held her tight, knowing it was not all right at all. By the Sisters, Jilian thought, don't let them hurt Ceeley. Please, don't let them hurt Ceeley.

They sat that way a long time rocking back and forth on the deck. She soothed the child as best she could, smoothing her curls, patting her back and murmuring softly.

The wind shifted and the deadly smoke wafted over the boat in thick black waves. They lay low on the deck and tried to dodge it, but it seemed to follow them.

Coughing and heaving, Jilian picked up her pack and the girl, and carried them both ashore. From the clear dock she could see the cloud hovering over their boat. No good would come of staying nearby. They would have to join the others sifting through the remains.

When Mut woke late in the day, his dizziness had returned. He couldn't have left now if he wanted. He could barely stand.

The witch arrived not long after, just as the sun was sinking behind the mountains. Mut tried not to feel disappointed. He'd known all along it would be the elfwitch herself, not an underling, not her double. He'd have to do something now, perhaps even escape with the boy in tow.

He watched her from his hiding place amid the goats everyone but the boy avoided. She crossed the long shadows on the far side of the meadow with a near mystical grace which did not surprise the dragon. But she came alone and wore a coarse robe that could only be seen as humble. Her troll attendants and fine clothing were nowhere in evidence.

The dragon didn't believe the elfwitch was truly able to completely debase herself, but the others seemed fooled. They gathered round her, talking all at once in their excitement as if they welcomed home a beloved and benevolent aunt. They called out 'teacher' and 'mother'. Every elf from child to adult jostled the others for position to show-off some well wrought trinket or bit of embroidery. They brought heaping piles of gifts, laying them at the foot of the chair they had placed in the center of camp to honor her. She accepted the chair with an overplayed bow, or so it seemed to Mut from his vantage downwind. He was eager to hear her response but she made no effort to project her voice and he dared not move closer.

It was plain to Mut they knew a completely different side from that which he'd seen. He trusted this new aspect even less than the more straightforward one he knew. He itched to get away. He must convince the boy that both of them had to leave tonight. If she caught him again, she would be sure not to lose him this time.

Mut did his best to conquer the dizzy spells as he slid through the tall grass sniffing for trolls, but at last he gave it up for useless. The smell of highly spiced food and the goats themselves masked all other scents.

The joyous laughter, eating and singing continued far into the night while Mut dozed off and on. Even the exhausted goatherder didn't come to curl against the dragon until nearly dawn.

As the camp quieted down, Mut began to feel a familiar pull. He wasn't fooling anyone but himself. The elfwitch knew he was there, but had chosen to let him play it his way for now.

Ceeley went limp in Jilian's arms the instant she stepped off the boat. The mercenary worried that the child had passed out until she heard her crying softly. She adjusted the pack on her back, then hitched the child higher and cradled Ceeley's head against her shoulder.

The girl was right. They never should have stopped. No one could have survived this. 'All right, Ceeley. OK, curly top. The sooner we find Maarcus and Walther, the sooner we can be rid of this place.'

Her only answer was a hiccup and renewed sobbing.

There was nothing left of the town but an ugly black carpet. No chunks of wood, no bits of metal, or even pieces of bone. Everything, living or not, was reduced to a fine ash.

Jilian picked her way, careful not to step in an ash-covered hole. Voices echoed strangely here, sounding not at all like those of Maarcus or Walther. Still she followed them for lack of any other direction. The voices grew farther away and she began running. A stew of pain surrounded her and she couldn't tell if it were her own or those who had lived here.

Finally, she stumbled upon Maarcus and Walther. Maarcus hovered restlessly around Walther, waving his arms and trying to get the dwarf's attention. Walther's back was to her and she followed his line of sight to the vision which held him transfixed. Jilian moved closer involuntarily, then recoiled at what she saw.

Before her the witch upon a hill raised her arms, calling down death and destruction. Trolls tromped through the tiny village, while dwarves screamed and ran when there was nowhere to run. Trolls ringed the outside of the village. Oblivious to pain themselves, they turned the people back into the flames even while they burned along with their victims.

There was only swift, excruciating death as their bodies caught fire and seemed to melt in the flames like so many dabs of cooking fat frying the morning's breakfast.

The scene played over and again until Jilian couldn't tell whether she watched the same few deaths or the entire village one by one.

'What are you doing here?' Maarcus hollared inches from her face.

His voice pulled Jilian back to the horror of the aftermath.

Seemingly no time had passed though she felt as if she had lived through hours of torture. Maarcus looked angrier than she'd ever seen him. 'I . . . We . . . The boat,' she stuttered.

'You were supposed to wait for us.'

'We couldn't . . . The smoke.' Jilian could barely speak. She glanced over his shoulder to Walther, who hadn't moved, then down at Ceeley, who seemed to be sleeping.

Maarcus looked at her strangely. 'Are you two all right?'

The mercenary concentrated. Answering slowly, she explained why they had left a haven no longer safe. 'We'll have to travel on land from here on in,' she concluded without a hint of doubt.

The Shoreman nodded taking her at her word, for now at least.

'But first, we've got to rescue Walther.'

'What's wrong with him? He's been that way for much too long.'

'Can't you see it?'

'See what?'

'The flames, the . . .'

Walther slipped to the ground in a sobbing heap. The scene was gone as if it had never been. And from Maarcus's behaviour, it seemed it hadn't.

Maarcus held his arms wide. 'Want me to take Ceeley?'

Jilian relinquished the limp child, who never looked up to acknowledge her surroundings. The mercenary crouched down to the dwarf. She put her hand on his shoulder and he flinched. 'Walther, Walther, it's all right now. I'm here.'

He leaned against her still crying.

'It was so . . . so . . . h-horrible.'

'I know, Walther.' She wrapped one arm around him in a reluctant hug.

'You, you saw?' he asked between breaths.

'Yes, I saw.'

'Maarcus didn't.'

She looked back at Maarcus. He was absorbed with Ceeley, crooning and rocking, and paid them no attention. 'No, I don't think he did.'

'But it was right here. How could he not see it?'

'Magic is funny that way, Walther.'

'It just never occurred to me that only some could see my visions.' He shook his head, half in awe, half in dismay. 'Maarcus didn't see it,' he repeated. 'And now he probably thinks I'm spineless or feeble-brained for staring off at nothing that way.'

'Maarcus has led a royal life. He can't always understand what it's like for ordinary men.'

'But you saw it. And Maarcus must have seen plenty of magic growing up in the Cliffs.'

'True,' Jilian answered. 'But I have a feeling Sir Maarcus the Seventh is rather attached to looking at things the way *he* wants them to be, not the way they are or might be.' She looked hard into his eyes. 'You're special, Walther. The Sisters spared you for a reason. You can fight the elfwitch.' Jilian didn't know what came over her to make her say such a thing. Just the same, it was as obvious to her as knowing that a stick breaking in the forest almost always means an assassin stalks his victim.

'You really think so?'

'Absolutely. Come on, Walther. Let's get out of this graveyard.' She pulled him to his feet.

He slipped in the ash as he rose and stumbled to find secure footing. When the dust resettled, a half-buried medallion poked through. Together the two leaned down to pick it up.

'You recognize this?' she asked.

'Yes. And you?'

'I've found a couple over the years and have been studying them.'

'I've seen two as well. Amidst the ruins of my village and on the boat just before we left. That was what set Ceeley against me.'

'Guess we'd better not tell her I've got them too.'

He cocked his head, apparently deciding whether she mocked him, and if he could trust her.

Jilian made his decision easy. 'Sorry. I know how you feel about her.' She went on, 'The first was the only intact artifact when my parents were killed. The second lay beneath the dust of a human town where I spent time after my parents died.'

'We must look at these all together. Find the pattern.'

Jilian nodded. 'But not now.'

'Later,' he agreed.

Jilian rubbed her thumb across the nearly familiar pattern. 'Do you want this one?'

'One is more than I need. Please keep it for us.'

Maarcus had wandered away, the dwarf still in his arms, but came back once he saw they'd found something. 'Anything interesting?' he asked.

'Yes, but we'll need to discuss this later. We need a refuge for Ceeley now.'

'And perhaps a healer.'

'How far are we from Twin Gates?' Maarcus asked the other two.

Jilian shrugged. 'Three days on foot, maybe two.'

'With good luck and good weather,' the dwarf amended. 'Why?'

'There's a woman, an elf, closer to me than my own mother was. Good woman through and through, could have taken lessons from the first of the Seven Sisters. Ceeley will be safe with her.'

The others nodded. 'Consider it done.'

* * *

The witch had tied Mut to a tree, his human arms wrapped behind him and his dragon legs hobbled. She circled and floated, whispering, soothing, cajoling, threatening him to accept his true nature. He flicked at her with his tail, but she dodged lightly, laughing while she did so.

'Haven't you always wanted to be a man? Haven't you always wanted to speak with more than barks and yips? Haven't you always wanted to repay those who stole your mother?'

His stomach twisted tighter and tighter until it ached more than his rope-bound wrists. How did she strike a chord he didn't have?

When Mut woke he couldn't be sure if he was still gripped by the dark dreams, but he knew he was very ill. His legs could not hold him to stand. He could not eat or drink. The struggle exhausted him. He dozed.

Someone lifted his head to drink water. Thinking Jilian had finally found him, he cracked open his eyes to find an elf boy he did not remember. Startled, he jerked his head away from the child. It landed with a jarring thud on the ground that made his ears ring. Rather than force the fluid, the boy patiently raised Mut's lower jaw and grasped it gently until the dragon drank his fill.

He lay on a cloth outdoors under a tree. The boy carefully removed the soiled mat and slid a clean one beneath him. The motion was smooth and even as if he had performed this same act many times before.

When this was done, the elf sat nearby patting the animal's head, rubbing his back. Mut welcomed the touch. It calmed the nightmares and made him feel safe. He would rest now and find Jilian as soon as he was better.

The foursome shuffled through the dust of the town on their way out. Maarcus carried Ceeley who couldn't be roused to walk or even stand. Jilian dragged behind. She'd been too late, again. Why did she even try?

As they passed under the welcome arch that had somehow remained complete, Jilian took one final glance over her shoulder.

A boy with dragon's wings rose from the ashes, a ghost the color of a midnight that knows no stars. He stepped toward her, his arms reaching out for balance like a toddler learning to walk. 'Mama?' he asked, his voice the sound of two dry sticks rubbing together.

Who was he calling? Jilian looked back to the others, but they had gone on down the path. No one was there.

She twisted back to the boy. His foot was raised to take another step, but it did not land. Instead he fell forward, down and down, into the ashes face first.

She ran to him and knelt beside him. There was nothing but ash.

Jilian didn't realize until much later that the boy had been human not dwarven as she had supposed.

Chapter 10

STORYTIME

'Uncle, I've been thinking.'

'Dangerous work.'

Ginni gave her father's thigh a playful punch. 'About those bones.'

'Absolutely not,' said her father.

'Want to push her over the side?' asked the dragon. 'Nice long drop to some craggy rocks coming up.'

'Too late for that. We missed our chance years ago.'

'Uncle!'

They rode on in silence, scanning the ground for Willam.

'Uncle, about the bones.'

'What bones?' he asked, pretending he'd already forgotten.

Ginni ignored his feint. 'Don't you want to know whose they were?'

He kept his voice flat to cover his own interest. 'I've seen plenty of skeletons. They look pretty much the same without flesh on 'em.'

'Not that. I mean who was being transformed and into what.'

He shrugged. 'Sure, that could be useful knowledge. Don't see how I can come by it. Likely get us all killed trying. Bad risk.'

She nodded to his back. 'Risk, yes, but worth the odds, I'd wager.'

'You're wagering more lives than just your own.'

Ginni fell quiet long enough for Tom to hope she'd genuinely dropped the subject this time, but when she spoke again the words held an unfamiliar edge. 'That's always been true, Uncle. And under Roslin's direction. Think about that for a minute.'

His answer didn't take a minute. 'I already have.'

'And?'

'And nothing. She's always known more about this sort of thing than we have.'

'Sure, but can it really make sense to do this all alone? You're a soldier—'

'When I can't avoid it.'

'Father, what sane soldier would go into battle armed only with his two most trusted companions?'

'Spies do with less.'

'Yes, but their duties are part of a larger, *organized* effort.'

She put a little too much emphasis on 'organized' for the mercenary's peace of mind, but he let it go. Unfortunately the dragon was feeling chatty.

'Told you she'd figure it out,' he mumbled.

Tom gently nudged Grosik's flank with his boot toe.

'Well,' said the dragon.

'Well?' asked his daughter.

'Well nothing,' answered the mercenary.

'You and Roslin aren't exactly the "joining" kind.'

Wanton Tom sighed and gave in. Ginni and Grosik would

spell each other nagging him until he'd wish he'd settled down with a talky woman instead of these two. 'True enough,' he said, 'but we *are* the fighting kind.'

'And?'

Maybe he could tell her just enough to damp her curiosity. 'Some time back a couple of men convinced Roslin and then me there were some very bad times ahead. We were already out and about and they figured we were perfect "information gatherers", as they put it.'

'And no one told me?' Ginni's voice rose in indignation.

Tom put a hand on her shoulder and she shrugged it off. 'Ginni, this started years ago. You were just a girl.'

'Roslin doesn't seem to think so anymore. She's been sending me out to do her dirty work for months.'

'Yes, and you saw my reaction to that. I still think you're too young. This is dangerous work.'

'What do you suggest I do instead? Enter a convent?'

Tom sighed. In all seriousness he said, 'I tried. Ros wouldn't hear of it.'

'I'll have to thank her when we get back.'

'Gin, it wouldn't have been that bad. I wanted someone to teach you things I can't and Roslin won't. Besides, I'm worried for you. Those who live by secrets usually die by them.'

'People die from falling in rivers when they can't swim. I always make sure I have the necessary skills to cross the river.'

'Yes, but this is different.'

'How?' Her shoulders hunched in defiance.

'This has an enemy, individuals who go out of their way to throw you in the river with hands and feet bound and rocks tied about your waist.'

'As if I've never had a presumed well-wisher try to knife me where I stood?'

Tom grunted then was silent. She had him there. Traveling with a mercenary had hardly been the pampered life of the Great King's children (before his death anyway), nor had living with a mage who never saw welcome once the villagers discovered her calling. He'd known whores with an easier time of it.

'Uncle, you need me.'

'Tom, we need her,' echoed the dragon.

'There's nowhere else for me to go.'

He hated to agree, but even more than having come to depend on her he couldn't picture leaving her with anyone else. As long as she remained sheltered by his sword arm or Roslin's magic, he could fool himself into believing she was safe. 'All right, Ginni. You're in.' He paused. 'But don't tell Ros you know about this. She was very adamant that we "protect you from the truth". She'll likely be furious with me and she tends to break chairs over my head in this mood.'

Ginni laughed. 'Oh, she does not. She just threatens to turn you into a frog.' In a whisper, she added, 'But it's too late for that. Ribbit, ribbit.'

'Go on, have your fun.' He laughed with her. 'One of these days, someone will turn you into one of those ghastly trolls.' He dangled his fingers in front of her face and feigned the sound of a monster.

'You can't scare me with that old story. I stopped believing in bogie creatures a long time ago.' She paused, perhaps considering the bones she'd found. 'I think.'

Tom hadn't meant his joke to turn serious, but found himself empty when he dug for a sharp retort.

Finally, Ginni settled more comfortably on Grosik's back. 'So out with it. What have we been up to?'

He was quiet a moment longer, picking among the facts and still hoping to give her enough that she wouldn't ask for more and yet couldn't guess the rest. If anything happened to him or Roslin he didn't want her chasing after them and endangering herself.

Despite his better judgment, he couldn't let loose of the string of a wish that he could shield her with ignorance.

Wanton Tom took a deep breath and began. 'They came to us years ago.'

'Who? When?' Ginni interrupted.

'Ginni, it's a long tale and you've got to let me tell it in my own way.' His voice sounded tired even to himself. 'All right?'

Ginni nodded.

'All right?' he asked again.

'All right.'

'The magician came to your mother not long after she left you with me. I don't know what he told her. I wasn't there and she spoke very little about it. A few years later the Great King's physician sent someone to fetch me to an audience. I'd never been called by anyone in or out of power before, not to mention someone with the reputation the old scientist still has among the men who've lived long enough to know better. I guessed it was Grosik that attracted Sir Maarcus. I've never run across another fighting man who travelled with a dragon.' He smiled, proud of their unusual relationship, then continued.

'Hospitable, the man was. Had himself fixed with a nice little cozy cabin in a clearing well off the main trails. Kept a few guards posted discreetly. Blended in with the forest, they did. Probably had the magician mask it from wanderers while he was at it. "Come sit down," he says. "Have a cup of refreshment."

'I looked at the teapot, picked up the cup and sniffed. Smelled like plain old tea. I stared into the cup and shrugged. It looked ordinary enough, so I took a sip and it tasted like one of the fancy brews I don't go in for. I figured then he was probably legit. If he'd been trying to poison or hex me, he would have found something more suited to a rough man. Ale maybe. "Tea's a bit refined for my palatte," I say, trying for polite. "But I will sit a while and hear what you have to say." I pulled back a chair, sat down, leaned it back on two legs.' Tom laughed. 'I just didn't want him to know I was in awe of him. Fool. Maarcus the Sixth had been around worse than me. He saw through the whole thing but only tipped his head, put his elbows on the table and began.

'"I understand you've recently come into the care of a young girl."

'"What's it to you?"

'"It so happens I have been looking for a female child for the past ten years."

'"Not mine," I say, unable to hide my relief. "This one's barely out of diapers. Thank the Seven Sisters she was past that when – " I realize I'm babbling like a nervous fop and stop talking.

'He looks me over, sure I must be lying but then maybe not. "Would you be willing to introduce me to your . . . *niece*, is it?"

'"Any time," I answer, all swagger now. He doesn't want you and he's always been called a man of honor. 'Sides, Grosik is watching over you and not likely to let anyone near enough to do you harm. "My niece is back with the dragon not far from here."

'"I'd be delighted to meet her," he says, with a pointed casualness.

'"Anytime."

'"Now would be excellent." He waits for me to answer but I can't think how to respond. I'd really gotten used to having you around and I'm not completely convinced this guy means you no harm. "Since she's so close," he continues. "I wouldn't want to inconvenience you at a later date." He looks at me with steely eyes and square jaw. It's plain I've got no way out but to fight. This is not the place or moment to do that. I'm outmanned and almost unarmed. Better to show him where you are because Grosik is there too. The dragon'll cover you and up my odds of survival while he's at it. So we tromp through the wood to the clearing, followed by a few crack guards. They were sharp enough to keep out of sight and quiet. I couldn't get an exact count, but I knew there had to be enough to protect someone as powerful as the physician. Maybe one for each of the Seven Sisters – or two hands' worth if he wasn't a religious man.

'But, Uncle, it could have been a trap for us all!'

'Ginni, the danger came from the first when he summoned me. We could have run, but he'd be keeping track. I'm not a thief – despite what some say – and wasn't about to start hiding like one. Grosik and I had our own defenses at the ready. I wouldn't have let them have you if I could help it and Grosik was there to make sure either way. We'd already agreed he'd leave me in the hands of the physician if need be to get you someplace safe.'

'But Uncle!'

'When did you become such an old maid?' Tom asked, echoing her earlier sentiment.

'Well, it's just that I've never seen you in that kind of situation before.'

'I should hope not. I go to great pains to avoid being surrounded by well-trained guards.'

Ginni laughed. 'And I'm not sorry that you do. Then what happened?' she asked, her voice betraying her eagerness to hear the rest.

'We'd found a small cave, of course.'

'Of course.'

'I led them to it in a roundabout trail, same way I'd gone to meet the old man. The cave was a bit small for Grosik's liking, but perfect for our purposes. He filled the entrance and no one was getting by without his say-so. You were behind him, probably stirring up as much trouble as you could manage. I tipped my hat to the dragon, our signal that I was OK, but he needed to be wary.'

'As if I wouldn't have known regardless,' the dragon huffed. 'Even the child understood that much.'

'"She's in there," I told the physician. "The only way you're going to get a good look at her is to go inside."

'"Then I shall," he answered, all formal but without a second's pause.

'"Your men'll have to stay out here."

'He gave me the once-over just as I had him back in his hovel in the woods, weighing whether he was on the road to becoming the dragon's bacon.

'"Not a lot of room in there."

'"I see," he says, still skeptical. "Then you won't mind staying out here with my men."

'No fool, that doctor. And so civil, he made me want to improve my manners.'

Ginni laughed. 'Oh, Uncle, you can't be serious. No one could do that.'

'He could. I swear by the Sisters, he could.'

'Well now, you *were* impressed.'

'You will be too.'

'*I* will?'

'The old man's still mucking around in things. No question. Once you get used to his style, you know when he's been by. You'll get another chance to meet him. I'm sure of the tale.'

Ginni didn't say anything to that, which set Wanton Tom to chewing on what his daughter could be plotting already. 'So you want to hear the rest?' he asked, more to distract her from her scheming than because of any rush to finish it.

'Yes, yes, please do.' Her voice sounded far away, but she shifted on the dragon's back to get more comfortable.

'So I bowed, very politely with only a trace of mockery. "I would be charmed to keep your men company." He let it go, but his guard didn't look too pleased. They hate it when the job becomes sticky. Protecting Sir Maarcus from Grosik wasn't just messy, it was impossible – and we all knew it.

' "Grosik," I called.

'He opened his lazy eyes, as if he'd slept through the entire conversation.

' "Sir Maarcus the Sixth, the Great King's physician would like to meet the child. Could you let him pass?"

'Grosik stood to show off his height and further intimidate the gentleman.'

'Nonsense,' the dragon said. 'I don't need to stand in order to make my presence felt. They were all scared spitless but had enough backbone not to show it. I was merely letting the man by. It was either that or have him crawling up my leg and over my backside.'

Together Wanton Tom and Ginni laughed.

'So he gets by Mr Charming here and then I can't see. I shift positions but the dragon is blocking the entrance. The royal guards are circling with me, partly to make sure I don't try anything, partly 'cause they can't see any more than I can.

'It's so quiet we can hear a pebble bouncing down the hillside. Suddenly, you scream and then the physician screams. Pretty soon we're all crowding the cavemouth. Grosik flicks his tail once like a contented cat. The ground shakes, but the men are prepared and keep on their feet. Sir Maarcus comes out, nods to me, motions to his men and he's gone.'

'But why did I scream? Why did he scream? And when did you get called into his service?'

'Grosik'll have to tell you about the screams.' And maybe

by then, Wanton Tom thought uselessly, she'll forget about this mission.

Grosik cleared his throat. 'Well, Mistress Ginni, daughter of mage and son of mercenary, it happened thus.'

'Grosik, you've been calling me that from the time I was a small child and I have always wondered why. For months I thought I was a changeling, or a neutered male. Now, I am reasonably certain I am female and female alone.'

'Do not interrupt the storyteller. He tends to eat such annoyances.'

Ginni carelessly slapped the dragon's flank as if he were just a large playful dog. It sounded much harder than Tom would dare regardless of all their years together and he was astounded by the behaviour Grosik tolerated from his daughter but no one else.

'Oh nonsense. Come on, Grosik.'

'I forget,' he rumbled.

'Well, double nonsense. You've never forgotten a thing in your life.'

'I could drag through my old dragon brain and try to remember or . . . I could tell about the king's physician.'

Ginni sighed dramatically and looked out over the dragon's head to stare at the mountains below. When Grosik kept quiet, she made another show of sighing and settling onto his back. 'All right, you win.'

'Well,' the dragon began in a voice that reminded Tom of a busybody washerwoman he'd known as a child. 'Sir Maarcus the Sixth – he was the first that counted. There's another one running about now, but I agree with the old man here that the markedly older coot hasn't put away his parchment and guards just yet. Sir Maarcus looked one shade paler once he got past me to you, but perhaps that was just the light.

'You were further back, rubbing sticks together and

challenging yourself to build a bigger fire.' He twisted his head around to bring himself eye to eye with the girl. 'You have always shown an inordinate and unhealthy interest in things that burn.'

'Triple nonsense.'

Grosik stared without blinking for a long moment. 'You are young,' he said and turned back to face where he flew. 'Your life has had complications, though it has been more carefree than many others. All of us have limits. I don't wish to observe you the day you learn this.'

Tom had long since grown used to the dragon's talk of impending doom, but this – like his reaction to the bones in the cave – seemed to hint at something more dire than the usual gloomy outlook. He'd have to find a time to discuss things when Ginni was out of earshot.

Grosik resumed his story. 'The physician circled you once, twice, three times, then bent over, snatched you by an ankle and hung you upside down.'

'That was the physician? I thought that was you.'

Tom tried to stifle a laugh but failed.

'This time Sir Maarcus provided the honors. Though it was strange to watch because he did poke and prod much the way I had several years earlier on our first meeting. I've never met a man who thought like a dragon, but he appeared to come close. What really made you mad, though, was when he snatched away the stick you thrust at him. You screamed at him and he yelled right back without a trace of anger or irritation.'

'But none of us outside knew that,' Tom said. 'I was the only one willing to climb across the dragon so the rest crammed the entrance. Maarcus turned to me with you still dangling by one leg. He pushed up your sleeves and your pants legs and checked around your neck, obviously looking for something.

' "She's not the one." He set you on the ground. "But if I were you, I'd watch what you leave in her reach. It'll likely end up cinders." He nodded with one of those expressions that I figured meant we'd hear more from him, but he left us alone . . . for a while.'

'A charming tale,' Ginni said, 'but then what?'

'Some time later, he requested our help. We dickered over the fee and now I do spot work for him when I must.'

'What kind of "spots" do you work on?' she asked, undeterred.

Wanton Tom opened his mouth and nothing came out of it. He just couldn't tell her. 'Why don't we let Roslin answer that.'

No matter how much the girl pleaded and wrangled, he simply shook his head. For once, the dragon kept his peace. At last Ginni announced that a few hours this way or that made little difference to her. Tom smiled at her bravado and tried not to fidget like an old maid.

Chapter 11

CRISSCROSS

From Shoremen to highlanders, all the peoples of the One Land – by whatever name it is currently known – understand about the mountains. It is their heritage, part of the blood. One does not walk the hills; one climbs. Legs stretch and arms pump simply to visit a friend. In the high hills, rivers are the literal connection for all. They carry goods, information, surprises. Townspeople in the river cities welcome visitors because they bring the same rhythms of newness as does the river itself. A city at the nexus of two rivers embraces strangers twofold. And at least in the inns, they are cause for celebration, however minor.

So it was all the more surprising that the reception awaiting two humans and two dwarves was stone cold.

Twin Gates was seductive relief after the dead dust of the earlier towns. People, *live* people, stood talking in doorways and buying the night's meal at market. The three stumbled through the streets, overcome with the breathing aliveness of a place that moved and functioned.

Even Ceeley seemed to come back to herself and squirmed to be let down. It had been a while since Jilian had taken over from Maarcus and she gladly released the girl. As the child eagerly slid to the ground, the mercenary noted a frightening glint in her eyes. She glanced at the others with her eyebrows raised in question, but they were too delighted with the sights and sounds to notice such a tiny moment.

The four were past the outskirts and into the center of town before they finally noticed the strange quiet and the barricades. They had expected a jumble of activity in the One Land's most hospitable city, but everyone was hunkered down, waiting for what they knew must come, waiting for the seasonal rain to suddenly become snow or drought, for the thick black smoke to float downriver heavy with the smell of charred bones.

Where once a small group of humans and dwarves would have felt more at home here than anywhere else, today they became cause for all to stop their business and stare. The whispers raced ahead of them to spread across town. Two dwarves with two humans as traveling companions, what could such as these want?

Jilian shook her head to rid herself of such ridiculous notions. She told herself she was too jumpy from the last dreadful stop. There was no need to panic. They could be safe among the crowds here.

Maarcus confirmed her suspicions with a grumbled, 'Not as friendly as I remember. Not as well kept either.'

Jilian allowed herself a polite look around. They had come through the main part of Twin Gates and now stood close to the docks. She had to agree the buildings seemed to lean a little further toward the water and the colorful paint of previous visits had faded and given way to a grey-white.

'And the bulwarks along the river,' said Walther. 'I'm surprised they let us in at all.' He thought a moment and added, 'Probably weren't expecting us on foot. Not too many people travelling the trails these last weeks.'

'Or maybe they saw us and decided to pay extra close 'tention,' Ceeley piped up.

Jilian wanted to laugh off the dwarf's fears and assure them both, but found she couldn't.

'Honest,' the child said when no one responded. 'Someone's been following us since before we got to that big fountain.'

'Did you see what he looks like?' Maarcus asked, trying to sound no more than casually interested.

Ceeley shook her head. 'No, I never saw him all at once, only pieces of his clothes poking out.' She wrinkled her nose. 'He, I think it's a he, has this ugly shirt with lots of little squares in different colors. Ugly, ugly. Bleh!' She stuck out her tongue and the others laughed.

'Plaid, huh? Well no self-respecting dwarf would wear that,' Walther agreed.

'Not so fast,' Maarcus said. 'Someone, even a dwarf, in the employ of another might.'

Jilian caught a bit of a grin hiding at the corners of his mouth. 'You look like you know something.'

He looked around him, apparently trying to spot their tracker. Still studying the ramshackle buildings and harsh frowns of passersby, he shrugged and said, 'Could be my aunt. She has a peculiar sense of, um, humor for an elf. For a human too, now that I think of it. And of course everyone knows that dwarves have no sense of humor.'

Walther grunted, too distracted to rise to the bait.

Ceeley gave a half-hearted 'Hey!' but like Walther, she seemed to have something else on her mind.

'She wouldn't have known you were coming, would she?' the older dwarf asked.

Maarcus tapped his lip with a finger. 'Hard to say. Still—'

Jilian had enough of the idle chat and decided to cut to the point. 'So now that we've established we're being followed by someone with poor taste in clothes who may or may not mean us harm, what say we visit this elf aunt of yours before we find out the hard way?'

'I'd like to, but elves have serious rules of etiquette. I can't just arrive on her doorstep with a crew of people she's never met and walk right in unannounced.'

'Why the kings' assassins not? Aren't you as good as family?'

'Jilian, how many elves have you known well?'

'Not many,' she admitted. 'Too much magic floating around for my peace of mind.'

'Then please believe me when I tell you that especially now protocols must be observed.'

Jilian never had much patience for the niceties of diplomacy under the best of circumstances, but the events of the past days had sapped what little she possessed. 'Sisters, save me from ambassadors,' she muttered.

'He's right in this,' Walther assured her.

Jilian frowned at him, but let it go. She couldn't bring herself to challenge the dwarf. Though he'd kept a good pace with the rest of them, his face remained drawn and his hair an unhealthy yellow grey. 'You do have a plan, I hope,' she told the Shoreman.

'Clearly I have to speak with her alone and smooth the path for all of you.'

'Clearly,' she repeated, but her sarcasm was wasted. 'And how long will this take?'

Maarcus continued to study his surroundings. Distracted, he answered, 'No telling. A few hours at least, much longer if she's away.'

'Then *clearly* I need to find the rest of us a room for the night.'

He nodded absentmindedly. 'Yeah, good idea.'

'Maarcus, did you hear what I said?'

'You said you were going to find a room for the night,' he said, still not looking at her.

The mercenary turned to Walther, who gave her a weak smile. 'Fair weather ambassadors,' Jilian said, but the dwarf shook his head 'no'.

'Let's find that inn. Come on, Ceeley.'

'But I'm going with Uncle Maarcs, right, Uncle Maarcs?'

Maarcus finally broke off his searching to speak with the girl. 'Ceeley, my auntie doesn't like surprises, so it's better if I go ahead. She'll be happy to let us visit once I explain things.'

The girl's lower lip started to quiver, the first sign in hours of her exhaustion. 'But what if she doesn't like us? Will we have to leave?'

'Don't you worry about it. I'll fix everything. Besides, won't it be fun to stay in an inn?'

'Well . . .'

'I'll wager you've never done that before.'

'I've never seen a real live elf's house before either.'

He ruffled her hair. 'But you will tomorrow.'

'Do you swear?'

He drew a circle around his heart. 'My most solemn oath.'

Jilian didn't like splitting up, but his promise to Ceeley appeared genuine. 'We'll be at the Crisscross,' she said.

'The Crisscross. Got it.' With that he was off, leaving the three to fend for themselves in a hostile town.

'Where does his aunt live anyway?'

'Didn't say.'

'In a big house,' Ceeley said. Hopping on first one foot and then the other, she sang, 'We're going to an in-n. We're going to an in-n.'

'Hope it's still in business. Twin Gates doesn't seem to be

getting too many adventurers of late.'

The child paid no attention. Her song echoed down the alleyways and came back eerily changed.

Ginni'd always enjoyed flying with Tom and Grosik. Each trip was an adventure led by the dragon's odd, unpredictable sense of humor and balanced by his cantankerous desire to protect his own scaly skin. But the restlessness she'd felt caged in with Roslin only got worse after the find in the cave. She had no patience for the dragon's superiority and moodiness now. The vision of the pile of bones itched at her and wouldn't let go.

Suddenly she realized Roslin was right. They were wasting their time looking for the storekeeper and his wife. They needed to find the source of the magic. They needed to go into elf country.

'No, absolutely not,' said Tom in his most unyielding voice. 'It's a foolhardy action that'll get us all killed.'

Grosik answered it more succinctly. 'You can find yourself another dragon, Ginni. Elves abhor us even more than humans. I haven't lived this long just to be driven mad and sent crashing into a cliffside.'

And still Ginni could not put it from her mind. She considered the mental locked box trick Roslin had taught her, but she never used it voluntarily and wouldn't bring herself to do so over such an intriguing puzzle. In the end, she sat squirming on Grosik's back, poked and prodded with the unquenchable, unignorable need to do something, while Tom grunted at her and the dragon growled threat after threat to dump her over the side.

The inn was just an inn. Jilian immediately felt at home. She could already taste the beer. But with the child holding her hand, this kind of rough and tumble place seemed much uglier than Jilian remembered. She suddenly wished she'd kept the child outside.

Ceeley squirmed and yanked on her arm, suddenly restless and grouchy with too little sleep. 'Only babies hold their mother's hands. I'm bigger.'

Jilian relented. This was no time for a family battle with a six-year-old. 'But keep close to me and Walther,' she whispered.

Ceeley nodded, but it was all too new and irresistible. Walther wasn't much better despite his recent travels. Perhaps he'd never dared such a place on his own.

Dwarf clanholds had no use for inns or hostels. Family visited each other or stayed with friends. There was always a spare sleeping mat on the floor, an extra mug in the cupboard. Here were rough hewn tables and benches, and loud but jolly men. The place held the air of celebration. Both of them gawked and lagged behind as Jilian worked her way between tables and grasping hands. Though she'd never before walked into a tavern without Mut standing guard at the door – if not following her in – she couldn't bring herself to show her swaggering side in front of the girl for fear of alarming her.

Jilian glanced over her shoulder to check on Ceeley. Assured the awed child was safe within arm's reach of Walther, she asked one of the more sober looking patrons to point out the tavernkeeper. She approached a bearish man indistinguishable from his guests but for the stained grey apron, and began to dicker. 'We'll need two rooms.'

He leaned over the mercenary to see the dwarves behind her, then gave her an odd look. 'Only got one 'vailable.'

'I have one more companion outside. Two rooms.'

'Four friends, or five enemies. Matters not at all. Got one room.' The words came out harsh and broken, as if he spoke in an unfamiliar dialect – or couldn't be bothered to use one sound more than necessary. The foul-smelling, bad-breathed innkeeper held up one finger. 'One room. Twenty coin.'

'Twenty! I could sleep in the palace for less! Ten.'

'Don't see a palace here. Twenty.' He held out his hand for payment.

Jilian looked at him suspiciously. 'You don't seem overly eager to rent this room. Why is that? Somebody die there lately?'

'Not in the last couple days,' the man said offhandedly, but his gaze flicked past her and back again. 'Bad business to let your customers die where the other joes can smell the rotting body,' he added, showing a gap-toothed smile.

'Huh,' Jilian grunted. This is just a negotiating tactic, she told herself, but she'd never heard of an innkeeper trying to talk a traveller out of renting an empty bed – unless he had a problem letting to dwarves. She took a closer look at the grease spots on his apron and vowed not to eat the food no matter how tempting.

'Fifteen.'

'Twenty,' he repeated with no sign of budging.

'Fair prices and good service,' Jilian muttered, removing the requested coin.

He snatched it out of her hand.

The mercenary repressed a shudder. She'd dealt with worse slobs than this one. Yet everything about him set off her suspicions. The town had surely changed since her last visit.

'It's up the stairs outside, 'round the back.' He gestured toward the door. 'Number three.'

Jilian gave him a hard stare before turning to go. 'Be warned. My friends and I know what to do with a blade. We will not treat intruders kindly.' He didn't respond right away and she waited.

''S 'at so?' He wiped his hands on the filthy apron, showing no hint of being cowed by the likes of Jilian or her dwarven friends. 'Do tell.'

An outburst of laughter snapped her attention to the crowd. 'Hey, old man,' a loud, drunken voice called. 'What will you give me for your daughter?'

'She's my niece.'

The drunk chuckled. 'Even better. You won't mind if I take her off your, um, hands, for one night.' The voice turned menacing. 'Will you, old man?'

'I most assuredly will mind.'

Two tables away, a human ruffian perhaps slightly more distasteful than the rest was caressing Ceeley's arm. Her head shook back and forth but didn't deter the man.

Jilian drew the knife from her leg strap, but the man suddenly dropped his hand and went back to his beer. Around him, his fellows laughed and slapped the table. 'Just y'ur fortune to get a chicken 'at's already been plucked. M'be you'll 'ave better wit' 'er.'

'Yeah, honey, how 'bout it? What ya doing wit' these two pieces of elf-bait?' All eyes turned to the approaching Jilian.

The mercenary nodded tightly, not yet trusting herself to speak. She'd been among such men plenty of times, but not in the company of a child. She simply could not look at them in the same way. She began to clean her fingernails, slowly and deliberately, with the tip of her knife to buy time to settle on what she would say. Finally, though, she decided to speak as she always had at moments like these and hope not to lose Ceeley's trust in the process. 'Gentlemen.' She lowered her voice to its most sultry and raised her eyes and the knife to the crowd. 'This blade makes an excellent boning knife. The last man to act as you suggest woke without his. The man before that did not wake.' Now her words were clipped and precise. 'Which shall it be?'

No one moved; no one spoke.

Jilian calmly ushered the dwarves out the door before the mob realized it had the force of numbers on its side.

Outside, Ceeley said, 'I think I'm tired, Aunt Jilly. Can we go to bed now?'

'Sure, honey, right this way.' She led them where the innkeeper had directed. She paused at the foot of the worn staircase. Jilian wrapped her arm around the girl's shoulders.

'Ceeley, I'm sorry about those . . . those . . . *men*. They drink too much ale, they say things . . .' She started to sheathe the knife then reconsidered. She looked sternly at Walther flanking her right as if he were somehow at fault, then shook her head with disgust at the male condition.

'But we aren't – ' Walther started, quieted his protest, then began again despite Jilian's unforgiving expression. 'Ceeley, they, we . . . That is, most of us are civilized.'

'A few,' Jilian allowed. 'A few of them are civilized.'

Ceeley feigned indifference. 'Hey, I just told him I was too tired and besides I have a horrible headache. And if that hadn't worked, I'd've told him I was on my monthly.'

'How could you be? You're only six!' demanded Walther, apparently forgetting his concern in his surprise.

Ceeley strutted, proud of her lie. 'What do humans know about dwarf girls? Besides, my aunt used to say that sometimes when uncle got too mushy. He usually went for a walk instead.'

Jilian had to chuckle at that, though Walther didn't appreciate the humor. 'Uh, right. Let's go check out our rooms. It should be up here.' She steered her upward.

At the third step, the child's knees buckled, but Jilian's arm braced her and she did not fall. The girl shuddered once then straightened her tunic. 'You OK?'

Ceeley nodded.

'Want to talk?'

Ceeley shook her head, paused on the stair, then asked, 'Why did he call me "elf-bait"?'

Jilian bit her lip to keep from speaking her mind. She'd never heard the phrase before but it didn't bode well. 'Don't know, curly top,' she said lightly. 'A new one on me.' She patted the girl's back and tried not to think about the difficult line between saying too much and too little. She didn't want to frighten Ceeley, but it was perhaps even more dangerous to coddle her. This child had seen her entire family, everything familiar, destroyed but she had not broken, had more than once crawled from her private, mental safe haven. 'Let's go count some goats and tomorrow we'll go dump some of that underbrewed ale on their heads!'

Ceeley giggled. 'Bedtime here I come. Mean guys better watch out. Charge!' she shouted, and dashed up the rickety staircase.

Together they climbed the wooden stairs while Walther lagged behind. Just below the top, the mercenary caught a sound barely heard yet out of place. Jilian quickly grabbed the child and put her behind her. She silently motioned for Ceeley to wait on the step next to the tiny landing.

The latch on the door hung loose. A common sight in this town on previous visits, it seemed out of sorts now. Jilian nudged the door with her boot and it swung quietly open to reveal a very large someone scrubbing the floor.

Jilian smiled back over her shoulder at Ceeley. 'Just the chamber—'

But Ceeley looked horrorstruck as below a man shouted. 'DOWN!'

A troll came barreling from behind her. His eyes were glazed, staring intently at the purse where she had hidden her token among the rest of her coin only just that morning. He held hands outstretched, reaching to snatch at the purse beneath her tunic.

Jilian jumped out of his path while kicking at him from the side. He was bigger than anything she'd ever hit before, but she had just enough force to knock him off balance and through the weak railing over the side.

Immediately Maarcus and Walther were leaning over him, relieving him of weapons. Ceeley kept her spot near the top of the stairs, but now she held a knife – where did she get that? Jilian wondered – and tried to look fierce.

'I guess our rooms were already taken.'

Maarcus was angry as he swore back at her, all trace of his earlier distraction gone. 'By the Seven Ladies, how can you joke about this!'

Jilian winced as she put weight on her bruised, left foot. The troll had been more solid than she'd expected. 'Better than foul words rolling off my tongue. What brings you back among the commoners, Sir Maarcus?' She nodded at their attacker, who lay motionless. 'And what about him?'

'Won't be getting up any time soon,' answered Walther.

Jilian thought she detected a smile behind Walther's very serious expression. 'Late or never?'

The dwarf kicked the troll once for good measure. 'I'd say never.'

The three nodded to each other. 'OK we leave him down here as a warning to others.'

Only Ceeley voiced the obvious question. 'Why was he here in our room?'

For a wind's breath of a moment, Jilian wished that Ceeley was still only a child and that none of this were happening. She inhaled and exhaled once, very slowly. 'On second thought, I strongly suggest we seek other accommodations. These no doubt have fleas. Don't suppose you found your aunt?'

'It's why I'm here. She bid me to come fetch you right away. Said you were in danger. I guess I arrived just in time.'

His chest heaved from running though he seemed reluctant to pause and catch his breath as he waved them forward.

'You missed the opening act.'

Maarcus ignored her comment in his eagerness to tell his own story. He launched in without preamble. 'To begin with, I couldn't guess if she were dead or alive, never mind living in town. Her house is as shabby as most of the others on the outside. When I knocked, the occupant – I think it was a he – said he's lived there all his life. Seemed unlikely to me.'

'Unless he was her apprentice?' Ceeley asked, cautiously descending the stairs.

Maarcus smiled. 'My thought exactly. So I—'

'Uncle Maarcs, why is the troll smoking?'

Jilian wagged her finger. 'Not funny, curly top. I've had enough troll doings for one night.'

'But look, Aunt Jilly.' Ceeley pointed at the smoke seeping from the body as if it were no more than a covered pit surrounding a great cookfire. Flames blackened edges of his clothing, but did not spread. The four watched with morbid fascination as the troll slowly sunk in on itself. Skin and cloth were charred in places though mostly intact. Only a wisp of smoke here and there hinted at anything unusual.

'I don't think he was meant to live if we did,' Walther ventured.

Ceeley moved in and kicked the body before the others could hold her back.

'Ceeley, careful! He might—'

She nodded with satisfaction. 'Nice and dead. Might what, Aunt Jilly?'

'Be dangerous,' Jilian finished lamely. 'We really don't know much about any of this.'

She watched the child prod the body with first her boot and then a stick. Finally, she poked it with her finger. There seemed to be no fear. That would come later, Jilian supposed.

'Hey, he's not even hot!' She stepped back and stared up at Maarcus. 'And he looks kind of like you, Uncle Maarcs.'

'Thought I was slightly more handsome than a troll,' the Shoreman said through a pained smile.

'She's right,' Walther added. 'Look at him.'

Obviously insulted but trying not to show it, Maarcus circled the body, studying it for some sign of resemblance. He rubbed his days' old beard. 'Well, I guess we do both look like something the dogs hunted down.'

'Uncle Maarcs, I'm serious.'

Jilian had been half-listening to the exchange, more amused than intrigued, but now joined in and bent to examine the body. 'She's right, Maarcus.'

'Not you too.' His face flushed in the moonlight.

'There is some resemblance. You both seem to be human males.'

Maarcus laughed. 'That's a relief. I thought I'd become one ugly—'

'But how did the troll become . . . whatever he is?'

Maarcus instantly sobered, putting aside his earlier embarrassment and subsequent relief to consider this new problem. 'That is a stumper. What say we go talk to the innkeeper?'

'Don't know if that's such a great idea. Some of us have had a very long day. What do you say we come back after a good night's sleep? You can tell us all about your aunt along the way.'

Maarcus remembered his urgency. 'Of course, absolutely. You'll love Aunt Zera.'

Jilian tried hard to listen to Maarcus, but found she just didn't have the energy to keep alert to attackers and hear his tale at the same time.

Chapter 12

BLOODLINES

It took longer than Walther expected to get to the elf's house. Maarcus must have lost his way, but he was too proud to admit it and the others were too tired to challenge him.

Jilian and Maarcus took turns carrying the sleeping Ceeley through the dark streets. The one time Walther tried, Ceeley shifted and slid about in his arms so that he nearly dropped her. He mumbled an apology but Jilian dismissed it with an expression that made the dwarf wonder who worried her more. He caught her whispering to Maarcus that 'his face seems even paler against the moonless night.' Walther would have blushed if he'd had the energy. Instead he simply stumbled after the two humans.

At last the Shoreman announced, 'Here we are.'

Shouldered in between its neighbours, the building was just like the others down to the flattened dried-up flowers in their pots on either side of the entrance.

A tall elf opened the door before they'd had a chance to

knock. He stepped back and motioned them in. 'Quickly, quickly.'

The group hurried inside.

The exterior gave no hint of the luxurious interior. Maarcus paid no attention to the richly carved furnishings, the tapestries and paintings lining the walls, the thick carpets underfoot, while Jilian struggled to remain unimpressed and failed. Walther watched as she shuffled Ceeley's weight to her hip and reached out to touch a weaving with her free hand.

'May we see her?' Maarcus asked the man.

The elf did not answer, but guided them down a short hall to a sitting room instead. Food and drink was set out on a sideboard. 'Rest and enjoy. The mistress will—'

The exotic but not unpleasant or overpowering scent of flowers Walther couldn't place flooded the room. Suddenly he was fully awake.

'Thank you, Harmon.'

The apprentice nodded acknowledgement and left the room.

Walther sat and nibbled a sandwich, appetite second only to his enchantment with the elf. She commanded the room by neglecting to claim it. Her regal bearing suggested grace rather than haughtiness.

She held out her arms to Maarcus. 'Nephew, are you well?'

He took her hands in his own, lightly kissed each cheek, then moved back a step. 'As well as can be expected. And you, Aunt Zera?'

Her smile suggested more pain than joy. 'About the same. And your friends?'

The dwarf nodded his appreciation but found his tongue a heavy weight glued to the roof of his mouth.

Jilian spoke primly. 'Very well. Thank you, mistress.'

Walther hid a grin and Maarcus laughed at her outright. Jilian flushed.

'That's enough,' the elf said in the gently scolding voice of a doting relative.

The Shoreman's face reddened to match Jilian's, and Walther struggled to contain his laughter.

'May I see it?' she asked Jilian.

Without hesitation, the human woman withdrew her medallion and handed it to Zera. She seemed completely to trust this woman she'd only just met, showing no doubt that the elf would return it safely after her study.

Walther glanced at Maarcus. Mouth grim but eyes wide, the Shoreman could not hide his astonishment. Apparently Jilian had not confided in him, but he wouldn't admit it in front of the others. Walther felt a swell of pride, petty though it was. Jilian trusted him.

Zera flipped the coin over and over. 'She will want it,' the elf said cryptically.

'I suspected,' Jilian answered. 'But why?'

'This is one of the originals.'

'Original whats?' asked Maarcus, feigning nonchalance as he moved closer to see.

'Have you had it all this time?' the elf asked Jilian, not answering him. She spoke as if the two women were the only ones in the room, or as if the others didn't matter.

'Only since shortly before my parents died. It was my mother's.'

'How did she come by it?'

'She would never say.'

'It wasn't your mother's.'

'I know. It was completely unlike anything else she ever cherished. But why did she keep it?'

'For you, of course.'

'But what would I do with it?'

'Just as you have. Keep it with you always.' The elf returned the coin and stared into Jilian's eyes. 'Know you nothing of your heritage?'

'Heritage?' She shrugged. 'A woodsman's daughter with a strange companion and a knack for finding trouble.'

'I'll say,' Maarcus interjected, but the elf ignored his comment. He closed his mouth but obviously didn't take the treatment well. He began to pace loudly, trying to draw attention to himself, consciously or not.

'Sit,' Zera directed and did so herself.

Only Maarcus remained on his feet. The women paid him no mind as Jilian placed Ceeley on a low couch and found her own comfort crouched on the edge of a carved footstool.

'You are one of the king's own.' Zera said.

'King's own . . . Guard? Which king? How can that be?'

'King's own *heirs*. It's the only possible way to possess such – unless of course it's stolen. But it must be rightfully yours or you would not have been able to abide its presence. Nor would you have ever been able to carry it so close to your skin all these years.'

'Aunt Zera, this makes no sense at all. What is a Shoreman king's heir doing beyond the outer reaches of his land?' Maarcus rotated his wine goblet, staring as the dregs swirled. Walther guessed the aunt had been hard on the Shoreman tonight and he seemed to be losing his stomach for it.

The elf finally addressed Maarcus but her steady gaze stayed on Jilian. 'Unlike the current "throneholder,"' she said disdainfully, 'the true king was ruler to all the One Land. His heirs could do worse than come of age out of reach of the usurpers, as you know. All but one of the Great King's documented heirs have been assassinated since his death. The bumbler has survived by affecting such uselessness that his royal blood can be waved now and again for show without threat that he will act on it for his own ends.'

'You said "heirs". More than one then?'

She nodded still watching Jilian. Walther saw the woman's disbelief slowly yield as the elf spoke. Her words were issued with a plain sincerity which convinced despite the facts as the others knew them. 'There were the Great King's twins, mysteriously taken in the middle of the night.'

Maarcus spoke slowly, looking at the human woman out of the corner of his eye as if she might attack him. 'But no one ever knew what became of them,' he protested.

'No one but your grandfather and the Magician.'

Maarcus shook his head. 'No, I don't believe even they knew the truth of that rumor.'

The elf woman chuckled to herself. 'Maarcus,' she said, not unkindly, 'naïveté is charming and has almost certainly helped to guard your life, but you'll soon need to throw away that crutch. Your grandfather has sought to protect you just as he has hoped to train you to survive the political upheavals. Still, you must realize by now that he and Abadan know all there can be known about the Great King's affairs. It's time you came to learn their secrets if any of us, let alone the One Land, is to overcome the witch's campaigns.' She stood. 'Enough for one evening. We will continue this tomorrow. Harmon can show you to your rooms when you're ready.' On the way to the door, she paused over Ceeley's sleeping form, crunched into a fetal ball. 'You are safe here, child. Sleep well.'

The dwarf's face relaxed as she stretched in her sleep and Walther felt his own tension loosen in response.

Willam hadn't so much given in to exhaustion as have it hit him on the back of the head like a highwayman. He was standing and then he was not with no memory of the transition.

He woke with dirt in his mouth and his arm in a sling, but a clear head. His fevered chasing of Lyda only to learn they had killed her seemed to him a delirium from which he might hope to recover. Maybe she wasn't dead after all. Maybe this was some sort of elfin trickery—

A woman's voice interrupted his thoughts. 'I'm sorry. You're wife is no longer as she was.'

He sat up, looked in the direction of the sound, found her sitting on the rock in the shadows barely distinguishable from the lush undergrowth.

'You are?' he asked, feeling plenty annoyed and equally tired of folks seeming to know more about him than he did himself.

'I am Roslin, mage and guide.' She stiffly tipped her head a thread's width in greeting.

Willam bit back a retort. He'd had his fill of mages and magic. Beyond that, something else about this woman set his neck hairs to rising.

'I can help you.' She remained comfortably seated.

'Out o' the goodness of y'ur heart. Thank you kindly, but I do believe I've 'ad enough 'elp.'

Smiling as if she knew he couldn't possibly *not* be convinced, she tried a different approach. 'We were fated to meet.'

He stood and brushed off his dusty clothes. 'Seen my share o' fate too. Don't 'ave any use for it.'

The smile grew wider with a touch of grim behind it. 'I can give you a child.'

Willam shook his head. 'Sounds like you've 'ad a worse time of it than I 'ave. Why don't you go on 'ome to wherever witches live and leave me alone.'

'But you do want a child,' she pressed.

'True I've wanted a child for years – and my neighbor wanted to be king. The Seven Sisters don't always see fit to give us our wishes. Now I need to be on my way. Good morn to you.' He bent to gather his few belongings and turned to face the trail.

'Your wife sacrificed much for you. Would you throw it all away?'

Willam strode up to the mage, sitting so superior on her rock. He lifted his arm with the palm flat. The woman flinched but did not cry out. 'You leave my wife out o' this. Magicians, elves, dwarves too prob'ly – all think you can risk 'er to get to me. Well, she's gone now and I won't listen to any more talk.'

The witch opened her mouth then closed it.

He dropped his arm. 'Now leave me alone. There's a long walk ahead o' me and I plan to get started.'

Willam stepped away from the rock where she sat, then hesitated. In his chase these last days, he had somehow got himself into an unknown land. The mountains were still his beautiful mountains and the countryside itself renewed his battered spirit. But here he was in a spot amidst all that should be familiar finding even the trees seemed wrong.

Willam had gone beyond his hills twice or thrice to the realm of the Shoremen, but the greenery was nothing like this. It was common enough. He'd returned because he couldn't stand to live with the sea so near. It was not the water – before Lyda, he'd often camped near violent waterfalls as tall as ten houses – but something about the endless sea itself he couldn't abide.

And now he meant to travel there? Well, he would see how far he got. In the meantime, he itched to *go*.

He spun back to face the woman. 'Where have—'

The witch and the boulder were both gone. He blinked and the trees once again became known.

'By the Sisters,' he swore, 'those wrinkled old, mage-cursed nags better leave me be.'

Laughter echoed in response, but the witch did not show herself.

He got his bearings and once again began the long trek.

Jilian woke in uncommonly comfortable surroundings. Soft pillows and thick blankets set off her suspicions and she sat bolt upright in bed before she remembered the night before and the elf's calm pronouncement. Impressed by Zera, she'd almost believed that a mercenary could be the Great King's heir. In the late morning light, the idea seemed ridiculous. Maarcus had been right to be skeptical of his aunt.

In the wake of Zera's departure, Jilian had found herself unable to look either man in the eye. Silence hung for long minutes until Walther said too loudly, 'Congratulations, your highness.'

Half laughing, half appalled, Jilian choked on the wine she'd been sipping.

Maarcus answered for her. 'Oh come now. She's not a princess.'

'I suppose you're right . . . for now,' Walther said, seemingly reluctant to let go of such a romantic notion.

They'd stared at the floor, at the furnishings, anywhere but at each other. In the end, there'd been nothing to do but call Harmon and ask the way to their rooms.

Now Jilian dressed and made her way back downstairs to the sitting room, where Zera, Maarcus, and Walther waited as if they expected her. Bread, cheese, and brewed tea sat on the sideboard. The dwarf, looking refreshed and nearly healthy, held an empty cup.

Zera said, 'We need to speak of your twin brother.'

Jilian turned from the food. 'With all due respect, Mistress, I have no brother, much less a twin.'

'What about your dragon?'

The cheese knife thudded against the board. 'Mut? How did you hear about – ' She looked at Maarcus, who returned her glare with quiet arrogance, his old self. 'If you harm my dragon . . .'

'So long as he is in the hands of Alvaria – whose followers call the One – he is in far greater danger than anything I would do.'

'And how would you come to know what the witch plans?'

Zera looked evenly at Jilian. 'I taught her everything she knows. She is my daughter.' Barely a pause and then she added, 'Just as you, Jilian, are her daughter.'

Guided by a personal compass she had trusted from that day in the pond, Lyda went to one town and another, on hillsides and in valleys, on riverbanks and inland. Worsening weather did not touch her. She moved through sleeting rain and driving snow, dressed only in the gay robes she'd worn since emerging from the pool. Through all her journeying, she sensed the elves' calming presence over her right shoulder, a reassurance never heavy enough to weigh upon her.

The towns were all alike. Closed against strangers, afraid and hungry. Still, so very still. Parents hushed their children until crying grew as rare as laughter.

When she came to the village of her birth, Lyda didn't recognize it. Both she and it had changed beyond either's reckoning.

As had become her habit, she stopped to rest in the town square. It gave the locals a chance to see her and judge her harmless. Sometimes hours would go by before the first greeting. These were usually the children, allowed out to play for a time when the sun was warmest.

The town square took her by surprise. The statue, the fountain echoed the others before them. But as she sat on the bench with her back to the stone, she felt a calling, hungry and unpleasant. Lyda resettled her shoulders, trying to rid herself of the crawling sensation. When this didn't work, she turned to examine the fountain.

Slowly, pebble by inlaid pebble she studied the designs until at last she realized this wasn't just the familiarity of town upon town. This was a place she had lived.

Then why was the statue rising above the quiet fountain that of an elf?

It jolted her as nothing had in so many weeks. For once, she could not wait until the people came to her. She had to go to them.

Lyda crossed the square and headed down one of the narrow streets leading away from the center. Here crowded on either side was the tiny two-story house where she had lived until the day she left to marry Willam. It seemed no more shabby than its neighbors, but somehow sadder than she had remembered it.

Lyda knocked on the door and stood back to wait. A curtain cracked on an upper floor then swung closed. Heavy footsteps thudded on the stairs and stopped behind the door.

'Strangers are not welcome here.'

'I am Lyda. I lived in this house a lifetime ago and had hoped you might point me to the way of my parents' graves, for I heard they passed on some winters back.'

'If you are of this village, then you know the way to the cemetery.'

'There is still only the one, then?' Lyda found this oddly comforting. Something had not changed. When the voice did not answer, Lyda gave a blessing. 'Peace upon your house. I will be going now.'

Retreating footsteps were her reply.

She walked the cobblestones, turned right then left and ultimately found her way to the graveyard behind the town chapel. Covered in snow, it seemed no different than she remembered. She let herself through the low iron gate and walked among the dead. There were more markers now, of course, and few of these held more than a wood marker with name, date, and the seal of the Seven Sisters.

Cold started to seep through her poor shoes until her feet grew numb. Lyda stumbled and landed on one knee, coming up to face the marker for mother, father, and sister. This last took her breath away. She had known about her parents; this same sister had sent the letter. But no one had thought to notify her when the sister died. Who would have known to tell the married sister of a spinster woman? Who would have cared?

Lyda settled onto the snow-covered ground and let the loneliness call to her. Did her sister have no friends at all?

She put her hand on the marker, ran her finger through the letters of her name. 'I cared,' she said softly. 'I'm sorry I didn't come before, but I'm here now. Peace, sister.'

She rose after a time.

Lyda walked the streets, murmuring a prayer she had put together. When she had touched each door, she stood in the square and waited until nightfall. When no one came, she circled the fountain one last time, and stood up facing the strange statue of the female elf. 'Peace.'

Lyda lowered her head. There was nothing more she could do for this town. She left as silently as she had come, but a bright trail streamed behind her and faded into the cobblestones.

Through the haze of receding fever, Mut could sense something terrible had happened to the child. His touch had shifted back to the wavering unsureness of a few days ago. His speech was quiet and halting. He gulped and paused so often that Mut could barely make out a word.

'. . . L-l-leaving.' Swallow. 'S-s-sorry . . . can't t-take g-g-goats. T-t-telling you, have to . . . have to hide.' Beneath the stuttering, his voice was urgent. 'T-they wanted m-me t-t-to . . .' He trailed off.

Mut struggled to understand. Who had to hide? The child? The dragon himself?

The boy hugged Mut hard. 'Can't carry you . . . Good f-f-friend . . . M-must hide. S-s-special . . . S-s-safe . . . S-s-s-sissterss' . . . l-luck.' The goatboy patted his flank one last time.

The child moved so quietly that Mut did not hear him leave. He could still feel the ghost warmth of the child's hand, though he knew the elf was no longer nearby.

The dragon struggled to stand and get his bearings. He lay on his side with legs spinning, but he couldn't get them under him. Mut panted a while and tried to gather his strength.

No use.

Lifting his head took too great an effort and he was dizzy from repeated attempts.

Mut concentrated and settled for sniffing at the air. He could smell water and pottery. The boy had placed a bowl within reach. The green of broken grass stems rose up from beneath the cloth mat he lay on. The different green of the leaves overhead and close around him floated on a gentle wind. Mut guessed the child had found a tiny clearing of trees to shelter and conceal him. A stray breeze brought the scent of goats. He would have noticed sooner had they been upwind, but he wasn't far from their pen.

He dozed and woke again. Come daylight he needed to be away from the camp. The dragon let out an involuntary whine. Mut had no hope of even crawling deeper into the wood.

He'd never felt so alone and hunted. From the approaching sounds of shouting and calling for 'Goatboy' –

had Mut ever heard the poor elf's true name? – the dragon didn't expect to be rescued.

His spirit broken, Mut lay limp and let them come to him.

A soft boot toe jabbed his side and a body went flying across. The dragon would have laughed at the clumsiness if he'd had the energy or the heart.

'Over here!' shouted a young voice he recognized as one of the elfboy's taunters.

Once they stumbled upon him, the noise dropped to a frightening hush. Not even the child's parents seemed to care about the whereabouts of the boy.

The elfwitch was not far behind. The dragon felt the crowd part to grant her passage. 'So,' was all she said.

Mut opened his eyes to look into the strangely swirling depths. There was nothing more to say.

She motioned and assistants rushed to pick him up.

The mat dipped and Mut's head hung off the edge. 'Careful!' she shouted. 'He is more precious than you can know.'

The jostling made his stomach lurch. Mut closed his eyes. As they gently repositioned him, he allowed himself the short-lived luxury of believing the boy might be left alone in the witch's excitement over her triumph.

Her next words killed that hope. 'Find the goatboy. He will not be excused for his betrayal.'

Chapter 13

HANDIWORK

Wanton Tom rolled over quietly on the rocky ground, hoping not to awaken Ginni and wishing for a patch of grass to soften their beds.

'Uncle, I'm still thinking about it,' she said without a hint of sleepiness.

He feigned a snore.

'Oh, come on admit it. You're as awake as I am.'

'M-m-m . . . frozen ground,' he mumbled, still trying to avoid the inevitable.

'I can't ignore it, Uncle.'

'Go back to sleep.'

'I haven't been asleep all night.' She threw off her blanket and sat up. 'Neither have you,' Ginni accused.

'Then go to sleep for the first time.'

'But the dreams, Uncle.'

'Forget about them. Dream something nice and calming like a battle between dragons and trolls.'

'Ugh.' She tried to punch his arm, but couldn't quite reach

him and the swing fell short in the dark. 'No wonder your friends used to tell me you roasted babies for breakfast.'

'I did. You just got lucky. We weren't hungry the day we found you.' He laughed softly with mock wickedness. 'Better watch what you aim for in the dark. It may see better than you do.' Tom inched his way toward his daughter, and whispered 'Boo' in her ear.

The resulting shriek echoed painfully and made him wonder if it had been worth trying to make such a minor point when all either of them really wanted to do was get some untroubled shuteye. He sat up next to her and rubbed his ringing ear.

Ginni laughed. 'You were saying, Uncle?'

'You saw me coming in this starless pit of a night?'

'No, heard you.'

'Impossible.'

'Suit yourself.'

'Arrogant girl.'

'Not at all,' she argued. 'Just the daughter of a mage and a warrior.'

Wanton Tom lay back down, feeling very old and every wrinkle the washed-up soldier. 'Not now, Ginni.'

'We're up. Might as well talk about it.'

'We're not up. I'm down, lying down here on the ground. Hush before you bother the dragon.'

'Too late,' Grosik growled. 'I thought humans liked to waste their nights sleeping.'

'Normally, yes, but those bones . . .'

'No, we won't discuss them,' Tom answered. His voice did not invite argument.

His daughter immediately changed tacks. 'It's time to rejoin Roslin. I think something is preventing us from finding that storekeeper.'

'Why would anyone care if we found him?'

'Not just us, Uncle.'

The dragon snorted. 'Who would care about such a puny man?'

'The elves trusted him with that bracelet for years,' she reminded him. 'I'm no mage, yet, but I spent enough time with him that I should've caught a stray whiff of him by now. There's been nothing. It's as if we'd never met or he'd never existed.'

'Maybe he's dead,' Tom suggested, accepting Ginni's theory despite himself.

The darkness seemed heavier while his silent daughter considered. A piece of jewelry jangled as she shook her head. 'No, I don't know why, but—'

'The girl's right. *This* time. He's not dead. I haven't detected the stench of rotting human flesh in this part of the hills since we began this journey. Trolls, yes, humans, no.'

'There must be some sort of protective cloak over him. I'd guess elves. Maybe the ones who trusted him with the bracelet aren't done with him yet.'

'You don't know anything of the kind.'

'OK, maybe it was a gift to the Great King and it found its way here in all the turmoil after his death.'

Tom sighed and lay back down. 'These fanciful dreams of yours are going to get you in trouble.'

'*Us* in trouble,' corrected Grosik.

Ginni didn't bother to respond to his verbal finger wagging. 'But we are going back, aren't we?'

He hated to agree with her, but he had come to believe over the years that she did have a healthy dose of the sight. Too bad Roslin had never seen fit to train her in it, but the woman had violently refused. He might have asked her to battle all Seven Sisters single-handedly for the response she'd given. 'Yeah, we're going back. Now get some sleep.'

* * *

Roslin dropped back into herself with a jolt. Her entire body ached, but that wasn't unusual after such a long session. Though she'd never left the room through all her conjuring, it took her a while to adjust to the inn's plain wood surroundings.

She stood, stretched, and unconsciously began to pack her magicks. For the first time in her life, she felt sympathy with the encroaching elves. Even the worst of them held more vision in her palm than the most talented human village contained in all its small-minded isolation. She was done with them.

Done with Ginni.

Done with Tom.

Done with Abadan and his scheming companion.

Done with unimportant shopkeepers who dare to deny destiny.

They would not find her where she was going – but she doubted any of them had the foresight to think to look.

After she left, the room seemed to alter, to close in on itself. For weeks yet to come, more than one customer would pass the door and refuse to enter.

They gave up the idea of sleep altogether an hour before dawn. Ginni and Tom were packed and ready to climb aboard the dragon's back the moment he condescended to allow it. Finally he assented at first light for reasons only Grosik knew.

Once decided, the trio traveled quickly. The dragon didn't bother with playful dips and dives and the humans left off their usual joking small talk. Each knew he was preparing for battle, perhaps with Roslin, perhaps with someone more hostile.

Grosik took them as close as they dared then settled into the same cave he'd used on Tom's earlier visit to the Cups.

The march down from the cave took longer than flight would have, but all agreed it would not be wise to bring a full grown dragon into the village. They were going for stealth not panic.

It was late morning when Ginni and Tom by-passed the innkeeper with a mutual shrug and headed directly to their old room.

'A few days, a week, where else would she be?' the girl asked.

Knowing his former lover's explosive nature, Tom didn't answer. It wouldn't help to consider what she might have been doing while they were away.

They climbed the stairs with caution. Ginni put one hand on the door and held the other up to halt her father. 'The binding spell has been changed.' To Tom's raised eyebrow, she said, 'We're no longer welcome.'

He scratched his beard. 'Guess she was madder than I thought.'

'I knew we'd have to bow and scrape some with utmost sincerity – ' Ginni's expression suggested anything other than sincerity – 'But this? Do you think she'd lock us out for good just because we were gone a few days?'

'Maybe she's not in there and she didn't want visitors, even us, in the meantime.'

Ginni placed her ear toward the door without actually touching it, then looked back at Tom behind her in the hall. 'Hard to tell. I'm going to knock. OK?'

He fell into a fighting stance, knife in hand. Tom nodded.

Ginni lifted her hand just as the door cracked open. 'Do come in,' whispered a hoarse voice.

'Ros?'

'Mother?'

'Not—'

Two arms roughly yanked Ginni into the room.

' – good,' Tom finished to the air. Feeling every shred the fool who walks into a trap but unable to leave his daughter to defend herself, Tom kicked the door wide open. It slammed against the wall, snapped the top hinge, and came to a crooked rest.

All eyes were on him, as he stepped into the room. One oversized troll, one elf, and Ginni. No Roslin. The odds were off – but in whose favor?

The troll held onto Ginni. She struggled convincingly against the elf and spat soldier's insults to complete the image. In truth, she calmly awaited a signal from Tom – or at least he hoped she did.

'Where's Roslin?'

The troll moved to attack Tom, but the elf waved him into stillness. 'We thought you could tell us.' Tom wanted to accuse them of trickery, but suspected the elf was on the up and up right then. Elven honor seldom stooped to frivolous lies, though it welcomed the duels to prove it.

'We've been out.'

The elf nodded. This much was obvious. He waited for the average slow-witted human to fill in the silence with more useful information. Tom wasn't feeling average. He kept quiet.

He looked around the room. Things seemed orderly. He watched Ginni out of the corner of his eye. Whenever the elf looked at Tom, her gaze slid over to Roslin's table of magic. Apparently something was out of sorts there, but he couldn't guess what. He scratched his nose to let her know he'd received the message.

'When did trolls become so well mannered that a cultured elf might choose one as a traveling partner?'

The elf shrugged as if to suggest no particular talent was required, or else the entire matter was beneath his notice. 'There are ways for a civilized people such as mine.'

Too civilized, by Wanton Tom's reckoning. Always let someone else get the grime under the fingernails, someone like this troll. The whole unnatural business with the troll made Tom uneasy. He looked at Ginni, made sure she understood their peril.

His daughter spoke up for the first time. 'What do you want from us? We know even less than you do.'

'I gather information as my queen commands. How can I be certain which small detail will be worthy of her praise?' He circled the room as he spoke, forcing Tom either to lose sight of him as he moved or to succumb to the intimidation and spin about. Tom let the elf walk. Ginni could watch his back.

The elf was dressed in traveling clothes, ones that disguised his race to the casual human eye. Nothing could disguise a troll – an outsize beast who seldom achieved conversation beyond grunting, though this one seemed exceptional at least in its hugeness. Undoubtedly part of the troll's purpose would be to draw attention away from the elf.

Wanton Tom knew sleight of hand when he saw it – a favorite pastime of the elves. The entire war reeked of it. There was more going on than land claims and border disputes. The campaigns of terror held a separate, more sinister but still undeclared purpose.

And one of the biggest clues stood in the room with him.

Someone needed to see what these two were up to, and Tom looked like the unhappy volunteer. He swore mentally but let nothing show on his face. He preferred a straightforward battle with fists and swords. Sneaking around ran against his knuckles-in-your-nose attitude – never mind that this was what the old physician had paid him to do.

So he'd have to convince these overgrown, over-polished dwarves to take a live passenger and find a way for Ginni to

escape first. Tricky that. One of these days his overprotect-
iveness would cost them both . . . and they both knew it.

Before Tom could settle on a plan, the elf decided it for
him. 'Take the girl,' he told the troll. 'We don't need the old
man.'

'Old man!'

The elf gave Tom the once-over with a show of fastidious
distaste. 'By human reckoning, you are old.' Suddenly there
was a knife at the mercenary's throat. 'But even old men have
been known to argue against the odds. Go.' He waved at the
troll. 'I'll be a child's step behind you.'

Ginni genuinely tried to pull free this time but the troll
held her fast. Maintaining a cool attitude, she called over her
shoulder, 'Do take care of the Grouch for me, Uncle.'

'Count on it, Runt.'

The troll jerked her through the door. He could hear them
thudding clumsily down the stairs. 'Behave yourself,' he
whispered, half prayer, half admonition. No heroics.

The elf pressed the knife against Tom's neck. 'I should kill
you now . . .'

The mercenary stiffened in readiness to defend himself.

He moved the blade to within inches of Tom's face. 'But I
won't just yet. That dragon of yours would make a useful
pet.' He sheathed the knife and moved to the doorway. 'You
can follow us, but it won't do any good.' He paused then
added, 'Old man.' He turned away, leaving the door hanging
askew.

Tom kicked the dangling door and snapped off the lower
hinge in his rush to get outside. The street was nearly empty
of traffic. There was no sign of the elf, his troll companion,
or Ginni. 'By the Seven!' he swore. 'I'll show them an old
man. My hair hasn't even begun to grey . . . much. Hang on,
Runt. We'll get you out of this.' He took off for Grosik at a
dead run.

* * *

Walther had never seen the likes of such a dinner. Celebrations among his people were a haphazard affair, the most formal banquets requiring only that the revelers put on clean, pressed shirts. True each family spent days cooking their clan's specialty, but they presented it with all the humble flair of the most revered dwarves. Children dodged about the long table and weren't shooed away unless their high spirits threatened the food.

Yet here he sat stiff and polite at a table with more dishes and flatware than he would have thought it possible for four adults and one child to use.

The dwarf tried not to scowl at Maarcus. The man was completely in his element. He'd managed to dig up fresh lace and fluff attire and now waved his wine glass as if *he* rather than the adoptive aunt hosted the party.

Jilian too withstood the regal test much better than the dwarf. Perhaps somewhere in her travels someone had taught her to hold her teacup in such an uncomfortable position without wincing.

Ceeley, well, Ceeley was a child. No one seemed to mind as she darted around the table eating tidbits off everyone's plate but her own and keeping up a constant string of chatter. At least in this Walther felt at home. And seeing her so energetic went far to balance his own unsettled mood.

The adults ate in silence, all but Ceeley unwilling to voice their thoughts. Walther watched the others choosing one fork for this, another for that. The rules held to an unknowable and frustrating pattern. He sampled each new dish only to find the vegetables steeped in odd, bitter sauces and the meat served cold and bloody. Finally convinced no one paid attention to him anyway, he chose the utensil of his fancy to pick at the strange courses and push them around his plate while he waited for the others to finish.

The door opened and the most wonderful aroma floated in. 'Ah, perfect. Thank you, Harmon.' Zera waved her apprentice forward. He stepped into the room carrying a magnificent soufflé. 'A dwarven specialty,' the elf explained to the humans. 'Known across the One Land for desserts beyond compare, rightly so, and this is their most extraordinary culinary achievement. Walther could you do the honors?'

The dwarf found he was shaking as he took the lit candle. He felt an important honor had been bestowed on him just as it would have been had he been feasting among his kin. Carefully he waved it over the chiffon until the white topping had seared to golden brown. He snuffed the flame with his fingertips and replaced the odorless stick in its holder.

'Well done, well done!' the elf exclaimed.

Walther blushed and returned to his seat.

The apprentice stepped forward and served dainty portions round the table beginning with Jilian. Here it comes, Walther thought. Here's where we pay for our lodging.

But instead they continued to eat. The humans tasted the exotic food cautiously, just as the dwarf had done with the earlier course. Walther found himself smiling with the elf in a rare moment of kinship as the other two tried to decide whether they liked the soufflé's foreign texture and flavor. In the end, the dessert won them over and both had an extra serving.

In his amusement, Walther lost track of Ceeley and only belatedly noted she hadn't touched her dessert. Concerned she might be ill – or equally likely, exploring where she shouldn't – the dwarf turned in his chair to find her.

'She is well, Walther,' the elf said, seeming to know of his concern the same moment he did.

Indeed, the elf spoke true. The child had fallen asleep,

curled happily near the burning fire as content as a family cat.

'Shall we retire to the sitting room?' the elf invited.

Walther would have just as soon retired to his bedroom, but he held no illusions. The female's gracious suggestion was not to be denied. Maarcus and Jilian were already following Harmon from the room and down the hall. 'No need to worry about Ceeley,' she added. 'My apprentice will see that she gets to her bed.'

Two elderly, human royals were leaning close in excited conversation when the dinner party arrived. Walther didn't recognize them, though he didn't care much for politics. If the truth be known, he had become even less interested now that the skirmishes seemed to have turned into full-scale war except as to how it bore on his ability to avenge his clan.

'Grandfather! Master Abadan!' Maarcus exclaimed, utterly surprised.

Walther's wandering thoughts snapped to the matter at hand. This could well prove vital after all.

Maarcus gave his senior a manly handshake which was warmly returned by a hearty back-pounding. By comparison, the greeting between magician and diplomat was a formal and brief mutual nod. Old wounds there, Walther guessed.

'And you must be Mistress Jilian,' said the elder Maarcus. 'Your highness, we have looked long and longer for you. It will be my pleasure to serve you the rest of my days.'

'If she proves worthy,' groused the magician.

'Oh, she will,' inserted the elf. 'But please allow me.' She turned to Maarcus. 'Nephew, you of course know everyone present. Jilian, may I present Sir Maarcus the Sixth, counselor to kings, and Master Abadan, the One Land's most powerful human magician. Gentlemen, my granddaughter.'

Maarcus and Jilian stood with their mouths hanging open.

Had she introduced Walther with such airs, he would have been equally dumbfounded. The dwarf suppressed an urge to joke only to find Abadan staring at him with undue intensity.

'Do you do that often?' he asked.

What had he done this time?

'And may I present Walther Shortdwarf, a wizard of unknown talents.'

Walther bowed to hide his embarrassment. A wizard? Surely the elf took this too far. He straightened to find the junior Maarcus looking as if his superior position among the peasants had just been usurped by one of his subjects.

'But you can't mean him?' the man asked Zera. 'I've been traveling with him for days and never caught a scent of—'

'Nephew, your family has no talent whatsoever for magic.'

'She's right,' his grandfather said. 'It's part of why it took me so long to trust Abadan. Also,' he added, 'it's part of why our family has risen to prominence. We can not be swayed by others' illusions.'

'Enough old history,' the magician grumbled as he took the most comfortable chair. 'Let's get on with it.'

'As charming as ever,' Maarcus the Seventh remarked, regaining some of his composure.

'Yes, now that we're all here, let's begin,' Zera said, ignoring Maarcus. She took a seat and waited for the rest to do the same.

'Begin what?' Jilian asked, standing with her back near the wall and legs apart. To Walther already settled in his chair, she seemed very much the deadly mercenary she claimed to be.

On the opposite side of the room the younger Maarcus had taken up a similar stance – bookends of anger, Walther mused. 'What has he talked you into this time, Grandfather?'

'Nephew, must I remind you whose house this is?'

No one missed the steel in her soft voice, Maarcus least of all. He found a stiff-backed chair and perched on its edge.

Jilian remained standing but relaxed enough to lean against the wall. 'I'm listening.'

That left only the senior Maarcus, who chose the overstuffed chair next to Abadan.

'Now that we've all sniffed each other over like hunting dogs, maybe we can get down to business,' the magician muttered.

The room was silent as the elders waited for one another to begin. They stared each down until Abadan let out a long suffering sigh. 'Always me to deliver the difficult news.'

Zera smiled. 'Don't go on so. You enjoy being the voice of doom.'

Abadan allowed a slight grin in confirmation. He settled more comfortably into his chair and arranged his robes about him. The magician closed his eyes and did not speak for a long moment. Walther felt himself drifting with exhaustion when at last a storyteller's voice broke the quiet.

'Some say the royal twins were only a legend. A few know differently, but even fewer would dare to tell their tale. And among these, there are no heroes, only desperate folk who hoped to see the land survive intact.

'In the time before any of us were born, the One Land was seven lands, one for each of the Sisters. The talking species claimed territory for their own and left the other clans to do as they would. Eventually they grew apart and could no longer speak one another's language.'

'Wait a minute,' Jilian interrupted. 'Are you telling me I share kinship with that troll who nearly kicked my head off?'

The magician shrugged. 'Trolls are a difficult matter. We haven't quite sorted them out yet.'

The implications were clear to Walther. For generations his own clan had passed down a less far reaching version of this story. And he had to admire the way Abadan answered her question without answering it.

'As I was saying,' he continued. 'These peoples no longer trusted each other or intermarried, but they slowly came to trade with the neighboring lands and ultimately to respect one another's customs . . . for a time. This too passed and the wars began.'

Shuffling noises came from the corner as Jilian shifted her weight and finally decided to sit in another of the stiff-backed chairs near Maarcus. 'I thought you'd heard enough of old history. Why then bring up even older legend?' she asked without trying to disguise her impatience.

'You'll see.'

'I've heard more than I care to already.'

Abadan turned to Maarcus the Sixth. 'Are you sure she is who we think?'

Maarcus laughed. 'You don't remember his highness in his younger days. No one could tell him anything.'

The magician nodded. 'Couldn't tell him much in his latter days either. Very well.'

Jilian frowned and toyed absently with a knife. Beside her Maarcus was expressionless. Whether he'd heard this story a hundred times or this was the first, Walther couldn't tell.

Harmon came in with a serving tray, distributing tea to all but the magician, who sipped a snifter of liqueur.

Abadan licked his lips, making every show of enjoying his refreshment. 'As I was saying, the wars began. And with every battle won or lost, prophecies sprouted like casualties. It grew harder and harder for anyone to know which fore-sights might be true. Many spoke of twins, but it seemed unlikely. Only one spoke of the birth of marked twins conceived during a respite from the fighting and this seemed the most unlikely of all.'

He turned to stare at Jilian and everyone present followed his gaze. 'But you were born and you were marked.'

'I was not a twin.' Jilian spoke resolutely, despite the elf's revelation the night before.

'I thought you told her this much at least?' Abadan asked the elf.

'So I did. Should I also have bespelled her food to assure she believed me?'

'Without the girl's cooperation we are nowhere. No, we are worse than before with the One, as she calls herself' – here the magician made a face – 'run amuck.'

Zera winced but said nothing.

'The girl, as you call me, is sitting in the room with you and does not appreciate references as if I were not. Spit it out, what do you want from me?'

Abadan looked surprised at her question. 'Isn't it obvious? To accept your destiny.'

Jilian laughed. 'You sound as if you believe your own ballads.'

'Number one,' Maarcus said, taking over while Abadan sipped at the dregs of his liqueur. 'You are the royal twins – you Jilian, and your brother, Nikolis. We know this to be true for several reasons, the coin you have kept with you primary among them. We fashioned it as a sort of protection.'

'Didn't help my parents much.'

'It wasn't possible. We could not be certain you would spend your entire childhood with them. And we couldn't increase the risk of having the spell detected,' Maarcus explained.

'Just like a royal cold fish, aren't you?' Jilian said, disgusted.

'Some think so, but we've labored long to preserve what the Great King built and keep this world from becoming much colder,' Abadan said without remorse. 'Back to the subject. Given your brother's state—'

'Yes, care to explain how he came to be a dragon? If he's my brother, I'm sure he wasn't born like that.' Jilian's face showed more challenge and skepticism than belief.

Maarcus the Sixth turned grey.

'Grandfather!' the younger Maarcus said. 'You couldn't have—'

'Couldn't have what?' Abadan asked. 'You've always known we do what we must.'

Color began to return to the physician's cheeks. He sighed. 'That's a tale for another time.'

'We couldn't expect him to carry a token such as yours to guard him,' the magician continued, 'even if it compelled him the way yours did, so we hammered a silver collar.'

Jilian shook her head. 'He's never worn a collar.'

'Are you sure?' the physician asked. 'Not back in his youngest days?'

'Never. I'm sure I would have noticed it when we clipped his fur in the summer.'

The two frowned. They looked at each other and then at Jilian. 'Think. This is very important. You never saw any metal anywhere on him? A bracelet perhaps encircling a paw?'

She shook her head again. 'He would have hated that.'

'Not good,' the doctor muttered. 'Not good at all.'

'Could be worse,' the magician said.

'How?'

'If the prince doesn't wear the charm, then the elfwitch can't claim it.'

'True. That is encouraging.'

'Still, we must get him away from her before she attempts to transform him.'

'Transform him into what?' Jilian asked.

'Human most likely,' Maarcus said. 'Though there are other possibilities . . .' He trailed off in response to her expression.

'You are serious about this, aren't you?'

'You must be the king's daughter,' Abadan said, exasperated. 'No one else would so persistently refuse to accept the obvious.'

'See here. Bring out the dragon's head token.'

Jilian did as requested.

'Now place it in my palm.' The magician held out his hand. 'Go on.'

She hesitated but finally gave it to him.

'Now pay attention. The coin grows warm already. Soon it will be uncomfortable and if I hold it long enough it will scar my flesh.'

The mercenary reached out to touch it but pulled back her hand as if indeed heat radiated from it as the magician suggested.

'It's all right. It won't harm you,' Abadan assured her. 'However, despite the fact that I minted it, I am not its master.'

The dragon's head began to glow and Jilian snatched it from Abadan before it could do him damage. The magician's hand was red but hadn't begun to blister. 'How do I know this isn't a trick?'

'To what purpose? Try it with anyone. Try it when I'm in another building or another town and can't possibly have a finger in the results.' He waggled all ten at her.

'Who knows what a mage can do?'

Abadan slapped the table top. 'We are wasting time. How can we teach you if you will not learn?'

'Mistress Jilian,' Maarcus said, his calm measured voice a tonic to Abadan's hot one. 'Have you ever shown the token to anyone?'

'Other than Mut? No.'

'Why did you go to such great pains to hide it?'

'Obviously I didn't want it stolen.'

'But from the start, you tried to keep it with you, didn't you?'

'Well yes . . . it reminded me of . . . someone. It reminded me of someone.' She crossed her arms across her chest and Walther doubted she'd say more on that subject.

The others took the hint and didn't dwell on it. 'Ever mention it to anyone?'

'Of course not.' Her tone said the very idea seemed absurd.

'Anyone at all,' Abadan prodded.

She thought hard. 'Walther, but that was after . . .'

'Yes?'

Walther spoke up. 'After we found a similar coin amidst the ashes of Three Falls.'

'And?'

'And nothing.'

'Did you show him yours?'

'No. Should I have?'

'No. Precisely my point.'

Jilian stood. 'This is all quite interesting, but I really am quite tired.'

Abadan held up his hand. 'Five more minutes?'

'Three.'

'Do you bargain everything?' the magician asked.

'No, sometimes I just kill what's in the way and take what I want.'

The physician coughed at her crudeness.

The mercenary smiled. 'Two and a half.'

'Very well. Close your eyes and concentrate.'

She shrugged. 'Your time. I'm already quite good at this. Otherwise I'd be dead,' Jilian added, but shut her eyes.

'Now tell me where the coin is.'

'It's in my pock – It's moving! How?' Jilian opened her eyes and spun about in the direction the token had gone. It hung suspended in mid-air near the door.

'You will do well to remember that though no one else can bear its touch, it can still be stolen. Any thief powerful enough to take it from you is not someone you want to possess it. Guard it well.'

The elf ignored the dragon's head coin, but both Walther and Maarcus seemed drawn to it.

Fascinated, Walther was the first to speak. 'This is yours, isn't it, Jilian?'

She took it from the air. It didn't resist her touch as she put it away. 'It is.'

'It's different from the one we found.'

'There were only two originals forged to protect the king's twins,' Maarcus the Sixth explained. 'But when word began to spread that the king's true heirs could be identified by them, a few ambitious royals began imitating them. They claimed to have found them among peasant children which were in truth their own carefully seeded offspring.'

'But what are they doing in the ashes of burned-out villages?' Walther asked, curious despite his memories of shoveling through the wreckage.

Abadan made a face as if he'd eaten sour fruit. 'She uses the weakest ones as a reminder.'

'But how does she come by them?'

'She collects them. One by one, their owners are snuffed out and she keeps the only thing of any use to her.'

'But why?' the junior Maarcus challenged. 'My grandfather just said they were only imitations.'

'Yes. Still, some were convincingly made, imbued with enough magic to fool the less schooled.' The senior Maarcus looked over at his companion with an unreadable expression. 'It would take a magician of Abadan's ability to recognize the most successful copies.'

Walther felt a chill run down his spine. 'Do you mean the elfwitch can draw strength from these?'

Zera spoke up. 'To varying degrees. She has been studying them the entire length of your lives. Without doubt she knows more about them than any of us. You must therefore be all the more cautious around her, Jilian, for you hold the lodestone to all the others.'

The mercenary nodded. Walther guessed this was one warning she would take seriously.

'Tomorrow we'll begin your training,' said Abadan eagerly.

'Yes, tomorrow,' Jilian echoed, but it seemed to Walther her heart wasn't in it.

Lyda's mission did not include death. She could do nothing for those already resting in the palms of the Seven Sisters.

So she couldn't fathom why she had been guided to this wasteland formerly bursting with dwarven life and laughter. She could hear the echoes of children playing, their elders working. An entire village unworried by rumors of invaders and war, all snuffed in a single morning's flash of terror. No one survived the attack. No pulse beat beneath the rubble.

Pain lay heavy atop and below the ashes. She gave a few half-hearted pokes, but understood this was not her calling. She fought the urge to flee this place and its screams drowned in flames. She needed to unearth her purpose amidst the charred bones.

She tried, oh she tried, to see the hope that must yet linger in the puffs of fine, black dust that rose around her feet. Death greets each and all in the proper time; and his Sister consort does not allow exceptions.

In the end, there was no enlightenment, no way to reckon the lesson to be learned. The elfwitch mocked both Death and his Sister with her willful destruction. Her moment too would come, as it must. The Sisters would not ignore her hubris. Lyda strove to feel pity for Alvaria's fate, and found she could not manage it.

She whispered a prayer for the dead and another, which begged forgiveness for her own cold heart. 'Peace,' she choked out. 'Peace to us all.'

Lyda fled with the remains of their lives clinging to the soles of her shoes, burying the wondrous, colored trail behind her.

Maarcus the Sixth paced the length of the sitting room, much too annoyed to remain seated. Only Abadan and Zera remained. 'You nearly frightened her away with your talk of destiny,' he told his old friend.

Abadan shook his head. 'I don't think so. She needed to be shaken up. Just watch. She'll come around to our way of thinking.'

'And if she doesn't?'

'There's still her brother.'

'Not very useful in the hands of the elfwitch.'

'No, but we only need to delay her long enough to give her a few skills. Then we'll be able to rescue the boy.'

Maarcus crossed his arms and snorted. 'When did you become the optimist?'

Abadan smiled the broadest smile Maarcus could ever remember seeing on his wrinkled face. 'Oh, just since I met the girl.'

'You really must stop referring to her that way. She could well be your queen one day,' the elf reminded him.

'If the Sisters are willing,' the magician whispered as if in prayer.

'You are serious. What did you see in the Princess Jilian that I missed?'

'Oh, you saw it. You've simply forgotten how to recognize it.'

'And?' Maarcus prompted, still pacing.

'Backbone. Unlike all her half-siblings – living or dead – the girl has backbone.'

The physician stopped in mid-stride and spun to face his companions. He had suggested as much himself earlier, but dismissed the observation without realizing it. 'Why so she does!' A wholly unfamiliar feeling welled up in his throat and a hearty laugh escaped. 'We actually succeeded. After all these years, she's proven we were right.'

Maarcus had never known the magician to gloat over his greatest achievements and he didn't now. Abadan sat calmly sipping his liqueur through lips pursed in a subtle grin. His eyes were bright with delight in his triumph. 'And she had enough sense, manners, or curiosity to listen to my little tale. She'll be back in the morning and then we can truly begin.' He lifted his cordial and saluted them all.

Chapter 14

PETITIONS

Roslin sat by a pond and dabbled with her scrying bowl. She didn't quite trust it after the recent episode, but it still responded the way she expected. She had to assume its absence was part of her vision, however strange it struck her.

With no particular objective, she let her mind wander across the landscapes of the broken One Land. Refugees fled from the hills to the lowlands with no more thought about what they would find than a goat might worry over a grazed-out field.

Idle curiosity led her among the streams of dwarves but there was nothing of interest there. They feared the elfwitch and with their limited talents it was no wonder to Roslin that they should. Humans joined the flow though they held her attention scant minutes longer than the dwarves. Here, too, they carried what they could manage and stumbled forward in blind cowardice. She wandered by a stray ripple that might have been Willam the shopkeeper and ignored it. He deserved his short-sighted fate.

The scatterings of elves most intrigued the mage. Here were the lowest, most contemptible of all. The others ran out of ignorance; by contrast, the elves rejected knowledge and power. Here were a people who had been offered a great destiny and foolishly denied it.

Disgusted at the tides of waste, Roslin flung out her arm and jostled the bowl.

And so it was that as the ripples cleared she happened to see the elves who took Ginni away while her father looked on helplessly. The mage laughed aloud at the frustration evident in every muscle of his face and body. She'd warned him years ago when he left her that the Sisters would make him pay for his mistreatment and baseness. Now they finally had.

But unlike Wanton Tom, Roslin wasn't deceived by the minor magic which cloaked an elf, a troll, and a human girl. She watched their hurried progress from town to woodland while Thomas went whining to the dragon.

Ginni conducted herself with far more dignity than her father and Roslin felt a rare pride in her daughter. Perhaps the girl had taken in a tenth of what she'd been taught after all.

They continued on through secondary narrow paths while Ginni casually studied each turn and carefully pinched a leaf now and then. The mage didn't recognize most of the trails. She didn't need to. Their easterly direction was plain. They must be headed back to the elfwitch's stronghold.

This called for action. She couldn't let the child's training be squandered by simply handing it over to the witch. Then too the elf might just be talented enough to unlock certain carefully hidden secrets in Ginni's mind. No one was entitled to know what lay within her daughter's memory unless the mage herself permitted it.

Roslin did not go chasing after wayward apprentices, but

she knew someone who would, someone foolish enough to think even the lowest magicians were worth cultivating.

Abadan.

Abadan, who still believed she did his bidding. Abadan, who would be indebted to her after she dropped such a useful bit of information in his scrying bowl. If she could contact the court magician without letting on this would be a favor to her, she might yet see the child rescued without risk to herself.

The mage allowed herself a luxurious stretch and considered the different approaches to Abadan. Should she flatter him? He'd always struck her as the sort who lapped up praise. No, she'd never seen it influence his decisions. Should she appeal to his pity? No, too personally degrading. Further, she'd never known him to show mercy.

The obvious and simplest was likely the best. Abadan still espoused the need to fight the elfwitch – a cause Roslin had come to be less sure of herself. Probably the witch did some good by thinning the herd and leaving only the strongest. However, not the point at present. This opinion surely wouldn't aid her now, even though the royal magician often behaved as if he felt the same way.

Roslin bent forward to look into the pool now cleaned of any images other than the fish in the nearby pond. She'd follow Ginni a while longer yet, then report back to Abadan their desperate need to rescue the girl before the elfwitch extracted vital intelligence.

Tom ran full out all the way back to Grosik, cursing the whole while about the foolishness of stealth. He didn't care who saw him or what they might do about it. Ginni was his responsibility and he'd let her down.

Grosik didn't wait for Tom to reach him before showing himself. 'Bring the navy with you?' he asked.

'Huh?' Tom had no patience for the dragon's cryptic sarcasm. 'Ginni, they've got Ginni,' he spat out between heaving breaths.

'And?'

'What do you mean "And"? We've got to save her.'

'Agreed. And?'

The mercenary stopped to stare at the dragon. 'What's sticking in your thick hide? We don't have time for children's games.'

'Wrong. We don't have time for panic.'

'I'm not –' he started angrily but didn't finish. Grosik was right. He was behaving like a boy in his maiden battle. They'd all known something might go wrong. It had simply taken an unexpected jag to the left.

Tom looked out at the Cups from his vantage on the hill and back at the dragon. 'Thanks.'

'Next time, don't tie your shorts so tight. It cuts the blood flow to your brain.'

The old joke didn't strike Wanton Tom as particularly funny just now, but he gave a half-hearted chuckle anyway to show Grosik he'd calmed down.

'So?'

'Between "so" and "and", I do all the talking here.'

'This is news. Anything helpful you'd like to add?'

Wanton Tom paused, remembering the scene at the inn. He described it as clearly as he could.

'Since when do well-mannered trolls accompany elves, mannered or not?'

'I was thinking the same thing.'

'What about Ginni's nod to Roslin's magicks? Any ideas now that you've had time to think about it?'

The dragon never could resist a barb in the side. It helped remind him he was still superior despite the fact that he'd spent more than twenty years with a human. Tom focused on the table in his mind's eye. He started to shake his head 'no' until he realized the reason he couldn't remember anything is that *nothing* was there. 'The table was empty,' he said with a triumphant smile.

'Hardly good news.'

'Hardly bad news either,' Tom said to cover his gloating over such minor successes as memory recall. 'This confirms that Roslin wasn't there when the elf arrived.'

'Any clues to where she went?'

'Do I look like a fortune teller?'

'Too ugly for fortune telling.'

A chill wind blew and small rocks skittered down the hillside. The two stood silently listening to tenacious birds who remained in the face of irratic weather.

It took the dragon to speak the thought aloud. 'We won't be able to find her without the mage.'

'But she's gone.'

'You might stake out the room.'

'No, she wasn't planning to return.' Tom stared into the darkening horizon without seeing. There had to be another option. 'There is another mage.'

'Taken up a new hobby?' Grosik asked with the same voice the pious might have said, 'Consorting with the underworld?'

'No, Roslin was enough for a lifetime.' He laughed overloud. 'I mean Abadan, the master magician.'

'You deceive yourself in your old age.'

'Why is everyone calling me old these days?' Tom asked, not really wanting an answer. 'Grosik, this makes sense. The *esteemed* physician wanted our help and we gave it. He owes us a favor.'

'Did he ever promise such?'

'Well, he did tell us he'd be back. Why not go to him first?'

'Nothing good ever comes out of the capital, regardless of

what goes in. Too many squabbling functionaries to see common sense when it lands on their porcelain dinner plates.'

'True enough, but this is important. And I do have the means to contact Sir Maarcus without traveling to the Cliffs.'

The dragon didn't argue. Wanton Tom just had to remember where he'd put the babble box and how to work it.

Lyda wandered the frozen countryside. Behind her trailed the bright colors of spring, of festivals, of renewal and celebration. She brought hope to those who saw her and word of her passage began to grow. She'd never meant to be a prophetess. She worked no miracles other than bringing smiles here and there. Yet the people began to see her as a counterpoint to the increasingly horrifying rumors of trolls on the rampage, or worse, trolls with a leader who kept them under tight rein and let them free only to kill.

After Lyda left the ashes of the devastated town, she thought of Willam for the first time in weeks. Did he follow her? Was he home grieving? Did the elves find him? Did he know she was well? Was he well?

This last thought stopped her. She stared at the vegetation bowed low with icicles, marveling at how she'd come to be at her ease in such a strange land surrounded by refugees. Men, women, children, humans, dwarves, a few elves, all carried whatever they could manage as they moved in a great tide.

A small girl was tugging on Lyda's dress. 'Mistress Lyda, Mistress!'

Her aghast mother pulled her back. 'My apologies, Lady. She's so young, she doesn't—'

Lyda's smile was wholly genuine. 'Children are always

welcome.' For once she did not envy others for that which she had been denied. She bent down to the dwarf while others surged past. 'What is it, dear?'

'Where are we going?'

Lyda smoothed the child's brown curls. 'To safety. We are going to safety.'

The dwarf smiled and her mother grabbed hold of her before she could take up any more of Lyda's time. 'Thank you,' she said. 'Thank you so very much.' There were tears in her eyes. The woman bowed low and the two fell behind her.

Lyda choked down the urge to laugh. The absurdity was too much and she allowed herself a discrete chuckle.

But where was Willam? Could he be out here among these hundreds upon hundreds? She shook her head. Lyda could not see into other minds. They would cross paths when the Sisters willed it. 'Peace, Willam,' she wished quietly, just as she had for countless others.

Alone in her room in the deepnight with her head full of nonsense she half-believed, Jilian felt the sharp jab of Mut's despair. His situation had turned for the worse.

She couldn't bring herself to care about the heir to this or that when Mut was at stake. He was linked to her in a way that dug deeper than their years together. She had to do something *now*.

The royals and magicians could sort it out for themselves. The answers they gave her only added more twists to the maze that made up her life. As it was, she'd never had this much at stake before. With all her past assignments, if she died, she died; if her charge died, it would be unfortunate but not without precedent. But if Mut died . . . She wouldn't finish the thought. Mut was irreplaceable.

Jilian snatched her bag from its place in the corner,

checked to see that the essentials were intact, and slung the
pack on her shoulder. In her haste, she tipped over a chair
near the door. She caught it just as it hit the floor. Carefully
she righted it and stood waiting to see if anyone would feel
obliged to check on the noise.

Minutes passed and no one came. The mercenary let out
her breath. She needed to calm down. She ran one last
orderly search of the room and found nothing she needed.

Jilian considered leaving a note of appreciation to the elf
– for the bath if not the banquet – and farewell to the rest,
but decided against it. Chances were they'd know where she
was going. If not, she didn't want to risk giving hints and
have them chasing after. She worried over Ceeley but finally
had to trust that Maarcus, Walther and Zera could care for
her.

In the darkest of night, she let herself out the front door
without a whisper of goodbye to anyone. It was the sort of
exit she'd done many times in her life and the familiarity of
it slipped on perfectly, like the mercenary's favorite knife
resting against her thigh.

An hour or so before dawn, she stopped to nap. The
nocturnal prowlers had gone to ground and only a few,
cautious early birds stirred. Jilian climbed a tree and settled
against the trunk. No one would be looking for her ten feet
up. She shut her eyes and commanded sleep to come. It did
not arrive without a price.

'Do what you will,' said the elf, blocking the mercenary's
way. 'But know that you are not prepared.'

'It's Mut and the witch,' Jilian found herself admitting.
'I—'

'We've each and every one seen loved ones suffer at . . . her
hand.' Zera seemed reluctant to call the elfwitch by name.

'But we can't conquer her by chasing in unready. Please you need—'

'With all due respect,' Jilian interrupted, 'I need to find him before it's too late. He's all I have in this world.' The mercenary knew she sounded like an impatient child, but she could not ignore the pain twisting in her stomach.

The elf spoke calmly and convincingly. 'I don't deny Mut's place in your heart, Jilian. But you have many friends who would offer more than wishing you well from a safe distance. There are people who would die to spare you from the fate my daughter intends.' She leaned forward in earnest. 'I swear to you that any who have walked with you this far are as bound to you as if they'd sworn a bloodoath.'

Jilian waved a hand. 'Nonsense. I have never been anything more than a woodsman's willful daughter grown into a stubborn woman who knows how to throw a knife. It's all I'll ever be, even if I would like to believe your grand stories of royal birth and abandonment. Where were any of you these past twenty-five, thirty years?' The last slipped out without her meaning it to. She swore under her breath. Now she'd let herself be pulled into an argument that couldn't be won but was sure to squander time.

'Looking for you,' the elf answered sincerely.

Jilian stared at her hostess for a long quiet minute but finally looked down at her worn boots. 'That may well be,' she said to her toes, 'and you have been very gracious indeed. It is therefore with great regret that I take my leave.' She faced the elf, willing her to understand. 'I must rescue him if I can.'

'And if you can't?'

'Then I'll die trying. He would do the same for me.'

'And many more will die with you . . .'

Jilian awoke with Zera's presence thick in the air around

her. 'By the Sisters,' she swore, 'I have to do this. I have to.' But all the most colorful curses in the One Land would not put her mind at ease that she had chosen the right path.

Maarcus the Sixth couldn't perform the simplest form of magic. It was as Zera had told his grandson. The talent did not run in his family, plain and simple. Nonetheless, he was not above a few conveniences so long as they worked independent of his own abilities. One of these was the babbler, which Abadan had fashioned for certain persons to contact him. Among these was the reluctant spy Wanton Tom. Each babbler had its own code and only the intended user could activate it.

In better than ten years, Tom had never so much as tested it.

When the signal sounded, Maarcus couldn't recall it. But rather than blame an aging memory, a likely source these days, he immediately roused Abadan. The magician was none too happy about it, but the physician could count on one hand the number of times Abadan had been happy about anything.

'I'm sleeping. Do you mind?' he whispered fiercely. 'Untroubled sleep, a thing I have longed for for months and only just tonight achieved. Go away.'

Maarcus mercilessly ripped off the top covers. 'Someone has used the babbler.'

'Someone? What do you mean someone?' He snatched back the blankets and buried his head under the pillow for good measure. 'Come back when you know who it is and what he wants.'

'Abadan, this is serious. I don't recognize the sign. Listen for yourself.' He lifted the pillow and held the babbler against the magician's naked ear.

Abadan slapped it away from him. It flew out of the

physician's hand and bounced to the floor. 'It's that spy of yours, what's his name? Has a dragon. Fathered a child on that vicious woman, Roslin. Never lie with a mage, that's my advice,' he muttered. He burrowed under the remaining sheet. 'Why doesn't anyone use normal names anymore? Running Jon or something, he goes by.'

Maarcus almost smiled. He knew who petitioned his attention and he had a means of waking his friend as well. 'Abadan being among the most common names, of course.'

Abadan sat up, his face red with annoyance – or perhaps lack of air. 'That's different. I'm the king's magician born into a respected line of same.'

'Abadan, we don't have much of a king at present and aren't likely to ever again if we don't find out what Wanton Tom wants.'

'Wanton Tom. Right. That was his name. All right.' He pulled on a heavy robe over his nightclothes. 'Let's get this over with.' He crossed the room to a desk set out with his most ordinary magicks. There was nothing worth stealing here but enough to alert him should anyone decide to experiment. The scrying bowl he yanked from the air, at least as far as Maarcus could determine. He busied himself for several minutes while Maarcus paced.

Truth to tell, magic bored the physician. He didn't understand it, knew he never would; and things he couldn't decipher no matter how he tried were ultimately tedious beyond his patience to endure.

'Stop that,' Abadan said. 'You're stomping hard enough to bring in the trolls.'

'Hardly that,' Maarcus countered.

'No, but sufficient to vibrate the desk.'

'Hello, hello!' Tom yelled. 'Anyone home?'

'We're not deaf, young man.'

The relief on his face was evident. 'Oh, there you are.'

'Sleeping, I might add.'

'No time for that.'

'Says you.'

'Never mind. What does he want?' Maarcus asked over his shoulder.

Abadan waved as if trying to dislodge an annoying fly. 'You've awakened half the household. This better be important.'

'They've taken Ginni,' he said without so much as a nod toward manners.

'And she is?' Abadan asked, with growing menace.

'Stop trying to intimidate him,' Maarcus whispered. 'He's normally as unflappable as a dead bird.'

'Ginni, my daughter!' the man shouted. 'How can you not know who she is? You nearly took her away from me ten years ago! Where's the physician?'

'You needn't shout. He's right beside me. Wave to the people,' the magician said to Maarcus, knowing the mercenary couldn't see them.

'Go on. I'm listening,' the physician told Tom.

Wanton Tom cupped a hand to his ear. 'What was that?'

'He said, "Go on, we're listening." More to the point who took your daughter and why should I care if you can't keep track of your own offspring?'

Wanton Tom's face went red, but he didn't rise to the bait.

'Got more control than you have,' Maarcus whispered.

'He better. I didn't wake him up before dawn to whine about a lost child.'

The mercenary spoke slowly and distinctly as if to a difficult student. 'As you must know, Ginni is not only my daughter. She is also the daughter of Roslin the mage. The girl has considerable talent, fire being among her gifts. Her mother was using her for reconnaissance work, the nature of which neither Roslin nor Ginni explained to me in detail. The elf and troll who took her—'

'Elf and troll together?' Abadan interrupted.

'Yes, together. That's what I've been trying to—'

'We'll look into it and let you know.' Abadan severed the connection.

'You might have let him finish his tale. There may be more to it.' Maarcus began pacing again.

'I have the most important piece, the elf and troll. If Alvaria is willing to send them out together, she must be planning a new offensive, something that will make her past look like a parlor game. We need to accelerate the girl's training. We've got to get her ready to confront the worst.'

'I'll wake Zera.'

Someone knocked on the door.

'It seems we don't need to,' Abadan told him. 'Come in, Zera.'

She entered quickly and closed the door behind her. The elf didn't seem surprised to find them both fully awake at the early hour. 'I couldn't sleep. Finally after hours of promising I would not overstep, I went to check on my granddaughter. Her room's empty. She's gone.'

Chapter 15

STORM-WARNING

'Do you have to keep tripping over my tail?' Grosik asked.

'Do you have to take up the entire cave?' Wanton Tom countered. The interior seemed smaller than before as the mercenary tried to pace around a reclining dragon. 'They didn't even let me finish,' he fumed.

'You were expecting them to give the hired help cordial conversation?' Grosik asked.

'No, but the physician did gather up some respect that time we met in his forest hideaway.'

The dragon sneered at Tom. 'Or so you thought. Must I state the obvious? He wanted something from you. Now you want something from him.'

The mercenary walked to the entrance. The dragon did have a point. 'That's all well and good, but it doesn't tell me whether they'll go after Ginni.'

'Since when have you desired assistance from the government or its drones, most especially those self-absorbed magic wielders?'

Right again. Dragon sense was finally sinking in. It was part of what made them such a good team. In more instances than not, the cooler head ruled the hotter one. The trick was admitting whose was the most reasonable at the time.

'We'll need to go ourselves.'

Grosik's jaws snapped closed on a rabbit that had dared to make a break for outdoors. 'I'm delighted to concur,' he said around crunching food. 'The sooner we find her the better.' He swallowed the morsel. 'Otherwise, I'll have to get used to eating my meals raw again.'

Tom couldn't help but laugh. 'A facility with fire does have its upside.'

Grosik joined the mercenary at the cavemouth. 'What are you waiting for?'

When it came to magic, Zera was nearly as devoid of ability as Maarcus himself. Her talent seemed more as a teacher – she always had an eager apprentice – and a carrier. Clearly she had passed on her mother's great talent to her daughter and the daughter in turn to the granddaughter – though how strong the magic was in Jilian remained to be seen.

The three, Maarcus, Abadan and Zera remained gathered in Abadan's bedchamber planning, discarding then re-plotting their next step. The conversation circled in on itself with all courses of action equally uninspired until the elf said, 'Why not bring in your grandson and the dwarf? They've travelled with Jilian and may well have insight into our proper move.'

The men readily agreed. It was decided to reassemble in Abadan's workshop. Zera had donated the room to the magician's use and he'd long since transformed it into a magical chamber that rivalled his original in the Cliffs.

Maarcus hated both places even after so many years. Surrounded by unknowable and strange potions, he could never shake the feeling that a bottle was about to explode or another was slowly seeping around the edges of its cork stopper to poison them all. Still the magic was here and it made little sense to waste more time carting what might be needed to Abadan's bedchamber.

Reluctant, the physician dragged and fell behind the magician. Abadan didn't bother to wait. He knew Maarcus would arrive before he finished laying out his materials.

The scientist held his breath as he opened the door. Somehow the magician had tapped into the elfwitch's activities and the room tended to reflect her most recent tortures. Today the room smelled of dead things and sweet overripe fruit. He winced and tried to breathe shallowly. At least it wasn't as bad as last time when it had reeked of burning flesh and flowers out of season.

Zera arrived with the physician's grandson and his dwarf companion while the elder Maarcus was still getting acclimatized. His grandson's face went white but he kept his thoughts to himself. To the royal scientist's surprise, Walther did not seem unduly affected by the odor and instantly began to explore the lab.

Abadan gave no sign that he noticed the arrivals while he worked. Experience had taught Maarcus otherwise. In the magician's domain, more than anywhere else, he tracked the movements of others with a precision that frightened some of his guests.

He set the scrying bowl in the middle of a round table. 'Come, come.' Abadan beckoned with waving arms. The magician took the only chair and left the others to crowd around the table. He raised a hand to the assembled group. 'I will offer just this warning.' Abadan paused to look into their eyes one by one to be certain each heeded him. 'It is forbidden to gaze into the present. Doing so can unwittingly shape events. Generally the Sisters assure such alterations run counter to that which the seer would have hoped. For this reason, we must guide the magic elsewhere and seek insights indirectly. Now we begin.' He closed his eyes and bowed his head.

Walther followed Abadan's example as if it were second nature while the rest glanced from each other to the bowl to the magician.

Abadan uttered words from a language forgotten by all but a few journeymen mage-scholars. The fluid seethed and boiled in response and then calmed. Abadan's eyebrows went up in surprise though he said nothing. The vision appeared not within his scrying bowl but above. It held not an image of the past or the future as he'd directed, but the present. Abadan's mouth dropped open in utter amazement.

Maarcus felt his innards clench. Through the years of acrimony and friendship, he had never seen the magician caught so off-guard. But more astonishing than this was that Abadan turned to stare at the now open-eyed dwarf. He rose from his seat, walked around to Walther, then guided him to take his chair.

Maarcus tried to shake the unease. So many firsts could only bode ill.

Abadan paid no attention to the others. Walther himself paid no mind to anyone at all, for he was caught in the grip of the vision. The rest could follow along or not. Nothing they did would influence it.

A beautiful and young human woman was being led into a camp by an elf and troll. She seemed to move of her own will and to be completely at her ease. Whether this was in fact so, however, was unknowable. Likely she was the one called Ginni, daughter of the mage and the mercenary.

The crowd parted and the elfwitch stepped forward. Her face held the smile of the cat who has cornered her mouse. She raised an arm and pointed toward Ginni while the girl stood defiant. Alvaria turned her palm skyward. A wind picked up the human and set her down hard enough to jar knees. The girl regained her balance without so much as a blink.

'Where is the bracelet?' the witch yelled. 'I know you have it. I saw when you uncovered it.'

Ginni did not answer and the vision popped as if a bubble burst.

'Bring it back!' shouted Abadan and Zera.

Walther sat shaking his head within cradled arms. 'I have never had any control over the visions, least of all now.'

'But the bracelet. We need to see this bracelet!'

Maarcus understood Abadan's urgency though he couldn't bring himself to shout at the dwarf. Despite his marvelous talent, the poor wretch understood the ways of magic no better than the physician. Still, if the bracelet were somehow related to Mut's talisman . . . It was too much to hope for.

Abadan sighed. 'That was really most extraordinary. How did you do it?'

'I told you,' said the distraught dwarf, his voice muffled by his arms, 'the visions come when they will and release me when they're finished.' He raised his head. His eyes were red and troubled. 'I have seen such terrible things these last months. Is there nothing we can do but watch?'

'What?' the younger Maarcus asked. 'What have you seen?'

But Walther only burrowed his head back in his arms and refused more questions. The others looked at each other, unsure what to do.

A strange chirp sounded loudly in the tense silence.

'What's that?'

'Oh, just another of my babble boxes,' Abadan said. 'But what an interesting interruption.'

'Why? Who is it?' asked the elf.

Abadan laughed as if he'd won a private bet. 'The girl's mother. Roslin.'

Nearly a day had passed before Roslin settled back at the scrying bowl. She'd considered her wording over and again to be sure she had the best combination of urgency and importance without admitting her own weakness. Then she'd waited for the sun to be decently risen to contact the magician. Abadan wasn't known for his early hours.

Roslin set the foolish box Abadan had given her some years ago next to her scrying bowl and glared at it. She'd used it only once before in the dark hours after she'd had to leave Ginni in the mercenary's care. When she realized Abadan could see her even though she couldn't see him, she'd vowed never to use it again. Just the same, she kept the device among her belongings because a good magician never squanders an opportunity to learn about a competing magic. This time she hoped her own much advanced ability with the scrying bowl would allow her an equal view, unbeknownst to Abadan.

She prepared the bowl minus the elven serviceberry. That she'd add once she'd reached the magician. Next she arranged her friendliest smile and patted her hair into place – both likely wasteful gestures, but good impressions could be useful and one never knew what appealed to such twisted men as Abadan. Finally she ran her fingers across the runes around the edge of the babble box in first a counterclockwise then clockwise motion. The wood box grew cold and clung to her skin as if she'd touched frozen metal. Despite the discomfort she repeated the motion and gently called the magician's name.

Abadan answered almost immediately. 'Why, Roslin, what a delightful surprise to hear from you.'

'The pleasure is all mine, I'm sure,' she answered with equal insincerity. She looked down with mock humbleness to cover her action as she added twin drops of serviceberry to her scrying bowl. The potion clouded and reformed to show Abadan's sharp-nosed face. He seemed to be surrounded by others, but she couldn't make out their features. It worked! She had him now.

'Do speak up,' he prodded. 'We're rather short-handed and time-pressed here at the capital. They'll have me serving the king's breakfast next.'

Roslin laughed. 'I doubt that for one of your stature and talent,' she said, even as she realized he wasn't in the Cliffs but Twin Gates.

'Yes, well . . .' Abadan fussed. He didn't need to tell another magician he'd never be welcome near food. Suddenly he was all business. 'Since we are both in high demand at present, let me save you some trouble. I understand your daughter, a girl of some talent herself, has gone missing.'

So he'd heard from Wanton Tom. Roslin nodded then realized she wasn't supposed to know he could see her. 'I wouldn't call her missing exactly. After all, I do know where Ginni is. In truth, it's where she is that should concern us. I have every reason to believe the elfwitch has abducted her. Inasmuch as Ginni has been reconnoitering on behalf of the One Land for some months now, you might want to retrieve her before Alvaria discovers what you've been up to.'

'I'm sure you'll want to aid us in this quest.'

So he wasn't going to make it easy for her. Roslin had expected as much. Nonetheless, she would see the matter settled on her terms. She took on a troubled expression and let her shoulders slump.

'Certainly I'd want to help, that much more because she is my daughter.'

'Excellent. When may we expect – ' Abadan began before Roslin cut him off.

'However, as you know, I am currently engaged in important research work for the One Land at present. Though it grieves me, I must respectfully suggest that visiting Alvaria's lair will compromise all I have done for the One Land.'

In the scrying bowl, Abadan mouthed 'worse than a dragonlady!' but his tone was neutral when he spoke to her. 'As I know how greatly this pains you, I won't press the issue. Rest assured, though, we'll find your daughter with all due speed.' He severed the connection abruptly.

Roslin slapped at the babble box. 'Old goat.' She moved to cleanse the scrying bowl and was astonished to find it still held the image of Abadan's workshop. Fascinated, she watched as the magician turned to Maarcus the Sixth and three others whom she did not recognize. Surely the younger human male was the junior Maarcus, but the dwarf and elf intrigued her. What were they about? Suddenly the dwarf's eyes grew wide. Abadan looked over his shoulder and spoke a simple incantation.

The fluid in Roslin's bowl rippled and boiled. When it cleared, the surface reflected only her own expression. The mage tossed the contents of the bowl into a shallow pit dug for that purpose.

Now was the time to call a truce with Alvaria. The elfwitch was the only one worthy of allying with her own great talent.

'Two in one morning. We are popular.'

Maarcus spoke from the floor where he was crouched over an unconscious Walther. 'Or the girl Ginni is genuinely important. But her mother – ' He shook his head. He'd never understand women like that, his own deceased wife among them.

'First things first.' Abadan turned back to Zera. 'Jilian.'

'Is she truly gone? Couldn't she be somewhere nearby?' the elder Maarcus asked, already knowing better.

Zera didn't bother to respond. His grandson asked, 'Do you know how and when she left?'

'By way of the front door it seems,' Zera said, then added, 'On two legs.'

'By the Great King!' Abadan exploded. In truth Maarcus was surprised he'd held his peace this long. 'Why didn't you listen when I wanted to set a guard?'

'You know as well as I do the uselessness of that. If she's managed to elude us all these years, no ordinary magic is powerful enough to restrain her. Further we agreed that such coercion would make for an inept ruler.'

' – And we've had plenty of those,' the magician interrupted. He looked at Maarcus as if he were to blame. 'If only you . . .'

The physician ignored Abadan. He shared the man's frustration. To be so close . . . 'She must come to it by way of her own royal vision of the One Land's future,' Maarcus reminded him.

He hadn't felt so heavy since the day the Great King died. In the years since they'd spent all their time struggling to keep the One Land together – when they weren't simply fighting to stay alive. (Though the latter got somewhat easier once the long line of usurpers realized it was simpler to attack each other than the two senior advisors with their endless, and lethal, means of self-protection.) The physician forced his attention back to the dwarf who was beginning to stir. They couldn't lose the One Land to the elfwitch now that they were so close to establishing a strong and legitimate government.

'Maarcus,' Zera said, 'the magic is stronger within Jilian than you can know. She has a very good chance of achieving her task.'

There was an odd smile – part admiration, part embarrassment – on his grandson's face.

'What?' the scientist asked, hoping against hope for a thread of good news.

'She has remained quite single-minded about the dragon.'

Abadan looked down at the slowly recovering dwarf and shook his head. 'That satisfies *her* goal. But what about ours?'

Agony deeper than pain drove Jilian much harder than any compulsion she'd ever had before. Certainty that Mut hurtled toward a violent crossroads pushed away her lingering fear caused by the dream-vision of Zera.

When she'd awakened that morning, a beautifully carved walking stick lay at the base of the tree. Thinking it must be a gift from Zera, she'd claimed it with hardly a second thought.

Now hours later the sun rose high in the sky. She stabbed the newly acquired stick into the thick layering of dead leaves. Around her the forest felt thick with death. The mercenary peered into the gloom. 'Seven ladies and their seven sons! I'd like a moment's peace and a stripe of sunlight.'

In response the wood went noticeably darker. The sun had barely crossed its zenith, but the heavy canopy of trees cast forbidding shadows. Birds and animals seemed reluctant to breach the dank air. Jilian paused. She must be nearing the Lake of Mists. Many strange goings-on were suspected of beginning on the shore of this lake – no stranger than trolls perhaps, but more dangerous than those same behemoths run amuck.

It was not chance she'd come this way. It was a summons.

Despite its reputation, the lake was little more than a pond. To call it a lake spoke of the mysteries which shrouded it just as the trees which grew past the shore into the water itself obscured the boundaries. Jilian could easily have thrown a stone to the opposite bank if she'd been able to see it. Regardless of weather or season, mist was said to billow up in thick waves.

Suddenly drained of energy, Jilian sat on a rock jutting into the water and peered into the murk. She spoke aloud to keep up her spirits or maybe to let Mut know she was just resting and would soon be on her way. 'It only looks as if monsters lurk below because of the mist. In truth, I hear the water has been known to restore the aged and ill. Not that I believe it, of course,' she added. 'But there is a spring feeding into the pond . . .' Her voice sounded flat in the dense air. In the unnatural quiet, the mercenary shifted her weight on the rock and closed her eyes.

It pulled first at her mind, then abruptly, she was *under* the water. Jilian could see the surface of the lake over her and the trees looming above that. The mist had vanished.

She put out her hand and touched bottom – hard stone with a covering of fine sand, as if she were on dry land. To her right was impenetrable darkness. To her left, a light.

Walking toward it was a strange sensation. She seemed weightless while at the same time it took her full strength to move. Twin dragon coins burned against her breast. A warning? A welcome? She didn't know.

The light was sheltered within a cave. She stood at the mouth and waited. Nothing changed; no one beckoned her forward. The small candleflame filled her sight as it cycled from blue to indigo to violet to white then back again. She looked as long as she dared then turned her head to the side.

A voice from nowhere, from everywhere, said, 'Attend. You must watch.'

Jilian closed her eyes and steeled herself. She counted to seven then opened her eyes once more. Again the light was all that she could see. She watched the colors rotate until she felt as if she too were rotating.

Then the color changed to a deep red the shade of just spilled blood.

'No!' Jilian threw her hands up to cover her face—

And felt herself tossed away like refuse.

For a long breath, the mercenary lay with her face buried beneath her hands. When at last she had the courage to peer between her fingers, she found herself back on the rock.

Jilian sat up slowly, the vision of the pulsing blue light still filling her thoughts. Her left hand felt cramped as if she had held it clenched for hours. When she opened it, a stone the color of dried blood leaked fluid onto her palm. Horrified, she tossed it back into the water.

The stain would not wash off.

And her walking stick was gone.

Thinking it had rolled off the boulder, she looked in the water lapping against stone. She retraced her path along the bank. There was no sign of it – only traces of red.

Across the lake, someone had built a fire. She approached it to discover no one tended it. She stared at the ordinary oranges, reds, and yellows for a long time before she spoke. This time she knew it was to Mut.

'I have failed. Beware, Mut, please beware.'

Each agonizing minute seemed to stretch outside time as it had when she was a child awaiting a deserved punishment.

The loss of her parents ached as if it were only this morning that she'd mourned over their ruined corpses. Their path had always been straight and clear, while hers was twisted and overgrown, shadowed by mists and strange lights. Their way may have been easier, though she did not envy them. In the end, they had not chosen their fate; Fate had chosen them and discarded them when its mission was fulfilled.

She stood. Her body felt sluggish, loathe to depart. *I feel as if I've been drugged.* The thought came unbidden and unwelcome, but she immediately knew the truth of it.

Jilian forced herself onward away from the lake. She crashed through trees and underbrush, falling into an unexpected clearing. Maarcus and Walther sat motionless, frozen in place by an unknown force. *Where was Ceeley?*

Frantic now, Jilian ran from one to the other, poking, kicking, slapping, yelling, begging. Motionless as dead wood, not even an eye twitched in response. She tried to think what to do. She could not carry them to safety. She could not leave them here.

In the distance, lightning streaked the sky. The accompanying boom knocked her off her feet. A moment later, a second flash. She braced herself for the thunder. It was the third and loudest that told Jilian she was beyond hope. A power rivalling the Sacred Sisters was at play.

A thick mist like the one so often covering the lake had rolled in, obscuring her view. She hurried the few feet to where she thought they rested, but couldn't find them. Jilian stood stock still and reached. In her mind, she pictured the position of each in relation to the other and to her. Slowly she felt in the direction of Maarcus, who was nearer, then Walther.

They were gone.

Mut thought he was beyond caring. Alvaria had let him run out his strength and will. He'd never see Jilian again. The poor goatboy who hadn't even been afforded the dignity of a true name was surely being tortured or mistreated in another less well appointed tent. The dragon lay, facing the back of the tent and listlessly waiting to die.

The guards dropped someone on the packed dirt floor and ordered, 'Make sure he eats. The One says he'll need his strength to get through the ceremony.'

The dragon didn't turn around. He could hear the person stumbling to right himself, losing and falling against Mut. A gentle hand touched his flank. 'It's you!' said a human girl-woman. 'I'm sure of it!'

Too many had been too sure of too many things of late. Mut tried to maintain his careless disconnection. Still, he couldn't help but notice that her voice held awe as she asked, 'May I?' and paused for his consent before patting him.

Finally unable to resist and chiding himself that this was just what the witch wanted, he opened his eyes. A heart-shaped face framed by sun-brightened chestnut colored hair filled his view. Rich brown eyes, large with wonder, stared unblinking into his.

Mut gave way. His heart pounded in his chest. He couldn't stand against someone this beautiful. He would die rather than deny her whatever she wanted. Jilian would always rule his soul, but this girlwoman had taken an instant to settle into his blood.

She seemed to sense his change in mood and began to groom his long, tangled fur with her fingers. He'd never been able to tolerate such minute attention from anyone including Jilian, but now it calmed him. The witch's ceremony would likely kill him, but he'd die satisfied.

It must have taken hours for her to work her way through the knots. He listened to her talk of her travels, her troubles with a stern mother, her worries for her well-meaning father who would surely try to rescue her. Like her, the stories suggested more than the obvious. She left plenty unsaid, though she spoke from deep within.

Outside the sun set and the valley grew dark. Torches danced as they were carried about. Humming became singing. The crowd grew turbulent like a building storm.

The girlwoman rose and went to look out. 'Please eat. It's

your only chance to live. You can't escape if you don't survive.' Her voice was earnest, genuine. Besides, it was *her* voice.

He stood and padded over to the food bowl. The mush of yesterday had been replaced with fresh fish lightly seared. His mouth watered. She knew what he liked. Inches above the plate, he stopped. *She knew what he liked.* No one other than Jilian knew his diet. He sat back on his haunches.

'Oh, come now. I know this isn't a king's banquet, not yet anyway . . .'

How could the elfwitch know what he liked? And why didn't she give it to him earlier if she did? Did she have Jilian? No, he didn't think so. He would have known.

The girlwoman sat beside him, took a bit of fish, and placed it on her tongue. She tried to smile, failed, and only just managed to swallow it down. 'Food better suited to dragons, I'd guess.' She broke off another piece. 'Give it a try. If it's poisoned, at least we'll suffer together.' She held it under his nose.

He sniffed at the fish. He had nothing to lose. The worst that happened was that he died. A few hours ago that had seemed a good choice. Mut nibbled the food in the girl-woman's hand while taking care not to drip dragon slobber on her.

'There's a good boy.' She sat back and let him finish the plate and lap the water bowl dry.

As if on cue, a male elf and troll entered the tent.

'Good to see you gentlemen again,' she said in a voice that was pure swagger and not the least pleased.

The elf bowed graciously. 'The pleasure is mine, Ginni born of mage and mercenary.'

So that explained her parents.

The troll didn't speak as he gripped her arm hard enough to make her grimace.

The elf lifted Mut as if he were no heavier than a human infant, cradling him unbound in his arms. 'If you wish to avoid pain, you will not struggle.'

Slowly, so as not to alarm the elf, the dragon twisted to see Ginni. Though she didn't fight the troll, she'd squared her jaw in defiance. She hasn't given up yet, thought Mut. How can I?

They were brought forth into the frenzied chanting of the camp.

Chapter 16

TRANSFORMATION

Walther came to with a terrible foreboding. The mage in Abadan's bowl, Roslin . . . she was about to . . . What? Something dreadful, an act as evil as any the elfwitch might conceive.

Both Maarcus and his grandfather bent over the dwarf. Their identical expressions were oddly clinical, as if they'd been trying to decide whether he would live. Zera hovered a step or two behind, her carriage more openly worried. All three broke into smiles upon seeing a sign of his recovery. Abadan paid no attention to any of them as he attended to his magicks with considerable clatters and clashes.

Or so Walther assumed until he said, 'Feeling better? Good. Going to have to do something about that Roslin. She's getting dangerous.' He didn't look up from his work.

'What about her daughter?' Maarcus the Sixth asked.

'What about Jilian,' the younger Maarcus demanded.

What about Roslin? Walther thought. And what about me? No, he didn't matter. The Evil he'd felt before his

collapse had already been unleashed. It would be worse –
much, much worse – than his little home town.

The dwarf sat up and all four barraged him with questions.
He ignored them. 'Where's Ceeley?'

'Safe,' Zera said, breaking through the babble. 'You
needn't worry. We have more urgent concerns to tend to.'

Walther shook his head 'no'. 'Where's Ceeley?' he asked
again with more force, gritting his teeth.

Abadan held up a hand to silence the others. 'Why?'

'*It*'s on its way here and I don't want her to be abandoned
again.' He didn't say, I don't want her to die alone.

'It?'

'Alvaria, her trolls, Roslin . . .' He closed his eyes as if that
would shut out the approaching horror. In his mind's eye, elf
and human, female mages both, formed a union he didn't
understand. 'I don't know.'

Loud crying echoed at the door, nearly drowning out a
tentative knock.

'Open,' ordered Abadan.

Harmon brought in a visibly distraught Ceeley. 'I'm sorry
. . . I . . . she . . . I didn't know what to do.'

'It's all right, Harmon. We were just—'

A tremendous boom rocked the house to its foundation.
Ceeley screamed all the louder.

It's begun, thought Walther. I escaped the last one, but
there's no surviving this.

'If we can reach the tunnel, we'll be all right,' said Zera,
seeming to answer his unspoken thoughts. She winced as
another thud pounded outside. 'But Abadan, I don't expect
the house will last through too many of those. Someone is
determined.'

'Yes, I know.' The magician was already gathering his
most precious items.

The younger Maarcus took Ceeley into his arms, and tried

to comfort her with meaningless assurances that none of them believed, including the child.

Another bang shook the house. Plaster fell from the ceiling. Bottles flew from the shelves and crashed to the floor.

Abadan moved faster, spilling as much as he saved.

The physician pulled on his arm. 'Now, old friend. We've got to go.'

He ignored all but his magicks.

Zera spoke with more practicality. 'Abadan, you are no use to us dead.'

Heavy footfalls thudded on the stairs.

Abadan looked up. 'Maybe you're right. Don't think I like the atmosphere around here. Too much dust.'

Maarcus was still trying in vain to quiet Ceeley.

Zera leaned over and whispered, 'Hush now, Celia Sailclan. It is very important that you make no sound.' She put her finger to the child's lips.

Ceeley instantly stopped her wailing. Her eyes were big and round, but she kept silent when the elf removed her hand.

Zera nodded to her apprentice.

Harmon led the way down the hall away from the approaching footsteps. He turned down a corridor Walther had not noticed before and then another. The dwarf looked over at Maarcus and the eerily quiet child he carried. The man appeared grim but not unduly alarmed. But then, he probably knew where they were going. Walther, on the other hand, felt as lost as Ceeley looked. He almost wished for the excuse of his river dizziness rather than this blind run into the unknown.

Jilian raced through the trees as if her life depended on it — her life or Mut's. She paid no attention to the branches reaching out to snag her clothes and scratch her bare skin.

She tripped and fell, rose again and kept running. Sure of her direction, and that Mut was near, she never paused to confirm her bearings.

Her first thought when she smelled the smoke was, I'm too late. Her second was, This isn't possible!

She had come full circle and now stood on the edge of Two Gates.

She paused, hidden by the forest's edge. All the world before her seemed consumed by fire. She could hear screaming yet she saw no one fleeing her way. This evil torture was the elfwitch's doing – but how had the mercenary come to be here? Had Alvaria sent her astray? Had Zera summoned her help?

Zera, Maarcus, Walther, Ceeley, even the physician and the ill-humored magician – all caught. And Mut, more than that. Sick to the core and dying – or worse. Only Alvaria could devise a torment more dreadful than death itself.

Jilian viciously yanked down an overhanging tree limb and snapped off the smaller twigs. Her gut felt no less twisted for that she'd attempted to get to Mut and failed. The dragon remained foremost in her mind and heart, but she couldn't ignore the fate of her friends.

In her mind's eye, she saw her parents' cabin burnt to cinders with nothing left but the dragon token. Reflexively, she patted her pocket to assure herself it was still there after the episode at the lake. A needless action, she'd have known it was gone just as she knew something dire was about to befall Mut.

There were no good choices. Reluctantly, Jilian settled on the obvious path beneath her feet. The mercenary made her way through the streets as quickly as she could manage, dodging trolls when she wasn't ducking flaming refuse. How she found the house amidst the disaster she would never be able to explain.

Trolls guarded the main entrance. Jilian circled the building and its attached neighbors, employing all the stealth she used to foil an assassin. As far as she could see, no one had set the house afire, though the doors had been bashed in and the panes on the ground floor were shattered. In the alley behind the house, trolls watched over the glassless windows as well as both doorways. Jilian heaved a sigh of relief. So many sentries must mean the others were alive – and likely within.

For the first time since she'd run from the clearing, the mercenary stood still and listened with more than her ears. Underneath the villagers' terrified shouting, she felt the elfwitch tugging at her mind, trying to convince her of the death of everything she held dear. Jilian resisted. The devastation surrounding her set her scrambled thoughts in order. She recognized the fear for what it was now.

Jilian started to pull back and regroup when it occurred to her that the elfwitch had given her the quickest means to get to Mut. If she purposely allowed herself to be caught, she'd give Sisters' odds in her favor that the trolls would take her to the witch right away. She only needed to confirm the others' wellbeing to put her mind at ease.

Getting inside the elf's ravaged building would accomplish both.

Jilian knew she looked a sight from her recent ordeals and left it that way down to the twigs in her hair. Noting the placement of the guards while seeming not to, she approached the house head on so that even these slow-witted creatures couldn't miss her. She hung her head and stumbled up to the front door. A troll grabbed her hand as she raised it to the knob. Jilian feigned a wildwoman's rage, thrashing and shouting curses she'd forgotten she knew, especially a particularly vile one aimed at the elfwitch.

The troll stiffened as if slapped. Immediately an elf came

out of the house. Elf and troll each grasped one arm and pulled her into the entryway.

It was the last Jilian knew for hours.

Wanton Tom checked his knives and his sword yet again. Riding into battle with nothing on his mind but the anticipation of killing the enemy made him jumpy till he got down to work. This time, more than any other, he wanted to get to it. 'Can't you beat those wings any faster?'

'Certainly . . . if I lighten the load.' Grosik abruptly rolled onto his left wing then leveled.

'OK, you made your point.' Stubborn flying lizard, Tom thought. He swallowed bile that wasn't just a result of the dragon's antics. Knowing the truth of the transformation spell – at least as far as the magician explained it moments ago when he himself was fleeing with his companions – left the mercenary with more than a sour taste in his mouth. The elfwitch could do more harm to Ginni than she'd probably do to the dragon-prince.

'The elf camp is directly below us.'

Wanton Tom looked down but couldn't distinguish much from this height. 'Is she there?'

'Ginni or the elfwitch?'

'Ginni!' he shouted. In a calmer voice, he added, 'I guess I could stand knowing about the elfwitch as well.'

A strong wind rocked the dragon then circled around in a tight ring that threatened to pull them out of the sky.

'Got the answer to my second question.'

'Wrong,' Grosik said, his wings beating hard to fight against the whirlpool. '*That* is Roslin.'

'Roslin! How can it be Roslin?'

The dragon didn't take the breath to answer until they were beyond the maelstrom's reach. 'The wind tastes of the magewoman's magicks. Also, I cannot feel the elfwitch.'

Tom was almost afraid to ask. 'And Ginni?'

'I can't be certain.'

'We can't abort now.'

'No, but this will take some more thought. I suggest we reconsider briefly outside Roslin's sphere.'

Tom reluctantly agreed. 'Blind speed won't do 'er. We need something else.' He sighed. It seemed they had a new enemy, one who knew them intimately. Tom glanced over his shoulder at the calming air. Roslin could be unforgiving, but he'd never expected her to turn to such extremes.

They flew out a ways and landed in the nearest patch of frozen soil big enough to accommodate the dragon's girth. Tom's feet had barely touched dirt when Grosik's tail slapped the ground with a crack.

Tom turned his back to the great beast, sword in hand. Before him stood three elves – or at least he supposed they were elves. The colors of their cloaks swirled about them, reflecting sunlight in odd patterns that made it hard to focus for long. Their heads were unadorned but somehow even their faces were strangely distracting.

The tallest of the three raised a hand and Tom held up his sword to greet it. 'Peace,' was all the elf said. The air smelled of clean rain. All around them the world spoke of unseasonable spring, life, renewal.

The mercenary fought the desire to put away his sword but only succeeded in lowering it unsheathed. His gut relaxed involuntarily. It might as well have been the carefree days before he'd been told he had a daughter – a girl much too talented and fearless for her own good.

Tom didn't trust elven blessings, even less coming from such as these. He twisted around to the dragon. Grosik meanwhile held very still and the mercenary couldn't read whether the elves had managed the undoable – ensorcelling a dragon – or if the beast merely waited for the best chance to attack.

Tom was almost afraid to hear himself speak but he found his mind *and his voice* were his own once he dared. 'Don't know about peace. Not much 'cept war around here. Per'aps you're new to the One Land?'

'Quite the opposite, young Tom. We've been here a very long time.'

He smiled at the reference to 'young'. These elves had his weak spot pegged.

'Then you'll be informed regarding the witch's war,' he said neutrally, giving them an opening to defend Alvaria and claim sides.

The tall one didn't hesitate. 'We are and we do what we can to counteract it.'

'Such as?' Tom asked.

'Some other time. Now we must talk,' he said, not answering the question directly. He settled comfortably on a boulder Tom didn't recall being there and his fellows followed suit. When the mercenary didn't respond right away, he carelessly waved a hand and nodded. 'Please.'

'Prefer to think on my feet if it's all right by you.'

The one on his left whispered in his ear. There was no change in his expression when he addressed Tom. 'As you wish. This posturing wastes valuable time. Shall I begin?'

Maybe they're not trying to shill me after all, the mercenary thought. Or their court manners are rusty. He considered sitting but remained where he was and tipped his head slightly.

'You rush in blindly to rescue the girl-mage Ginni. It will not serve anyone's purpose and may harm the dragon-prince. We suggest another approach.' He paused and waited for Tom's acquiescence.

Or so Wanton Tom assumed. He had no intention of agreeing to unstated plans. 'And what might that be?'

'Leave an unimportant item of yours with us and then continue cautiously as you've planned.'

'Something worthless? Now what could that be? My sword? My—'

'They want the bracelet Ginni found,' Grosik cut in. 'Let them have it.'

'Why should I?'

'Because they are the rightful owners.'

'Says who?'

'The dragon is accurate . . . so far as he comprehends matters. We are more closely akin to caretakers than owners.'

Grosik snorted and gently slapped the tip of his tail, but uncharacteristically let the insult pass.

Tom stalled. 'The dragon makes mistakes now and again. We don't have it with us at present. Why don't you tell us your plan and we'll retrieve the bracelet for you once Ginni and the prince are freed.'

'You misunderstand me. We have no "plan" as you call it. Put simply, you will not be able to rescue the girl until the witch realizes the bracelet is beyond her reach. The only way to keep it in safe hands is to give it to us.'

'So you'll give it to the witch. I'm not that young.'

'They speak true,' Grosik said. 'We should listen.'

'You stay out of this. She's not your daughter.'

'No, but I have known her for all but the first months of her life. She trusted me enough to leave the bracelet with me when you both returned to the Cups to find Roslin.'

Tom couldn't hide his surprise. His mouth dropped open and he clamped it shut. Not only had Ginni deceived him, but the dragon had revealed the deception in front of unproven strangers. The mercenary found himself wishing he could call on the magician. Maybe he could . . . 'What use is the bracelet to you?'

'It holds the key to powerful magic,' the elf answered simply.

'Then why let it go to begin with?'

'At the time, it was a wise choice.'

'What's changed?' Tom asked, still wondering why he allowed himself to continue the conversation.

'Alvaria, who some call the One, has captured a human.'

'Yeah, my daughter.'

'Another human, of particular import to the entire One Land.'

'As opposed to a talented kid from the wrong valley.' Tom was feeling as impotent as a drunk after a seven-day spree. He was doing everything he could to draw out the elves' real purpose, but they hung in, completely unflappable.

'We do not weigh a person's value by anything beyond his – or her – ' he added smoothly, 'own deeds. Low birth or high will not guarantee peace in the One Land.'

Tom stood silent for a moment. 'This all sounds as sweet and smooth as a baby's powdered bottom.'

The elves waited.

'Which means it goes down as easily as a dwarven dessert.'

The elves waited some more.

Exasperated, the mercenary turned to his not altogether trustworthy dragon. 'Grosik, talk to them!'

The dragon shook his head. 'I have nothing to say to them unless you wish me to tell them exactly where to find the bracelet.'

'Will you help with Ginni?' Tom asked hastily before Grosik could say more.

'We'll do what we can.'

'Sounds about as promising as Ginni reaching her next

birthday.' Tom winced. He didn't want to consider that.

'She won't unless you trust us.'

Tom looked from the dragon to the elves. With Grosik ready to hand over the bracelet, he'd already lost the battle. Everyone was just giving him the courtesy of pretending to let him make up his own mind. Yet he was still missing something and he wanted to know what it was before he gave in.

'How do I know you aren't in league with the witch?'

'Ask the dragon.'

'Well?'

'Not her style.'

'All elves know how to employ underhand sweet talk.'

The three frowned.

'No offense,' the mercenary said with just a trace of sincerity.

'They will not betray you.'

'Any worse than *you* already have, you mean.'

The dragon slapped his tail against the ground and the land echoed his anger. 'I understand she is your daughter. Furthermore, your mouth has often spoken when your brain was not aware. Nonetheless, you go too far, Tom, my companion of many years.'

'Neither elfwitch nor woman-mage will be looking for you without the bracelet. You can safely reach your goal.'

'That word "safe" again. Doesn't seem too "safe" to me.'

The elf spread his arms wide. 'As safe as anyone can be on such a mission.'

Tom didn't have to think about that too much. If in fact they were on the level, this made sense. *If* they were on the level. 'All right, so we hand over this bracelet. Then what?'

'We put it someplace secure.'

'Fine as far as it goes. How does that help Ginni?'

'We will help you with Ginni.'

'As soon as we've taken care of the bracelet,' a second elf added.

'You won't need us before then.'

'Better and better. Pretty soon I'll be betting the next ruler of the One Land lives out a twin-year after coming into power.'

The elf laughed. 'You would be surprised at the possibilities.'

Worse and worse. Wanton Tom looked at the dragon. The beast had been his only friend for better than half his life. As much as he hated it, the mercenary had to trust Grosik. He nodded, unable to get out the words.

Grosik didn't rub it in. 'It's in the bottom of the left satchel.'

It remained for Tom to pull out the bracelet and hand it over. He rooted around in the bag, but realized it was surprisingly easy to give it away once he laid hands on it. The decision had been made. Besides, he'd swear the thing squirmed between his fingers eager to escape his touch.

They took the jewelry and ceremoniously passed it among themselves. All three bowed graciously. 'We will be back when we're needed most.' They floated away with less effort than it took ordinary men to breathe.

Row upon row of elves jostled each other in the dark. Each held a small candle that only made their faces seem more ghastly.

The trolls set Mut upon a polished granite altar with great ceremony. At the witch's instruction, they tied him so that he could see the proceedings but was helpless against them. When they were finished, no one bothered to reassure him he wasn't meant to be a sacrifice.

Elves stepped back from the altar next to him. An

unfamiliar woman struggled against her bonds and swore vile curses. Mut focused on her rather than think of his own fate, but was instantly sorry. Her eyes were cold and harsh, and along with ears and mouth, bore fresh scarring.

Trolls passed behind him with the girl, Ginni. She cried out, 'Roslin!' as they dragged her by, then went quiet and deadly still as they bound and gagged her.

Alvaria stepped up to the middle altar with her back to the crowd. She addressed the tortured woman so quietly that Mut had to strain to hear. 'Betrayal is always repaid in kind. Be pleased that your action will allow me to complete the transformation.'

'As you say,' Roslin spat. 'Your treachery will be returned sevenfold.' She began to chant.

Alvaria frowned. 'Do you take me for an untried apprentice?' She slit the woman's throat in one move, with little ceremony. Mut barely heard Ginni's muffled shouts. He doubted many of those gathered noticed them at all. She caught the blood in a painted skin sack, then turned to Ginni. 'A knowing betrayal of one's people is truly unforgiveable, regardless of race or reason. You, Ginni, have unintentionally served me well. Long have Abadan and Maarcus sought to keep the bones of transformation from me. Your discovery gave me the vantage I needed to complete my task. For this you will be treated well and perhaps have further opportunities to serve me.'

Ginni's eyes widened in horrified realization. Around the gag she said, ''idn't know. I—'

'Enough. Your time is not now.' She turned toward the crowd and took three steps forward.

Burning incense thickened behind Mut. Ginni's expression was bleak, but every muscle in her body said she had not given in.

Suddenly the girl's face went as hard as the dead woman's had been. Her lips began to move in silent prayer or incantation.

The elfwitch paid no mind to her captives, living or dead. She stood with arms raised on a moveable platform in front of the altar. Without preamble, Alvaria began a booming litany of the sins of those peoples who had wronged her.

'The hated humans who forced our migration back and forth along the river without rest.

'The hated dwarves who built their towns and blocked our passage.

'Illegal taxation to human kings to support their imaginary One Land.

'Destruction of our sacred places and seizing of our property . . .

'Only to be insulted by the return of small bits of river-bank, as if this could make up for the centuries of abuse!

'We could feed the centuries starved with the blood and flesh of our enemies—'

Mut's stomach tightened at the thought.

'But we are civilized, whereas our adversaries have barely risen from the mud from whence they came.'

Alvaria's charges droned on. Mut fell into a daze from the smoke, the flickering flames, and her chanting. He thought of Jilian, who had spent her life cheating untimely death; he thought of the girl Ginni, not ready to embrace it; of the woman Roslin, who already had. He considered whether he too was prepared to die.

In the end, it was a simple decision. He might yet be killed, but he would not go quietly as a sacrifice to Alvaria's evil. The dragon gathered his strength and cautiously tested his bonds. They seemed secure but not hopelessly so.

Abruptly Alvaria thrust bones before his eyes and shook them at him. Sticky warm blood rained down on him. His head was instantly on fire, the pain seared down to his own bones though he knew the blood itself could not have been the cause. The torture grew excruciating, beyond what any man could endure, and then worse still.

The witch's chanting grew even more frenzied. Her people answered the litany with frightening intensity. Beside him the girl shrieked.

Mut's neck popped. Suddenly his head weighed too heavy. Dizziness and nausea made it impossible for him to support his head at the strange new angle. His back snapped. The shock of each vertebra realigning along his spine was more than he could bear. Every bone in his body cracked, forced to refit a new, unfamiliar design.

How could he ever have wished for even an eyeblink of a moment to be human? Much better to stay an awkward failed dragon than suffer this slow death, a witch's amusement for her troops and believers. He whispered goodbye to Jilian. Praying to the Seven Sisters for the killing blow, he let blessed darkness swallow him.

Lyda placed one foot in front of the other and did not rest. All around her others did the same. Snowdrifts blew across their path, making dangerous rifts which appeared unexpectedly and maimed the unlucky. Man, woman, child, dwarf, elf, human, all prodded the ground ahead with walking sticks now.

They were tired. They were hungry. They were afraid.

She was tired. Hungry. Afraid.

Yet the ever-shifting crowd gained solace from her presence.

And she from theirs.

This passage was a trial. The people wouldn't succumb.

Nor would she.

Lyda did not count the steps behind, only the ones ahead.

She placed left foot after right, and wondrous colors trailed behind in the prints which snow could not obscure.

The dragon reawakened moments later amid Alvaria's crescendo of shouting. He writhed upon the stone slab as his muscles followed the reshaped contours of his body. The granite's coolness brought an odd relief of counterpoint to the agony. The leather cords had magically held fast but chafed against raw skin where fur had been.

He moved and his wings fell away with no more trouble than a discarded jacket. No wonder they had never held him aloft – but they were his! He lurched for the wings, snapping the bonds. Too late. They were beyond his reach. His hands felt foreign and weak, but more flexible. Had he been quick enough, he could have held onto the wings rather than merely stabbed at them with a claw. Where were his claws?

'Arise new man and know the great one who made you as you are.'

The words boomed in his head yet sounded very far away. Night noises echoed as if they came to him through wads of cloth stuffed in his ears. He opened his eyes, but images were cloudy. Shapes moved, but he could not judge their distance or their true forms.

'Arise,' shouted the voice again. 'Greet your queen.'

Queen? There was no queen in the Cliffs, had not been for generations.

A sharp prick to the abdomen. 'He bleeds, Lady Alvaria.' Others laughed.

'No, do not defile my work!' Light flashed and the elf collapsed. 'The next to touch him will be the first to take on his discarded body.'

Agony no longer wracked the dragon. Was he dead after

all, hovering in some kind of forsaken netherworld controlled by the witch?

'Arise now, man. Do not try my patience.'

This new form seemed not under the witch's absolute control then.

'Now,' she hissed.

He remained at her bidding as a captive nonetheless. Mut tested his limbs, flexed muscles, rotated joints. Nothing quite worked as he remembered. Still there were analogous parts.

Mut sat up with his legs stretched out before him, as if they remained secured to stone. He saw his nakedness reaching down to his groin. A man exposed, he covered his lap with his hands and thought longingly of his unruly fur. He made no attempt to stand.

A few in the crowd snickered, but none dared call out after the elfwitch's warning.

Alvaria circled the altar. 'You saw the power of transforming human and dwarf to beast. Now acknowledge one who can transform beast into any form I wish. Human. Dwarf.' She paused. 'Elf.

'Follow me to greatness.' Her voice hit a new crescendo, then dropped to barely audible.

'Those who do not will suffer this creature's fate. For any elf who betrays me will not just become a beast. No, I will change each and every traitor into the hated form of those they seek to join. Hear me and take heed.'

Mut closed his eyes and shut out the witch's sideshow barking. He concentrated on the stone bench beneath his nude flesh and let his mind come to know this new body, the body he realized intuitively had been his from birth.

Mut opened his eyes and his vision sharpened to colors and images he hadn't thought possible. He looked at the profile of the witch, saw at once that it was both more vulnerable and more fierce than their previous meeting in the clearing. She caught him studying her and smiled, a death's head grin colder and harsher than the worst mountaintop winter.

Alvaria flicked her fingers in a motion undetectable to those more than a twin-step away. Two trolls effortlessly lifted Mut and carried him off.

Chapter 17

STRATEGY

Free of the elves and the bracelet, Grosik wasted no time taking to the skies and bearing down on their target. His wings flapped with all their mighty power, disrupting smaller flying creatures in their wake. Tom wrapped his hands around the dragon's neck and mentally urged him on. Once over the camp, they headed straight down for the altar.

'Something's happened,' the beast told Tom.

'Ginni?' he asked through gritted teeth.

'She's . . . changed, but I think she's OK.'

'Transformed . . . ?' He couldn't finish the question. Tom couldn't bear to think the witch had turned his daughter into a troll while he was dickering with other elves. They would pay, oh, they would . . . But first the elfwitch. Alvaria was the One, all right – the one who spread misery wherever she could.

Grosik broke into his thoughts. 'No. Not that. Changed, but still human. There below us.'

The mercenary fought the wind to turn his head. From this

height, he could make out a lone form on the altar, but he would have to take the dragon's word that it was Ginni.

'She's tied. You'll have to release her. I'll hold off the witch – and her retinue.' He made it sound like a creature that lived in pond muck and ate spineless animalcules.

The dragon swooped over the crowd, breathing fire and batting them down with his wings. He landed atop several guards and Tom jumped off.

'No, you will not!' shrieked the witch.

Tom and the dragon paid her no attention as he quickly cut Ginni's last bond. The other straps were already charred to cinders. 'Up to your old tricks,' he whispered.

Her face remained stiff and her eyes hard. 'Glad you could make the reception,' Ginni said without acknowledging his joke.

'The prince is mine!' Alvaria yelled impotently, as if Tom cared about royalty.

He couldn't figure why she made no move to retaliate, and didn't stop to ponder the good luck. Maybe those pacifist elves had kept their promise and were hovering somewhere behind the bushes.

It was Ginni who defied the witch. As the last leather strap fell away, she turned magnificently to confront Alvaria. Her stature held all the haughtiness he both hated – and loved – about Roslin. 'For now,' his daughter said.

She mounted the dragon, yanking Tom behind her as she did so.

Grosik was off the ground before the surprised elves could scramble together a counter-offense.

It was a solemn crowd huddled in the woods beyond Twin Gates. Walther gratefully collapsed to the ground. The others, too, sank down, catching their breath. Only Ceeley seemed to have any energy at all, but hers was a leery wild kind that no one wanted to cage just yet.

After a time, Walther noticed that Abadan, Maarcus the Sixth, and Zera had been whispering among themselves for some minutes. He sat up to listen, still hesitant to presume the privilege of active participant.

The physician was saying, 'I agree with Abadan. We have to go to her. We've no choice now.'

Zera shook her head. 'And if she wins, she wins everything. Including us.'

'She won't win us all,' Walther said before he realized he'd spoken. 'Something drains her.'

The three turned to him with a mutually curious, analytical stare.

Before Walther bloomed a scene of the elfwitch's camp as a man riding a dragon swooped down to rescue the girl.

'Where ever did you meet Wanton Tom and Grosik?' asked Abadan.

'I don't know them,' the dwarf answered. 'I take it Grosik is the dragon?'

'What are you talking about?' asked both Maarcuses.

'Do it again, do it again!' shouted Ceeley, sounding nearly her old self.

'Hush!' whispered the adults at once.

Ceeley closed her mouth, looking slightly chagrined. 'That was exciting, Uncle Walther,' she said in a more subdued tone.

'What was?'

Abadan clucked his tongue. 'Just once, Maarcus, I would like not to have to elaborate on the ways of magic solely for your benefit.'

The grandfather and the grandson held identical expressions of confusion mixed with annoyance and frustration. 'Just once,' the younger Maarcus said, 'I would like not to be insulted for a lack which is beyond my ability to correct.'

'The dwarf,' Zera explained, 'had a vision. A dragon and a man, rescuing a young woman from a stone altar.'

'Was it Jilian?'

'No,' snapped Abadan. 'Probably the mercenary's daughter, Ginni?'

'You don't mean Wanton Tom, who contacted us this morning?' asked the physician.

'The same.'

The younger Maarcus fidgeted with the contents of his pack. 'What's this to us? One less problem.'

'Apparently the girl is quite *talented*,' Abadan said pointedly. 'They could be useful.'

Walther didn't like the sound of 'useful'. It was as if Abadan considered them all pieces to be employed regardless of risk.

'We could try Tom's babble box,' Zera suggested.

'The layout of her camp would be *useful*.' Maarcus stressed the final word.

So. Dwarf and human were together in their unease about Abadan's motivation. The dwarf grimaced at his friend.

Abadan extracted the device from his belongings without comment. He put his back to the others and began whispering into the box.

The physician moved to stand by his heir. 'Grandson, I know your heart. Please don't let it rule your head when it comes to the magician. He is a *good* man.'

'A good magician, no doubt. As to the other, I await proof.'

'You will have it by and by.'

'When?'

The elder's mouth tightened. Maarcus the Sixth could not answer.

The magician turned from his task. 'Odd. No one's responded.'

'Maybe the elfwitch recaptured them,' said the physician. Walther shook his head. 'I don't think so.'

'Nor do I,' Abadan agreed. 'This is something else. I'll try again, but first . . . I owe you an apology, Maarcus.'

'Me? Whatever for?'

'No, not you. Your grandson.'

'I don't succumb to flattery,' the man answered stiffly as if they had not just discussed this very subject.

'Good. I don't engage in it.'

'Nor does he ever apologize without considerable forethought,' said the elder Maarcus.

'My error is much older than our current squabbles. I distrusted and discounted your abilities, just as I once did your grandfather's. That mistake ultimately contributed to the Great King's dying sooner than the Sisters called for. *This* error eased the way for the elfqueen to capture the dragon-prince. We suspected she was about to make a dramatic move. We knew she was behind those dreadful raids *and* that she could mask her talent and deeds from you. We were nearly certain that Jilian and Mut were the lost twins.' He ticked off the four items on his fingers then flexed the entire open hand in frustration. 'All this we kept from you to protect you. We did you a disservice and we did the One Land harm.'

'You've always done the best you could. We all have.' Zera's voice held its own sad secret.

Walther studied his companions, seeking to read the truth of Abadan's revelation. The magician, the physician, and the elf all shared the sorrowful frowns of regret, yet each looked determined to carry on. Maarcus the Seventh had lost all his swagger to overwhelming astonishment. Ceeley had fallen asleep. Harmon watched over her with calm assurance.

'So we can't raise Tom on your box,' the dwarf said, trying to be practical. He alone seemed to remember the urgency of the situation. 'Any point in enlisting the mage?' He wanted to swallow the words as soon as they escaped his mouth. Abadan saved him the trouble of eating them.

'No, no, I don't think so. I say we go as we are, the seven of us.'

'We can't take Ceeley,' the doctor said.

'We can't leave her,' Walther objected. 'Besides, we are seven, the Sisters' number. How can we toss away such a portent?'

The others stared at him.

Then they bent forward to plan.

Grosik brought them to ground as soon as they felt safe. Ginni and Tom dismounted and stood giving each other the eye. The dragon feigned disinterest while father and daughter reassessed.

'Roslin's dead,' Ginni said, her voice flat.

Tom wasn't as sorry as he ought to have been. 'How?'

'Elfwitch cut her throat.'

Tom winced. 'She didn't deserve that.'

'Not many do,' Ginni answered, still stoic. 'Alvaria used Roslin's blood to transform the prince.'

'What prince?'

'The next king of the One Land.'

The mercenary hated conversations like this. Discussions with a witch never quite made sense. 'Ginni, what happened?' he asked changing the subject.

'Roslin died,' she said again, as if that explained everything.

'Were you there?' Maybe she was in battle shock and worse, from watching her mother used as a sacrifice.

'Yes, I was there.'

'Oh, Ginni, I'm sorry.' He tried to take her in his arms to comfort her. She didn't soften.

'I'm all right, Tom.'

'You're sure?'

'Roslin isn't important. She betrayed us. Father,' in her most serious tone, 'we have to rescue the prince.'

Back to that, were they? 'Haven't you done enough? I think we can sit this one out.'

'No. He trusts me. I can do it,' she assured him. 'I have the power . . . Uncle.' She almost sounded like herself and the coy smile reminded him of when he'd first found her.

'What power?'

'Roslin's.'

Roslin's? By the almighty dragon's tongue, what was she talking about?

'Everything she ever taught me, Uncle. It's all mine now. I am as powerful as Roslin ever was – and more so.'

They led Jilian to a tent where a barely clothed, sick man lay moaning. His skin was magnificent, as pink as a newborn's. His eyes were the same intense color as Mut's, as Jilian's own.

'Hello, Jilian.'

Instinctively, the mercenary reached for her knife and found she'd been disarmed. She let her hand drop. How could he know her?

'It's me. Mut.'

The buzzing in her ears reached a new pitch. No, this was the consummate trick. Mut, her most vulnerable spot. The dragon she'd always pretended was human actually transformed. Her head shook 'no' of its own accord and she

285

backed up involuntarily – right into the elfwitch.

Furious, she turned and struck out only to have the man grab her arm before she connected. His touch rang with familiarity. It reminded Jilian of mountain climbing, stick chasing, and assassin stalking. The smells of her life scented the close tent air. He let go of her arm and she let it drop to her side. 'Who are you?'

'Your brother.'

It was a seemingly simple answer. Two words. Apparently genuine. He did not embellish; she did not ask him to.

Behind her, the elfwitch stirred. 'Now that we've had this reunion, the prince is needed elsewhere.'

And then Jilian believed. Despite all the talk, it took Alvaria's casual use of the term 'prince' for her to accept all the rest.

'And where might that be?' Jilian asked, afraid she would lose him so soon after all her struggles to get to him.

Alvaria didn't answer.

Her brother made no protest as they led him away.

'As for you . . .' She smiled in anticipation. 'You missed a great opportunity at the lake. It would be a shame to do so again. Especially since I can offer much.'

'I have what I need.'

'Daughter, I know your heart.'

As Alvaria said it, Jilian thought it must be true. Even the buzzing in her ears had lessened. The desire to trust the elfwitch completely such as she had only believed in Mut was very strong. Jilian tried to remember why she fought.

'You could rule all the human lands,' Alvaria whispered.

But that was not in Jilian's heart. She had never wished to rule. It was the very reason she had resisted Zera. 'What about my brother?' she asked.

'He will lead my armies. You will make a formidable team – just as you always have.'

Jilian tried to picture Mut leading men into battle, but the image was laughable. Like herself, she knew this was not what rested in his heart. The dragon token burned against her chest. Jilian recalled Abadan's warning and covered the medallion with her hand.

The elfwitch slapped the mercenary's face between both hands. Her cheeks stung, but she'd known worse. Her ears rang. She ignored it. The witch and her magic no longer frightened Jilian.

Ginni was in deep meditation when the babble box sounded. Not having heard its call in years, Tom took some moments to realize what it was. When he finally did, he was about to tell the old physician they'd solved the problem – no thanks to him.

Ginni said, 'Don't answer it.'

Her voice held the eerie power of Roslin's and sent shivers down his spine. 'I was just going to tell him to take a hike up to the Dunav mountains.'

'Don't bother. He isn't trustworthy.'

Huh? More like Roslin every minute.

Tom looked over at the dragon, who only stared back with his usual enigmatic wide-eyed look.

'OK,' Tom answered, hoping his unease didn't show. 'Let him stew. He deserves it.'

Ginni smiled and this too reminded Tom more of the girl's mother than the girl. The upturned lips held a mean pettiness that Ginni herself had never been guilty of.

'Gin? You feelin' OK?'

'Uncle Tom, you keep wringing your hands like an old maid and I'm going to have to take away your weapons for fear you'll hurt yourself.' She'd looked more like the Ginni he loved when she said it, but he still didn't like the way she'd suddenly become the one who directed their moves.

All three joined in a good laugh, Grosik always happy to share a joke at Tom's expense. 'So, what are you up to?' he asked, not quite willing to let her strange behaviour drop.

'Thinking.'

'Never a good sign,' he teased.

'About the prince,' she continued seriously. 'The elfwitch transformed him from the dragon and I was only a hand's width away. The power that must have taken,' she added.

Tom thought he detected a note of envy, let that thought drift. 'How do you know he's a prince?'

'It's obvious. He's magnificent. You'll see.'

'Could be the witch,' Grosik suggested.

Or his strong, broad shoulders, the mercenary added silently.

'No, no he was genuine. I'm sure of it. We have to save him. It's our duty.'

'Now hold on there. The reason we're freelance is so we can decide when to worry about duty.'

'Father—'

She wasn't going to give in.

'Father, he was one of the lost twins.'

'Oh, that old rumor.'

'No, it was a prophecy, a much older prophecy than most people realize. The mages have known it for generations. Roslin gave me the power to recognize the twins. I tell you, this man was one of them. He must be rescued.'

Tom turned to Grosik. 'What do you think, old friend?'

'If she's right—'

'I am,' Ginni interrupted.

'If she is,' the dragon repeated, 'we have nothing to lose by helping him and everything to gain.'

'This isn't the proper spirit,' she admonished.

'Nothing to lose! What about limb and life?'

'Nonetheless, we go.'

Wanton Tom shook his head. It was the mirror of the debate with the elves. He could go or stay, but Ginni would go regardless. He couldn't let her face the elfwitch without him again. 'What'd you have in mind?' he asked carefully.

His daughter wasted no time on niceties. 'Here's how we do it,' Ginni said, and proceeded to tell him just that.

Chapter 18

RESCUE

Grosik came in at a steep dive. Ginni sat forward, holding on to the dragon's neck and allowing Tom the illusion of protecting her. He leaned over her from behind to grasp the same tough neck. The wind rushed past, pulling at the skin of his face. He smiled into it. He would have laughed if he could've spared the air. By the Sisters, he felt more alive than a handful of boys skipping chores on the first day of spring thaw.

Grosik set them down almost gently near the altar where they'd rescued Ginni. The two quickly dismounted.

A few elves milled about cleaning up the last remains from the celebration. The elfwitch was nowhere to be seen. An elf ran off when they landed and Ginni cut him down savagely with a fireball.

Tom hacked the others where they stood in shock and they fell limp and lifeless.

The dragon stood guard, waiting for a better challenge.

'This way,' Ginni called, and led them away from the

clearing to a tent set off from the others. This was her mission. Still, it felt mighty strange to follow her lithe figure as if he were chasing a coy maiden.

She stopped in front of a seemingly unguarded tent and motioned to Grosik. The dragon patrolled the outside and silently signalled all clear.

'Somethin's up,' Tom whispered. 'They couldn't've missed our arrival.'

Ginni waved away his caution and again he was struck by the resemblance to Roslin. Calm as you please, she opened the flap and entered the tent.

Tom shrugged, sword at the ready, and followed.

Inside, the man was plainly human though he wore elven clothing. He stood calmly as if waiting for something.

'Let's go,' Grosik rumbled from outside. 'Company.'

The man shook his head a barely perceptible 'no'. 'Not yet.'

'Your highness, it's me,' Ginni said. 'The one who fed you before the witch . . . before you . . . before Roslin . . .'

'I know,' he said. It was clear he did know, because his perfect aristocratic face held the sadness of one who can no longer trifle with those beneath him.

'But – ' Ginni started.

Tom felt his fist clenching to protect her against this royal puffball, who had the nerve to deny her.

'I must attend my sister.'

'That's all?' Ginni asked, with a derisive note. 'Bring her along. The dragon—'

'No, that's not all. There will be much more.' Throughout he stood motionless as the light from outside dimmed and he seemed to become more ethereal in the shadows.

The dragon let out a roar. 'Now!' he shouted. 'Bring him or leave him.'

Ginni turned to touch the tent skin. Suddenly the entire

thing was in flames, the only safe exit past Grosik. 'Your highness, we must go.'

But he was not there. His elven robe was a crumbled lump of cloth on the pillow covered floor.

Ginni spun about to stare at Tom as if he had set up the prince's escape. 'Where is he!' she accused in the voice Roslin had used when an unexpected event caught her short.

'Now!' Grosik repeated.

Tom took Ginni by the arm and yanked her from the flaming tent.

In the minutes they had been inside, the entire camp around them had erupted in chaos. Trolls and elves ran back and forth in confusion. Everyone screamed but no one seemed to know what to do. A bare few noticed the humans near the prince's tent, but none cared to challenge the dragon.

Ginni stubbornly planted her feet. She scanned the roiling crowd.

Tom tugged on her arm. 'We've got to go.'

She pulled it from his grasp with enough violence to twist his hand. 'No, not without him! He's still here.'

And then they saw Abadan and Maarcus the Sixth. 'No!' Ginni shouted to them. 'You can not have him. He's mine.' She raised her arms. Fire crackled from her fingertips across the panicked elves to ring the royal magician.

Finally Tom realized that Ginni was not just behaving like Roslin; she had somehow *become* Roslin.

Inside the tent, time lost meaning. The air thickened as Jilian's focus narrowed. Soon only Alvaria existed beyond herself. This view, too, constricted until the light the witch held was all that Jilian knew beyond herself.

She stared into the blue flame and felt the warming of the

token against her flesh. The mercenary was on the verge of understanding and she strove to reach . . .

Suddenly the flame flickered and died.

Jilian found not the elfwitch but her brother standing before her. But for the dragon birthmark, he appeared as fresh as he must have been on the day of their birth. She doubted she had ever been so beautiful or so flawless.

'The witch?'

He laughed, the joyous sound Jilian had always known Mut would make if he were human. 'Busy.'

The turmoil from outside broke through her haze of distraction. Screams, cries, laments, shock, outrage, defiance, disbelief. Above it all Alvaria boomed like the embodiment of death.

Jilian looked to Mut. Together they peered out of the tent flap.

The elfwitch called to her servants. They in turn gathered the trolls and the hapless elves. The wailing took on a single high pitch. The elves surrounded a small group. Alvaria stood atop the altar.

'Zera, bold one, lost one, mother of my flesh, come forward.' The crowd broke and Zera stepped forward.

'I give you this last opportunity to defeat your daughter.' She threw down an exquisite silver dagger.

Zera's eyes were filled with tears. She looked back to the others still penned in. 'I cannot. Forgive me friends beside whom I have struggled, but I cannot. I cannot raise a hand against my daughter or my people.' She kicked the dagger aside.

Alvaria laughed but there was no warmth or forgiveness in it. Jilian's gut wrenched. She knew what would come next.

She burst from the tent intent on protecting Zera, but it was too late. Already the elves were upon her, pummeling and kicking their own.

A dragon flew in, scattering the mob.

Jilian took her chance and ran to Zera's side. The elf's face was bruised. Blood ran from nose, mouth, and ears. One eye was swollen shut. As the mercenary cradled the woman's head in her lap, she felt Mut nearby, standing guard as he always had.

'For . . . give me, grand . . . daughter.'

'No,' Jilian said, 'nothing to forgive.'

'There is more,' she gasped out. Her clear eye stared at Jilian, willing the mercenary to listen. 'Trolls . . . like your brother. Trolls *not* trolls.' The eye shut and her body went limp.

'I'm sorry,' Mut said. 'Who was she?'

Jilian thought of several answers. At last not knowing how much he knew or what the elfwitch had told him, she said, 'A friend and teacher.'

He nodded. There was nothing more to say.

Maarcus watched Zera fall beneath the crowd and couldn't move. Spending so many years since the Great King's death dealing in intrigue, he'd forgotten the raw force of mob anger.

The dragon arrived carrying Wanton Tom and his daughter. Maarcus thought they might be able to fight their way out of it then, but Ginni turned to face Abadan and all reason fled from her. Her eyes held more, and less, than battle fury. Whatever its nature, it was aimed at Abadan. The magician was bent over conjuring their way free and saw nothing beyond his spell.

Beside the young mage, Tom appeared at a loss. He slashed to defend, but made no efforts to attack. Of the three, only the dragon acted as Maarcus might have expected. He let out a great roar that shook the ground beneath their feet while his tail slapped at anyone brave enough to come within reach. The powerful jaws clamped shut on a finely wrought elven sword and spat it out in pieces. Foreclaws casually dismembered a few more elves. Shortly no one challenged Grosik.

Intent on the dragon, Maarcus didn't notice the fireball until it was almost upon them. He dodged toward Abadan and missed. 'Down, old fool!' he shouted. 'Get down.'

'Leave me be,' Abadan answered. 'I've got more sense than to stand here unprotected.' The flames died in mid-air, not an arm's reach from his head. 'Cover your own skin and see what you can do for poor Zera.'

Zera. He couldn't find her in the turmoil. Peering through smoke, Maarcus spotted a human woman dressed in man's clothing. Jilian certainly. In a daze, he headed toward her. Someone caught his arm and shook hard.

'Grandfather. Grandfather!'

Maarcus turned to stare at the man who was both of his flesh and his finest protégé and barely recognized him. 'Zera,' he said. 'Help Zera.'

He coughed. 'Grandfather, I need to get you out of here.' Maarcus the Seventh tugged his arm.

The elder man pulled back with a physical strength he didn't know he possessed. 'Must help Zera.' He spoke slowly and distinctly as if to one of the Great King's imbecile advisors.

His grandson coughed again. 'I'll . . . help . . . her,' he choked out. 'You go with Walther.'

'No!' He whipped about and let the younger man follow. The smoke was getting thicker. He'd lost sight of both Zera and Jilian now. 'By the Sisters!' He rushed forward, tripping over bodies in the confusion but remaining upright. The dragon roared once more. The beast would be near his goal. He changed direction to head toward the sound.

Maarcus found them more by Sister's luck than through design of his own.

Jilian sat crouched over Zera. A man stood behind her. He bore such resemblance he could only be the lost twin, Nikolis.

'Jilian,' said a voice softly behind him. Walther bent down beside her. 'We can't help her now. We've got to go.'

She nodded and stood up.

Maarcus Senior felt himself slowly collapsing to the ground, taking the mercenary's place. In her time, Zera had been more than a friend and co-conspirator. He couldn't just leave her. Frantically Maarcus felt for a pulse, a faint breath, anything. He was the royal physician, the finest scientist in the One Land!

And he could never save anyone who mattered.

A ruckus grew loud behind him and someone jostled the doctor. He lost his balance and fell across Zera's lifeless body. A fireball flew past overhead and exploded just beyond.

A woman shrieked in anger and something hit Maarcus in the back of the head.

The crowd began to close in again once they realized the transformed prince stood among them. Walther concentrated, trying to conjure up something to frighten them into retreating, but nothing would come.

Jilian, the dragon-prince Nikolis, and Maarcus the Seventh triangulated the fallen bodies and prepared to fight. Fire streaked through the smoke and left eerie red trails. Trolls ran amuck, not knowing how or who to protect and so destroyed everything in their path as they'd been trained. The elfwitch bellowed orders, but her followers were too panicked to heed her.

Walther tried to see Abadan in the melee, but smoke and hysterical elves made it impossible. He bent to check on the fallen.

The elder Maarcus moaned and rolled over. When he saw the elf beneath him, he squeezed his eyes shut, then opened them to take in his surroundings and stare at Walther. He nodded as if to say, 'I'm fine.'

Suddenly all went quiet. Slowly the air cleared. Abadan stood barely steps away, facing the elfwitch still high on the altar.

They were locked in silent combat that Walther couldn't fathom but felt on some inner level. Around them stricken elves moaned, though few appeared mortally wounded. All in all, it was a very strange sight.

The girl mage, Ginni, suddenly appeared at the prince's side. 'Now, your highness, now is your chance.'

He stared at her uncomprehending.

She twisted round to look at Abadan behind her. Her face reformed into a savage grin. The mage raised her arm. A man yelled, 'Ginni, stop!' But he was too late. Her fingertips blazed with a frightening red light. She threw the flame with all her force and hit the magician square in the chest.

He fell without a cry.

The mercenary and the dragon pounced upon the girl. He grasped her arms, tied them at the wrist, and threw her across the dragon's back. He jumped behind and held her steady. 'Go, Grosik, go!' He didn't have to repeat the anguished plea. The dragon rose into the sky, carrying his companion as if she were a prisoner.

When Walther looked back to the elfwitch on the altar, she was gone. Jilian stood in her place, searching to no avail.

Jilian's dragon token burned against her chest. Her whole

body rang with the unfinished battle. She'd hardly managed to swing her sword though wounded bodies lay everywhere.

And then she noted a steaming troll, dissolving just as the one in town had done. The elfwitch seemed truly gone – for the moment.

The mercenary climbed down from her blood-stained perch and went to check on the others. Mut was smudged with ash, but otherwise not even a shallow cut marked him. Walther, Maarcuses, both younger and elder, seemed confused, but they too were intact. Zera was, well . . . Jilian already knew what Zera was. She did not try to fool herself. Abadan lay on the ground not far away.

She called the physician to her and together they began to examine him.

'Get those magicless fingers off me,' Abadan whispered. Maarcus continued to probe until the magician gathered enough strength to slap him away.

Everyone let out a tired, half-hearted chuckle.

A child ran at Jilian from behind, nearly knocking her over.

'Aunt Jilly! Aunt Jilly!'

So Ceeley and her guardian had come through. 'Mut, I'd like you to meet a friend of mine. Celia Sailclan, I am pleased to introduce you to my dragon.'

Ceeley giggled. 'That's no dragon. That's a man.'

'Indeed I am,' Mut answered. 'But I'm very happy to meet you just the same.'

Celia bowed a perfect curtsey as if she'd been born to it though Jilian had yet to see her perform such before now.

The mercenary turned to her brother. 'I always knew you'd have a way with females.'

His expression clouded. 'Maybe I would have if things had been different,' he answered seriously. 'There's no time for it now. We've won the day, but Alvaria won't give up so easily.'

'Prince Nikolis, you'll need to begin raising an army as soon as we return to the Cliffs.' Maarcus the Sixth spoke, but for once Abadan and the younger Maarcus nodded in agreement.

Jilian waited for her brother to deny their request and found she wasn't surprised when he didn't.

'I'll need intelligence,' he said.

'At your service,' Maarcus the Seventh offered.

'And you, Jilian.'

She smiled, slow and sad, thinking of the elfwitch's predictions in the tent mere hours ago. Maybe Alvaria did know Jilian's heart. 'We fight together as always,' the new princess told the prince.

'Always,' he echoed.

When news of the elfwitch's defeat reached Lyda, she could not quite rejoice. Marching amidst the refugees, her task was not complete until they had reached a place of safety.

Finally, though, she found Willam, trudging just a few steps forward with his head down and cradling one arm. Lyda smiled and hurried to catch up. This was one injury she knew she could heal.